TWISTED LOVE

MARC DANIEL

Text copyright © 2020 Marc Daniel

All Rights Reserved

To Olivia

Acknowledgements

The first thankyous are due to Katherine and Amy, my loyal beta readers, who soldiered through my rough draft and provided valuable feedback.
Sarah provided the professional editing touch the manuscript required and for which my readers will no doubt be grateful.
I will be forever indebted to Katherine, my proofreader, for the time she spent painstakingly hunting down typos and the like throughout the manuscript. Without her eagle eyes many errors would have gone unnoticed all the way to publication.
My last thanks are for my wife, Jasmin, who once again put up with me through the writing of another book.

Cover Design: Ivan Zanchetta (bookcoversart.com)

Also by Marc Daniel

MICHAEL BIORN SERIES
Michael Biörn

Shadow Pack

Unholy Trinity

Close Enemies

Twisted Love

Broken Alliance

ETHAN ARCHER SERIES
The Girl Who Went Nowhere

OTHER
Into the Woods

Prologue

The dilapidated shack stood in the middle of the Australian Outback, miles from the closest neighbor. It belonged to a witch. A witch who now lay lifeless in a corner of the room, discarded like the no-longer-needed tool she was. Her blood had been used to draw the glyph upon which the master now stood, hands raised, at the center of the living room, but the crimson fluid had been the witch's only contribution to the ritual.

The incantation, chanted in a tongue few alive would have recognized, held no meaning for either the man or the woman standing on either end of the glyph observing their master.

The acolytes were both warlocks, but they couldn't have been more different from each other. The male had the appearance of a tall young man and stood with a proud posture. Attentive to his master's every move, his ice-blue eyes were barely visible under the mess of auburn hair just reaching the collar of his equally unkempt layers of robes. The female, on the other hand, had her hazel eyes turned to her counterpart. As the atmosphere in the room subtly shifted, she felt her long flowing chestnut hair—half of which was intricately braided, while the remainder fell in waves to her waist—rising as if under the influence of static electricity.

Suddenly the air felt dry as all the moisture in the room was sucked out to condense at once into two massive architectural structures. The misty manifestations were perfect reproductions of the originals, accurate to the last detail.

The first one represented a massive Renaissance castle bordered by a river. Like all castles of this epoch, the six towers sticking out of the building's outside walls had been placed there for purely esthetic value. The numerous windows placed all around the towers allowed a 270-degree view from each one of the cylindrical structures.

The second fog castle was in stark contrast with the first. In this instance, the thick walls and towers had been designed with protection in mind. Narrow arrow slits stood in place of large windows, and the entire building was surrounded by a wide moat. A medieval castle dating from the Middle Ages.

Eyes darting from the first to the second misty manifestation, the master ceased chanting and addressed his two acolytes in a throaty voice. "The artifacts' fragments are in France. One held by its rightful owners, the faes." He pointed at the Renaissance castle before turning towards the fortified structure. "And another held by the vampires in their winter quarters in Périgord."

"Where's the third fragment, Master? Why wasn't it revealed by the spell?" asked the male warlock in a deferential tone.

"Are you questioning my power, Lotar?"

"Never, Master." The warlock's voice cracked with fear despite his best efforts to control it.

"The spell revealed the presence of all fragments, have no doubt about it. If you can't read the signs, your mind is the only one to blame."

Lotar bowed deeply but remained silent.

"Retrieving the fragments won't be an easy task, but I trust you will be able to handle it, won't you?" The master wasn't talking to either warlock in particular. The task would fall equally on both acolytes who would be forced to collaborate: something they had been growing accustomed to ever since the master had brought them together.

"I know someone who may help us retrieve fragments from both locations. He's a fae, but he has connections among all kinds of beings, including vampires. He's also notorious for his loose moral compass, a definite plus in this instance…"

"I appreciate your confidence, Demetra. Lotar, you'll follow Demetra's lead."

"Yes, Master."

"Demetra, I'd like to meet this fae of yours and decide for myself if he's our man."

"I will travel to France right away and bring him back with me."

Demetra's face lit up as the master nodded his approval. Her eyes closed and her hair danced in the wind a moment before she vanished into thin air.

Left alone in the room with Lotar, the master turned towards the warlock. "Have you figured out the location of the third fragment yet?"

Chapter 1

The fire roared in the earth of Michael's small cabin as he sat on the couch beside Sheila, sipping on a cup of black tea that would have tasted too sweet to anyone else on the planet.

Sheila had come to Yellowstone to spend Christmas with him but now the vacation was over. In a few minutes she would be heading out to catch her plane back to Houston.

This wasn't exactly how Michael had pictured their last day together, though. In his mind they'd been alone and more… naked.

"And do you remember Bill Thomason's face the time I rear-ended his snowmobile on the way to the Boiling River? T'was priceless," said Robert Spencer, crying with laughter from the armchair where he was sitting. The man had been laughing on and off but mostly on for the past two hours, reminiscing about the good old days when he and Michael had worked side by side as park rangers.

"I remember," said Michael, smiling. He hadn't seen Bob since the man's transfer to Denali National Park five years earlier, and he was truly glad for his old partner's visit. He just wished Bob had announced himself a bit earlier instead of calling that morning to tell Michael he was two hours away.

Back in the days, the two of them had been close, or at least as close as Michael got to anyone. A couple of the other rangers had even referred to them as the twins. A stupid joke, since Michael's brown unruly waves and chiseled features were in no way close to Bob's quickly vanishing hairline and chubby face. But like Michael, Bob was a force of nature and was within an inch or two of Michael's 6'4" giant frame. With his three hundred pounds of muscle, Michael had a good seventy pounds on his friend, though.

Sheila smiled politely and even laughed from time to time at the man's quaint sense of humor, but Michael could tell that she, too, would have preferred spending the last day of their vacation without company.

"And where did you manage to find this fine young woman, old boy? I can't believe you got out of the park long enough to meet someone." Bob's eyes were filled with playful sparkle.

"We met in Houston," answered Sheila. "Michael was in town helping the police and I was working on a story for my paper."

"Helping the police? With what?" asked Bob, his big hand reaching for the mug of coffee he'd placed on the floor beside the armchair's foot.

Sheila and Michael glanced at each other.

"An old army buddy of mine called in a favor. He wanted to identify some animal tracks and thought I could help," answered Michael, not wishing to discuss the matter further. Bob was probably one of very few people in the country who hadn't heard about the event on the news.

"I'm sorry, gentlemen, but I'd better get going if I don't want to miss my flight," said Sheila, standing up from the couch. "Aren't you glad I rented my own snowmobile, Michael? Otherwise you would have had to abandon Bob here to give me a ride." Her smirk wasn't lost on Michael.

In winter he usually picked her up in the town of West Yellowstone at the park's west entrance and she rode back with him to the cabin on his snowmobile, but this time the routine had been altered. He'd been busy rescuing a couple of cross-country skiers lost in the wilderness when Sheila had made it to the rendezvous point and after an hour of freezing while waiting for her unreliable boyfriend, she'd decided to rent her own snowmobile and surprise him at the cabin. Visitors couldn't typically enter Yellowstone on a snowmobile without a guide, but being Michael's girlfriend came with some privileges, and Sheila had no difficulties convincing the ranger manning the entrance to let her through.

"It was a pleasure making your acquaintance, Sheila. And if you're ever in Denali, don't be a stranger; I'd be happy to show you around."

Michael tried to picture Sheila in Denali and failed. She was a city girl who only came to Yellowstone because of him. She didn't feel particularly comfortable in the wilderness and since Denali was just as wild as Yellowstone and thrice more remote, Bob had more chances of bumping into her at a Veterans Day parade than in Alaska.

Sheila put on her winter coat, scarf, hat and gloves, grabbed her backpack and headed for the door.

"I'll be right back," Michael told Bob as he followed her out.

The weather was pretty mild for January, but the temperature was still below zero and Michael received no objection when he took Sheila in his arms and gave her a warm bear hug.

"Sorry again about that. If Bob had given me a bit more of a warning, I would have come up with a way for the two of us to spend the day alone."

"Don't worry about it. I'm sure you have more regrets than me," she answered, smiling pointedly. "I'd better get going. Love you, my big Teddy."

Michael ignored the remark and gave her a long kiss before letting her go. Once her snowmobile had disappeared around a bend in the road, he returned inside to find Bob standing, hands stretched towards the fireplace.

"Does she know?" he asked.

"She knows. She's known from the very beginning, before we even started dating."

"And she hasn't run away yet? Then she's a keeper. Good for you! And hot too!"

Michael ignored his friend's last remark. Bob had known about Michael's little secret for nearly ten years—ever since the day when he'd caught Michael effortlessly rolling a boulder that weighed nearly a ton to free the leg of a mountain goat. But Bob had promised to keep his friend's dirty secret to himself, and as far as Michael knew, the man had kept his word.

"I'm not in the neighborhood entirely by accident, Michael. I actually came to tell you something," said Bob, returning to his armchair.

"You have my attention."

"A few months ago, probably eight or nine by now, I was in Denali working a day shift when a tourist struck up a conversation with me. He started talking about all the parks he'd visited and mentioned having a friend working in Yellowstone. Who? I ask. And he tells me, Michael Biörn. I was so surprised I just blurted out that we used to work together. That the two of us were buddies…"

"What was the guy's name?"

"I don't recall his last name. His first name was Willy… or Billy, maybe. I thought nothing of it at the time—the guy looked perfectly harmless—but I thought about it over the months afterward, and the more I thought of it, the more the conversation appeared unnatural. The way he approached me, how quickly we got to reminiscing about you… I think the man played me for a fool. I think he wanted some intel on you."

"Did you give him any?" Michael's voice was friendly.

"No, I swear! At least nothing that matters. I didn't talk to him about anything personal, if you know what I mean. But still I've been feeling uneasy about it ever since and I wanted to tell you in person. I don't know what that guy wanted, but I don't think he was a friend of yours."

"I'm pretty sure you're right, but it's probably no big deal. Don't worry about it. Even if he wishes me harm, you know I can take care of myself." Michael tapped his friend's shoulder amicably, but inside his head, wheels were turning. The guy could have been the private investigator hired by Katia Olveda to dig into Michael's past, in which case there wasn't much to worry about… the threat had been neutralized, but this could also be something else entirely. Something that hadn't hit Michael's radar yet. "Are you staying for supper?"

"Sure, if you have enough for two."

"Don't you worry about that."

They spent the next few hours cooking, eating and retelling each other's stories from the past.

It was nearly ten o'clock by the time Bob finally left the cabin and jumped on his rented snowmobile to return to his hotel. "It was good seeing you, you old fart."

"Same here, Bob. Same here… Drive safe."

The snowmobile roared in the night and Bob was gone.

Michael returned to the cabin thinking about what his friend had told him. He cleared the table, did the dishes and by half past ten he headed for bed.

Sleep didn't come, however. He tossed and turned for an hour before finally getting up. He grabbed a well-worn Agatha Christie novel and headed for the couch. He'd probably end up waking up after falling from the couch in the middle of the night, but he accepted the risk.

Chapter 2

The cloud cover prevented any star- or moonlight from reaching the beach, but the giant bonfire blazing on the sand thirty feet from the water provided plenty of light for the four men and two women sitting on washed-up logs around it. Their laughs resonated on the deserted beach as they drank case after case of beer that had little effect on them. Their bodies metabolized the alcohol so fast that getting drunk represented a daunting task. They'd been trying for two hours and barely looked tipsy—something the men hiding behind the boulders a hundred feet north of their position realized fully.

The Alpha team leader, a man by the name of Ike Brown, checked his watch for the third time in five minutes. Timing was everything; the operation needed to be perfectly synchronized to have a chance of succeeding. He watched the seconds fly by until there were none left: precisely 11 PM. Show time!

He lifted his arm and gave his men the signal they'd all been waiting for. Without a sound they moved through the night, closing in on the bonfire like twelve shadows from hell. This wasn't their first rodeo; they'd been here before and had witnessed firsthand how wrong things could go if they committed the slightest mistake.

Ike knew that the Bravo team was moving in from the south at this very moment, but he found the thought only slightly comforting. The Bravo team wasn't as experienced as his own, and if they couldn't hold their line, one of the marks might manage to escape. That would be a disaster and, as senior officer, Ike would no doubt be blamed for it.

Crawling on sand in full tactical gear while holding assault rifles in front of them wasn't an easy task, but they were well trained and accomplished it with minimal noise. The marks had very sensitive hearing, but Ike counted on the sound of the crashing waves to cover the rustling of sand on their black military fatigues. They covered thirty feet without being detected and then forty, fifty, sixty…

They finally reached the thirty-foot line, a stone's-throw from the six aberrations drinking around the fire. Ike pressed a button on his digital watch and a second later three deflagrations filled the silence of the night. They'd been almost simultaneous, and the only reason he knew there'd been three was because there had been three snipers. The marksmen had all hit their respective targets and three marks were now lying face-down in the sand. But the job wasn't over; the three survivors had jumped to their feet at a speed none of Ike's men could have matched. Ike could still see them, though, and so could his men. They opened fire on the three marks with all they had while the Bravo team ran towards those who'd been hit by the snipers, their machine guns pouring bullets like water from a fire hydrant.

In the dancing light of the flames, Ike saw one of the marks starting to morph and concentrated his fire on that one until it finally stopped moving. Once he was reasonably certain the enemy had been neutralized, he ordered a ceasefire. The detonation from the last bullets echoed for a moment in the dead of night as the men got to their feet and cautiously headed towards the motionless marks lying on the blood-stained beach, their weapons trained on the bullet-riddled bodies. Two looked human enough, but the third was some sort of monster, a hybrid of man and beast no one could have identified. Ike knew what it was, though: a werewolf halfway through his transformation. The six targets had constituted the entire Santa Barbara pack; at least that's what the detailed report he'd read the night before had claimed.

One of the women was starting to twitch and she received a round in the head for good measure. They couldn't take chances with beasts such as these.

While three men kept their guns aimed at a motionless werewolf, a fourth knelt beside it to secure a collar around its neck. Within a minute all three monsters had been equipped with the sophisticated piece of equipment. On the other side of the bonfire, the Bravo team had done the same with the remaining wolves.

When the werewolves came back to life a few minutes later, having expelled the lead from their bodies, they found themselves facing eighteen assault rifles at very close range.

Anger and disgust were clearly visible in the eyes of the beasts, but Ike was unfazed. The monsters no longer represented a significant threat to him or his men.

"You'll notice you were all given a nice collar. High tech, very flashy… It's specially designed to guarantee your complete cooperation." Ike paused a moment for effect.

One of the males started to stand up.

"Sit down, Wolfie, now! Or lose your head…" Ike's tone hadn't been particularly threatening.

"I don't take orders from the likes of you," said the wolf without slowing down. He was fully erect now.

Suddenly his screams tore through the silence of the night as his neck started searing, the smell of burnt flesh accompanying the characteristic sound of meat placed on a grill. His hands went to his throat as the other wolves started crawling towards him. But before they could reach him, his head fell to the ground and his body collapsed beside it.

"These devices will activate automatically if you try to transform into your beastly selves, and we'll activate them for you if you try anything that could be remotely considered threatening," said Ike, pointing towards six of his men waving small remote controls. "I trust the five of you don't need another demonstration?"

He received no answer from the shocked wolves.

"Let's move, people. Bravo team, get these guys to the bus. Alpha team, back to the chopper. The night isn't over yet. We still have a package to pick up and this one's special!"

"What's special about it?" asked one of the men.

"It's a werebear, real tough apparently. He's hiding in a cabin in the heart of Yellowstone, masquerading as a ranger."

Chapter 3

Only sickly rays of light percolated through the grit-coated windows of the cabin, and although the sun shone high in the cloudless Australian sky, from the inside one could have thought night was about to fall on a cloudy day. The witch's body had been discarded, but otherwise the atmosphere of the shack hadn't changed a whole lot in the two days Demetra had been absent. She could still see the glyph on the floor of the main room as neither the master nor Lotar had bothered washing it off.

"So that's your fae…" The master stared at the man Demetra had brought back with her. "I can only feel the barest whiff of magic coming from him. Not very impressive."

"That's because he's a chameleon, Master. He only has one power: turning into anyone he wishes, male or female. His impersonations would fool the mothers of the originals. That's how good he is."

"I know what a chameleon is, child!" The sententious tone had cracked in the air like a whip.

"Forgive my presumption, Master. I meant no offense," said Demetra, falling to one knee, eyes turned to the ground. She could feel Lotar's gaze on her back and hated to show herself so vulnerable in front of him. But their master wasn't a benevolent one, and it was better to appear weak than to provoke a wrath no warlock could withstand.

"Get up, child, and introduce your friend."

Demetra rose and illuminated the man's face with a pointed fingertip. He didn't look like much more than a plump commoner. "This is Seemak. A chameleon attached to the court of Lord Vaalt. Seemak is a trusted servant and has access to nearly the entire estate."

"Do you now, Seemak?" asked the master. "And are you familiar with the object we are interested in?"

"I haven't mentioned the artifact to him, Master. I thought you might want to do it yourself," said Demetra.

The master gave her a look she had a hard time interpreting, something between irritation and pity.

"The artifact Demetra just mentioned is the *Eye of the Phoenix*," said the master.

Demetra saw recognition in the fae's eyes.

"I'm familiar with the artifact," answered the fae, "but it was broken in three pieces and nobody knows where they are. Certainly not in Lord Vaalt's castle, if that's what you believe."

"That's where you're wrong, fae. At least one of the pieces is kept in your castle, I assure you."

The fae proved smart enough to not contradict the master. "And you'd like me to steal it for you, wouldn't you? That's why you brought me here."

"You found a smart one, Demetra." The master's voice was humorless.

"What makes you think I'd betray my own kind, wizard?" asked the fae. He didn't look offended, just curious.

"You think I'm a wizard?" asked the master, amused. "Have you ever seen a wizard ordering warlocks around? Warlocks as powerful as these two?"

"I'm not in the habit of hanging out with wizards, Your Mastery." The fae's mocking tone hadn't been lost on Demetra but before she could decide how to react, Lotar had flung the poor fae against the wall where he remained suspended by the warlock's sheer willpower. For his part, the fae was clawing at his own throat in an attempt to dislodge the invisible fingers constricting it.

"Let him go," ordered the master, and Lotar immediately released the chameleon who collapsed to the ground, gasping for air. "Choose your words carefully, fae, for this is the only warning you will receive. The next time your tongue or behavior betrays the slightest hint of disrespect, I will kill you myself. Do we understand each other?"

Seemak nodded, but anger was clearly visible in his dark eyes.

"Now let me answer your question. You will betray your own kind and steal the artifact fragment from your master for two reasons. Greed is the first one. Faes like gold, don't they? I'll give you more gold than you can spend in a lifetime. More gold than you can carry yourself. And I will give you your first payment right away." The master's fingers snapped, and the lid of a trunk located in a corner of the room popped open, revealing row after row of gold bars, each weighing over two pounds.

"How does twenty of these sound? To get started, of course…"

Demetra quickly calculated the value of the twenty bars to be well over a million dollars.

"You'll get three hundred additional bars for each of the three fragments you will retrieve for me."

The chameleon eyed the master suspiciously but remained silent.

"I'll take that as a yes. Now let me give you the second reason you will accept my offer. A most obvious reason, really. This isn't an offer at all, actually, it's an order. Refuse and you die. Betray me and you die. It's that simple."

The master paused a moment to observe the fae's reaction, but Demetra knew that Seemak's face wasn't likely to betray any emotion. Even his eyes were blank now. The chameleon was in perfect control of his body.

"Now that the financial aspect is settled… Demetra tells me you have friends in the Eastern Covenant. Please do tell how this came to happen. Faes and vampires aren't in the habit of mingling."

In the blink of an eye the fae turned from a stout man in his fifties into a gorgeous six-foot-tall woman displaying overgrown fangs and a total lack of pulse. "Let's just say I have ways to get close to people."

"So your vampire friends don't know you're a fae?" asked the master.

"I wouldn't call them friends. They are more like acquaintances… And no, they don't know what I am. At least most don't. Only one knows my secret, and he knows that it's in his best interest to keep it to himself."

"And where is this acquaintance of yours at the moment?"

"Somewhere in France, I assume. Most of the Eastern Covenant leaves Transylvania during winter. They like to spend the colder months in their stronghold in southwest France."

The master nodded, apparently pleased with the information. Demetra knew why; it corresponded precisely to what the spell had revealed: the castle in France's Périgord region.

The master's eyes captured Seemak's, the fae faltering under the intensity of the stare. "It's time to get closer to your vampire friends, fae.

Because you will need to steal from them as well. And we don't want you to get caught now, do we?"

Chapter 4

The team's Osprey landed in a vast snow-covered meadow ten miles from their target's location. Ike was the first one out of the hybrid troop carrier. He checked his watch while his team jumped out of the aircraft and started unloading the gear required for their mission. His watch display indicated 3:04 AM. The V-22 Osprey had covered the distance from Santa Barbara to Yellowstone in less than three hours. Ike loved the bird whose tiltrotors combined the speed of a turboprop plane with the vertical lift capabilities of a helicopter.

One of his men handed him a pair of cross-country skis and he clipped them onto his specially designed boots. An instant later, the twelve men were sliding over the thick blanket of powder that covered the park. The meadow in which they'd landed had been specially chosen for its uphill position. Aside from a few stretches where they'd need to work to get over the hills, they'd be traveling mostly downhill by design. They couldn't afford to get to their mark in a state of exhaustion; their lives depended on it.

They'd covered nearly half the distance when snow started falling. The flurry only lasted a minute or two and quickly intensified into a full-on snowstorm. Visibility did not exceed ten yards, but equipped with their night-vision goggles, the trained men barely slowed down.

They soon made visual contact with the cabin that was their destination and halted to ascertain the terrain. They'd prepared for this during the afternoon's briefing, but one could only learn so much by staring at a topographic map. The real thing was a different beast entirely, one that deserved to be studied carefully before the assault.

Located two hundred feet from the edge of a heavily wooded area, the one-story structure didn't exceed four hundred square feet, a shack. A tool shed sat twenty feet to its east and constituted the only other building visible in the area. The hotel and campground located at Canyon Village three miles down the road were closed for the season, so the only witnesses to what was about to go down would be the owls and other nocturnal critters on the prowl.

In a hushed voice, Ike went over the plan a final time and the twelve men soon fanned out. Six of them would be watching the house from the outside to prevent any escape through a window, while the other six would be entering the premises.

The thermal-imaging technology incorporated in their goggles showed a single human form inside the cabin. The man—if one could refer to that thing as a man—was lying down on what looked like a couch at the center of the cabin.

The soldier in charge of placing the explosive on the lock checked the door for good measure and found it unlocked. The gods were smiling upon them; stealth was a definite advantage in this kind of situation.

They entered the cabin without a sound, six shadows in the dead of night, and found the man lying on his back, snoring heavily.

Ike pointed his industrial-strength Taser towards the sleeping lump while his men pointed their assault rifles at the monster's head, ready to unload them at the drop of a hat. The two prongs shot out of the gun and made contact with the man's chest, sending 200,000 volts of electricity coursing through his body.

The man looked as if he were having the seizure of a lifetime, his body flailing on the couch like a fish on a river bank, but Ike wasn't concerned for his wellbeing; he knew the beast could take it. When he finally released the button of his Taser, the werebear lay motionless on the couch, as limp as a wet towel, his open eyes pointing at the ceiling.

A collar was immediately placed around the beast's neck before he regained control of his body.

Ike jammed the barrel of his sidearm inside the man's mouth as he knelt at his side. "Good morning, Michael. Sorry to wake you up in such a fashion, but we needed you to be cooperative and we didn't think you'd have come with us if we'd asked nicely."

The man tried to say something, but Ike shoved the gun farther down his throat and the beast went quiet.

"The collar around your neck is a marvel of technology, a portable torch whose temperature exceeds two thousand degrees. Try to change into your bear or misbehave in any other way, and your head will roll off your shoulders faster than you can catch it."

Chapter 5

Seemak walked quietly along the dark underground corridors. To his left and right, the walls had been fashioned of countless human skulls, femurs and tibias piled atop each other to a height exceeding six feet. Paris' catacombs were a little-known tourist attraction. The famous ossuary harbored the human remains of nearly seven million Parisians whose bones had been assembled in true works of art at the end of the eighteenth century as a way to relieve the city's overflowing cemeteries.

Seemak no longer paid any attention to the peculiar artwork, though. He'd been coming to the catacombs for decades and was desensitized to its macabre atmosphere. Although a part of the catacomb was the object of daily guided tours, the part he was currently in wasn't accessible to the public.

Few were the humans in search of thrills who ventured past the section of the morbid maze open to visitors. And those who did often got lost, sometimes for days. Searching for idiots who'd gone missing somewhere in the catacomb's maze was one of the many duties of the Parisian fire department, and one they didn't particularly relish.

The clamor of voices told the chameleon he'd reached his destination. This was his first visit to the catacombs in over a year, but he had the feeling it wouldn't be the last one. He was unlikely to find who he was looking for on his first try...

He saw the light at the end of the tunnel and picked up the pace. He reached the underground tavern a moment later and confirmed it looked exactly the same as it had during his last visit. It wasn't much of a surprise, though; minor variations aside, the underground establishment hadn't changed in over a hundred years. The nymph who ran the joint clearly liked it that way.

If it hadn't been for her emerald skin and her hair made of vines and white irises, the nymph would have looked human enough standing behind her bar between two pillars made of skulls.

The same theme had been applied to the furniture. The bar was an assembly of human humeri. The tables were made of ulna and radius bones. The bar stools were assembled from pelvises and the chairs around the tables were a mixture of tibias and fibulas. Seemak didn't know who had designed the seats, but it was clear he or she had never bothered trying any of them. The bony monstrosities were even more uncomfortable than they looked and, with the exception of a couple of trolls and an ogre, everyone was standing.

Seemak ordered a Pixie Twist—a drink made of mead and a variety of berries that would have been lethal to any human—and went to sit on a particularly pointy chair in an alcove located at one of the tavern's seven corners. Being a chameleon came with some perks. A moment later, Seemak's reshaped bottom was sitting on a chair perfectly suited to his new anatomy.

He scanned the crowd but didn't find who he was looking for. There were three vampires present in the assembly, but none would do.

There was a time when faes, vampires and other werebeings could gather in establishments on the surface, but since Paris had become the tourist capital of the world there wasn't a single bar or club in town where non-humans could gather in peace. Only down in the catacombs, in the belly of the earth, did they feel safe enough to gather without attracting unwanted attention.

Seemak had been there two hours and was on his fourth Pixie Twist when a slender vampire with shoulder-length black hair showed up accompanied by two females, also of the bloodsucking kind. The girls were unknown to the chameleon, but that didn't matter, for once the three sat down, his suspicion was confirmed: the man was indeed Victor. The fae couldn't believe he'd struck gold on his first try.

He let the three vampires order their drinks and only approached them once the trio was sipping on their third Bloody Human, a mixture of human blood and fairy dust that bloodsuckers particularly appreciated.

"Evening, Victor, long time no see..." said Seemak, as he watched the fairy-dust-loaded vampire trying to place him. "Come on, I'm Seemak! How many of these did you have?" He pointed at the vamp's glass.

He finally saw a flicker of recognition in the eyes of the vampire. "Seemak? It's been a long time," said Victor, who was eyeing his two playmates worriedly.

"The next round's on me," announced the fae, heading to the bar.

He came back an instant later with four Bloody Humans. He handed the one free of fairy dust to Victor and gave the two females the glasses containing a triple dose of the good stuff.

Thirty minutes later, the two women were sleeping on a nearby table while Seemak and Victor stood against a wall a few feet away.

"What do you want?" The vamp didn't look particularly pleased to be left alone with the fae.

"I'm calling in my debt, Victor. It's time you repay me for the favor I did you."

"I was starting to think you'd never ask."

"You don't know too many faes, do you?"

"I don't! And that's not due to chance..."

Seemak shook his head, smiling. "Victor, my friend, you owe me and that's all there is to it. The fact you can barely stomach looking at my kind is irrelevant here... Have you ever heard of an artifact called the Eye of the Phoenix?"

Victor gave him a blank stare.

"I guess you haven't... It's a mighty fae heirloom that was drained of its power centuries ago."

"And what's so interesting about it?"

Seemak considered the question an instant before answering it. Like all faes, he was physically incapable of telling a blatant lie, but there were many ways to conceal the truth. In this instance, however, he decided honesty would probably serve him best in the long run. "The Eye of the Phoenix is one of the most powerful magical artifacts ever made. So powerful that the powers that be decided eons ago that it had to be neutralized, for if it fell in the wrong hands, it would spell disaster to the world. They couldn't bring themselves to destroy it, however, so they broke it into three pieces. The three most powerful high faes alive at the time were each given a fragment to protect and they swore an oath never to mend the pieces back together."

"Okay... And why should I care?" asked Victor, feigning boredom.

But his act didn't fool Seemak who'd clearly seen the glimmer in the vampire's eyes when he'd brought up the artifact. "You should care because the Eastern Covenant is in possession of one of the fragments, and you're going to help me steal it from them."

Chapter 6

The sun was slowly rising by the time Michael returned to his cabin after a night spent roaming the woods in his bear form. He paused at the entrance of his driveway and crouched to look at a track that the snow had failed to fully cover. He scanned the surrounding area but found no others. Odd since the indentation looked like it had been left by a cross-country ski. The track had probably been deeper than the others, which was why it was the only one left… the shallower tracks having been completely covered by the overnight snowfall.

He got back to his feet and headed for the cabin's front door, wondering all the while why someone would come to his driveway on skis during the night. The park's staff used snowmobiles most of the time, and they didn't come to visit after 1 AM, which was when he'd finally given up on trying to find sleep and had gone for a stroll in the woods behind the house.

He was twenty feet from the door when he noticed a smell that shouldn't have been there: gun grease. As a park ranger, he had a government-issued sidearm and even a shotgun, but the grease he was smelling wasn't a match for the one he used on his own weapons.

On the look-out, he carefully closed the distance separating him from the door, his suspicions confirmed before he even made it to the porch. The cabin had been visited in his absence. In addition to Bob's and Sheila's scents, he could detect at least nine or ten others, all human and all belonging to strangers. He slowly inhaled through the nose one more time for confirmation and noticed that two of the scents were much stronger than the others. Two of the men were still inside the cabin.

He slowly turned the handle and the door rotated without a sound on its well-greased hinges. The first thing he saw was two pairs of skis propped against the wall and two white assault rifles of a type he'd never seen before lying on the kitchen table. He cautiously crossed the kitchen and entered the living room to find two men in snow-white army fatigues rummaging through his meager belongings.

"If you tell me what you're looking for, maybe I can help you find it," said Michael in a booming voice that startled the two men.

They pivoted towards him and in the same fluid motion unholstered the guns strapped to their chests.

"Who are you?" asked the tallest of the two authoritatively, his gun trained on Michael's heart while his companion was aiming for the head.

"You don't know who I am? That's funny, given that you're in my house… The name is Biörn, Michael Biörn."

He saw incomprehension in the eyes of the tallest one but wasted no time wondering why his name came as a surprise to him. Michael rolled to the ground in a gracious motion just as the two weapons fired in unison. Unfortunately for the thugs, Michael's living room was tiny and his roll brought him straight to the first shooter before the thug had a chance to press the trigger a second time.

As the man lowered his gun towards his enemy's crouched body, Michael ripped it out of his hands, tearing his trigger finger off with it, and hurled the weapon towards the other man standing six feet away. The gun penetrated the man's forehead an instant later, but not before Michael felt the searing burns of two bullets penetrating his chest. One of them reached his heart, but as he collapsed to the ground, he made sure to take down his still screaming nine-fingered enemy along with him. He fell hard onto the thug, effectively pinning him under his weight as Michael's heart stopped beating.

The ranger regained consciousness thirty seconds later as the intruder had just finished extracting himself from under his three hundred pounds.

As always when he returned to the world of the living after a brief excursion to the other, Michael felt disoriented and confused, but he didn't need his peak mental capacities to know that the man in military fatigues crawling on the ground a foot away was bad news. Still lying on the ground, he grabbed the thug by the ankle and pulled. That brought the man right back to him, screaming and kicking.

Michael remained lying down a few seconds longer, regaining his strength while holding onto his enemy. When the man pulled a combat knife from an ankle holster hidden under his pants, Michael decided that rest time was over.

He took the knife out of the man's hand and used it to pin his left shoulder to the wooden floor while placing a gigantic hand on the screamer's mouth to muffle the sound.

"Who are you?" he asked, but the man just kept screaming. "We can do this one of two ways, pal. The hard way or the very hard way, it's your call. Personally, I'll enjoy both." As he finished his sentence, he pulled the knife out of the man's left shoulder and drove it into the right one. But this time no scream came out of the thug's lips; instead, there was the bitter smell of almond. Prussic acid… a poison commonly used by Soviet spies during the Cold War. The man had committed suicide.

Michael struggled with the implications. Why would a man have a vial of prussic acid hidden under a false tooth in the first place? And why would he choose to use it instead of answering a simple question about his identity? There was something very wrong with this picture. Something that stunk to high heavens.

Who were these people? Their equipment and training shouted special forces, but from which country? Michael hadn't noticed any foreign accent, but that didn't mean a whole lot.

What had they been looking for? That question was equally puzzling. It wasn't as if he owned anything worth stealing and he kept no incriminating evidence of any kind in the cabin, so what had they been after?

Now wasn't the time to try and solve the riddle, though. He had a more urgent problem on his hands. What was he going to do with the bodies? He thought about it for an instant and then realized he didn't need to do anything at all. He had killed these men in self-defense while they were robbing his house, and they bore no incriminating marks. At least if one overlooked the gun buried in one of the thugs' face... But Michael was a big guy and he doubted there would be many questions asked about it.

He went to the phone mounted on the kitchen's wall and dialed 911. His beloved boss, Jason Parrish, was the first to arrive on the scene forty-five minutes later.

Chapter 7

The underground detention facility was lost somewhere in the Nevada part of the Mojave Desert, thirty miles from any human activity. Since no road led to it, supplies and prisoners were airlifted into the facility by choppers and aircraft that landed on a runway dissimulated between two rocky precipices.

The werebear they'd picked up at its home in the middle of the night had offered virtually no resistance to Ike and his men, and although the team leader was grateful for the success of the mission, he couldn't help but feel slightly disappointed by the anticlimactic submissiveness of the praeternatural creature.

During his briefing with the director and their agent in the field, Ike had been warned about how formidable of an opponent Michael Biörn would be, and the captain had been ready for a fight worthy of his men, but there'd been no fight. Not the least bit of resistance from the creature. He'd even stooped as low as claiming they had the wrong guy before being sedated for transportation purposes.

An unbreakable six inches of bulletproof Plexiglas stood between him and Biörn who was seated on an aluminum chair much too small for him in the middle of an interview room whose reinforced concrete walls were lined with an inch of steel. The prisoners' wrists and ankles were secured to the concrete table in front of him by shackles thick enough to restrain a rabid Tyrannosaurus rex.

They'd been forced to give him an extra dose of neutralizer to reverse the effect of the sedative and Biörn displayed the haunted expression of a man waking up in an asylum with no recollection of how he'd gotten there.

"So that's our werebear?" asked the voice of the director.

"It is, Ma'am," answered Ike, turning towards the screen on the wall where an attractive brunette in her late forties sat behind a massive desk in an austere room apparently void of windows. He'd never met the director in person and received all his orders by secured email channels or through video conferences like this one. He didn't even know where the director's office was located. He imagined it to be in a forgotten hallway of the Pentagon, but it might as well have been in the White House or on the moon for all he knew.

His men were recruited from among the best the US armed forces had to offer, but he wasn't even certain whether his boss was a civilian or in the military, and he sure had no idea whom she answered to. He'd never seen her in a uniform, but that meant nothing. It could be a cover.

"Did he give you much trouble?" she asked.

"Not the slightest. Probably the easiest pick-up we ever did."

The director looked surprised. "Remain vigilant, Captain. Take no chances with this one. His rap sheet is quite impressive. Did you find anything useful inside the house? Anything we could use to track down more of his kind?"

"Not yet, but I left two of my men behind to conduct a thorough search."

On the other side of the Plexiglas, a man entered the interview room through a two-inch-thick steel door and sat down on the side of the table opposite the prisoner. He waved a remote control in front of the creature's eyes, while being careful to remain out of reach. "Remember this?"

The prisoner nodded and the man continued. "Then you know what happens if I press on the button... Good! I'm glad we understand each other. Now I'm going to ask you a few questions and you're going to answer them."

The prisoner nodded again.

"Name?"

"Robert Spencer."

The interrogator looked up, his finger hovering over the remote control threateningly. "You don't want to fuck with me, Biörn! You wouldn't be the first aberration of nature to lose his head on his first day in this joint."

"I'm not Michael Biörn, I'm telling you. I tried telling your colleagues back at the cabin. My name's Robert Spencer. I'm a US Park Ranger at Denali National Park in Alaska. I was just visiting Michael yesterday when you kidnapped me."

The fear was obvious in the man's voice, and his story rang disturbingly true.

"Quit lying, asshole! Our intel confirmed Biörn was alone in his cabin last night."

"He was for a while. But then my snowmobile died on me and I was forced to hike back to his cabin for shelter. I made it back there a bit after one in the morning, but Michael was nowhere around so I crashed on his couch and fell asleep. And then your friends came in."

Ike was starting to feel uneasy. Was it possible? Had they really arrested the wrong man?

"Get Parrish on the phone now!" ordered the director.

Ike grabbed his phone and dialed Jason Parrish's number. "No answer, Ma'am."

The director was maintaining her composure but her blazing eyes betrayed how pissed off she truly was. "You say he offered no resistance when you picked him up, Captain?"

"Not the slightest."

Ike's phone rang at that instant and he saw Jason Parrish's name appear on the caller ID. "Jason!"

"Who the hell did you arrest last night?" barked Parrish.

"What do you mean?"

"I just came from Biörn's house. Not only did I see him there, but the cops are on their way to put your two colleagues in body bags. He killed both of them, Ike! I warned you the man was dangerous, didn't I?"

"You also told me he was alone at home last night!" said Ike, before ending the call. "It would seem we made a mistake, Ma'am."

"It would indeed." The director punctuated her statement with a heavy sigh.

"What will you have us do? Should we release the prisoner right away?"

"Certainly not! Tell the warden to put him in a cell alone, away from the other degenerates, and lose the key for now. We have a mess to clean up, Captain."

"But, Ma'am, the man's innocent. He's done nothing wrong."

"Then you shouldn't have kidnapped him in the middle of the night. Now it's done, deal with it. Understood?"

"Yes, Ma'am."

The screen on the wall turned black and Captain Ike Brown found himself staring at the man on the other side of the Plexiglas. A terrified man sitting in a chair that had never been meant for him. Ike didn't like it one bit.

Chapter 8

Seemak and Victor's second meeting in less than twenty-four hours took place in the Bois de Boulogne, a forest west of Paris frequented by joggers and dog-lovers during the day and all kind of sexually-driven visitors at night.

Seemak had been surprised to hear from Victor so soon, especially since vampires typically rested during the day, but he hadn't been shocked. The offer he'd made the vamp was hard to turn down.

"I take you have news for me, my friend?" said Seemak in a honeyed voice.

"I do. I was able to locate the fragment."

"That's a good first step. And have you considered my offer? Are you going to steal it for me?"

"I have and I will. But it won't be easy and it will cost you much more than the erasing of my debt, *friend*."

Seemak made a show of considering the question for a moment, but in reality his mind was already made up. He'd fully expected Victor's counteroffer and had even counted on it. It was all part of the plan. "Very well. What else do you want from me?"

"If this artifact is so powerful, I want in on the action. We can share its power together. One day you, and one day me... What do you say?"

The vampire knew that Seemak couldn't lie and the fae was forced to agree to his terms. A binding agreement, but one Seemak had cautiously crafted ahead of time. "I, Seemak, agree with your terms and solemnly swear to release you of your debt towards me and share the power of the artifact with you in exchange for your assistance in retrieving all its fragments. This contract between us will hold true for as long as we both shall live."

The vampire appeared satisfied with Seemak's little speech. Vamps were so gullible. Seemak had no intention of breaking his vow, but he fully intended on getting rid of Victor as soon as the artifact was in their possession, thereby releasing himself from his obligation. Armed with the powers of the most powerful of all faes, not even the master and his warlock would be able to stop him. He would go back to Australia, kill them all, and then help himself to their gold. "So where is that fragment you located?"

Victor's thin lips twisted in a smile as he answered, "In Lord Zamfir's private vault."

Seemak was all too familiar with the name. Vulpe Zamfir was the leader of the Eastern Covenant. Probably the oldest and most powerful vampire alive. The fact he was the owner of one of the fragments was therefore not surprising, but retrieving the object wasn't going to be easy. "I imagine getting into Zamfir's vault will present a challenge."

"It will indeed, but it's nothing I can't handle. I have a plan, trust me."

Trusting the vampire was the last thing the chameleon was willing to do, but he kept the remark to himself. He simply needed to outsmart and double-cross Victor before the bloodsucker stabbed him in the back himself. Fortunately, Seemak's deception skills were significantly above average.

But before he could dispose of the vampire, he needed to answer one key question. Where was the third fragment hiding?

Chapter 9

The shadow moved stealthily along the hallways of the medieval castle. The vampires should all be sleeping in the middle of the day, but the enthralled werewolves and other creatures they used as guardians of their slumber would be patrolling both the grounds and inside the castle. The dark shape heard the sound of claws scratching against the stone floor and immediately sidestepped into an alcove. Two large wolves walked past the alcove a minute later but neither noticed the shadow hanging from the ceiling.

The shadow jumped back down to the floor, its shoes hitting the stones without making a sound, and continued its progression towards the objective. It reached its destination three minutes later after dodging a werecougar and two human slaves. The door was unlocked, and the shadow silently slipped inside Vulpe Zamfir's private quarters.

The medieval room was wrapped in darkness, but the residual light filtering through the curtains covering the small window looking onto the inside courtyard was more than enough. The shadow clearly distinguished every piece of furniture, the paintings on the walls, the rugs on the cold floor and each book in the massive library that covered an entire wall of the apartment.

A fireplace was stacked with logs and kindling, ready to be lit by the human slave assigned to the task, but this wouldn't happen for another two hours. The fire was to be lit thirty minutes before dusk, so that the room would be nice and warm by the time Lord Zamfir woke up.

At that thought, the shadow's eyes involuntarily went to the stone sarcophagus located at the center of the room. Underneath the three-inch-thick granite slab lay the ruler of the Eastern Covenant. Probably the most powerful member of his species, not only in influence and authority but in strength, too.

The shadow walked to the five-foot-tall family painting on the wall and pulled on the bottom left corner. The painting pivoted noiselessly on its hinges to reveal a large electronic safe. Without a pause, the shadow entered the eight-digit combination, and the safe sprang open.

Inside were four shelves covered with various papers, gold and objects of no interest to the thief who'd come for one thing and one thing only. The shadow found the coveted artifact in a small box lined with silk. A smooth, polished stone in the shape of a crescent moon extending into a semi-ellipse. It was entirely transparent, and its orange color was reminiscent of citrine. But citrine it was not. This small fragment of rock was worth a thousand times its weight in diamonds, probably even more.

The shadow pocketed the stone before closing the safe and returning the painting to its original position. It was about to exit the room when the door swung open and a female slave appeared in the frame.

"My apologies, I didn't know anyone was awake I was just com—" Before the poor woman could finish her sentence, the shadow struck her in the chest and she collapsed to the ground. Her head split open as it hit the stone floor and blood started oozing out of it, but the shadow didn't pay it the slightest attention. It stepped over the motionless body and exited the room without a second thought.

Chapter 10

Lucy's foot moved towards Irini's head at a speed far exceeding what a human could have seen coming, but the elder blocked it effortlessly. Lucy was progressing fast, but she was still years away from beating Irini. The two moved so fast it would have been hard for a human eye to distinguish which limb belonged to whom were it not for Lucy's ivory skin and red hair contrasting with Irini's copper complexion and raven-black mane.

The freshly turned vampire retreated before the avalanche of kicks and punches that her teacher unleashed on her until finally she found herself backed up against one of the courtyard's walls, pleading for mercy. Irini withheld her last blow and helped her apprentice up. Although the sun wouldn't rise for another few hours, the two women were the only vampires training inside the castle's courtyard.

Unlike the other vampires of the Covenant, they could have trained in broad daylight without fearing for their lives, but this was a little secret they kept to themselves. As far as Irini knew, the two of them were the only vampires alive immune to UV light, and this for a good reason. They weren't true vampires but vampire hybrids. Lucy was a wolf hybrid thanks to the bite of her sister Olivia, while Irini was a bear hybrid courtesy of Michael Biörn's fangs.

"Why did I beat you this time?" asked Irini.

"Same as always, you're too fast for me. You're unbeatable."

"Wrong! My speed isn't the answer. If I fought like you, you'd be able to beat me without increasing the celerity of your attacks. So let me ask you again, why did I beat you?"

Lucy considered the question a moment before shaking her head and shrugging her shoulders. "I don't know."

"I beat you because you don't anticipate your opponent's move. You only react and that's a lost cause. When by a miracle you anticipate an attack, you usually do a decent job of blocking or dodging it, but in most instances you don't start moving until my fist is already on its way and by then it's much too late."

Lucy looked defeated. Another teacher might have said something encouraging to her pupil, but that wasn't Irini's way. "You'd better start practicing this skill, girl, because I'm done holding back against you. You've had six months to adjust to your vampire condition. That's plenty! No more excuses!"

Deep inside, Irini was proud of her pupil, very proud even. Lucy was quite possibly the best student she'd ever had. She was well on her way to master thralls, was making significant progress in her swordsmanship and firearm training, and could already defeat most vampires who didn't have a century and a half on her.

Irini saw Cristos Kaczka march into the courtyard accompanied by three of his men and immediately knew something wasn't right. Cristos was head of security for the Eastern Covenant and older than Irini herself.

"Vulpe wants to see your protégée, Irini."

"What about?" asked Lucy, but Cristos ignored the question and nodded to his men.

Two of them placed themselves on either side of Lucy and grabbed her by the arms.

"What's this about?" said Irini, placing herself between Lucy and Cristos.

"A most unpleasant affair, Irini. You can come along but Lucy must come with us."

Wheels were spinning at full speed in Irini's head. What in heaven was going on? Vulpe had never talked to Lucy. Not even on the day Irini had introduced her to him a few days after she'd brought Lucy back with her to their Transylvanian stronghold, the historical castle where the Covenant's elders spent the summer. Something was very wrong indeed; Cristos' attitude didn't bode well.

"Go with them, Lucy," said Irini, as if the poor girl had a choice... "I'm coming with you."

Lucy, Irini and their escorts entered the castle's reception hall to find it occupied by a dozen elders and a couple of slaves waiting upon them. Irini recognized all the faces but she doubted Lucy would. Her pupil would no doubt identify Vulpe's wife Milena and his brother Vladislav who were seated at either end of a large settee in the middle of the room. But as far as Irini could recall, she'd never met the beautiful Anastasia, Vladislav's bitch of a wife who stood with her back to the flames dancing inside the room's massive fireplace. The two sisters-in-law's personalities were as different as their looks. With her distinctive hip-length jet-black hair, Milena was reminiscent of a blue-eyed Mortitia Adams, a stark contrast with the blonde Anastasia whose angelic face hid a ghastly temper.

In addition to the Zamfir clan, a half dozen elders could be found sitting on various couches and armchairs nearing the center of the room where Vulpe stood staring at the newcomer.

With his deep-set eyes and hollowed cheeks, the leader of the Eastern Covenant was intimidating on the best of days, and today wasn't a good day. Draped in a black silk robe with two lions—the Zamfir family coat of arms—embroidered in gold thread on the breast pocket, his eyes were trained on Lucy. Irini suspected he'd been pacing the room a moment earlier but he stood perfectly still now.

"What's going on, my liege?" asked Irini, her tone deferential.

"Why don't you ask that question of your protégée? She's in a better position to answer it than I am." Vulpe sounded calm, but Irini wasn't fooled. The ruler simmered with anger and could blow at any instant. Whatever Lucy had done, she'd better have a good excuse for it, or her life would be forfeited.

"I am sorry, my liege, I don't understand. You seem angry with me but I have no idea how I've offended you," stammered Lucy.

The ruler took a few steps towards her and the two men who were holding Lucy thrust her forward to meet the elder. Irini was relieved to see Lucy get down on one knee and bow her head in deference.

"Where is it? Where did you hide it?" asked Vulpe.

"Where did I hide what, my liege?" Lucy's voice sounded strained. She was terrified, and for good reason.

Vulpe bent down and grabbed her by the throat before lifting her a foot off the ground so that her eyes were at the same level than his. "The jewel you stole from me, child. And do not lie, I know it was you."

"I stole nothing from you, my liege." Lucy was struggling to keep her panic at bay.

"My liege, if I may say a word," started Irini, but she stopped when Vulpe turned his gaze towards her. "What is it you have to say, Irini? And I suggest you choose your words carefully before you speak!"

"I spent most of the night training with Lucy, my liege. If the robbery took place in the past few hours, I can assure you that she cannot be the one behind it."

"The jewel was taken in the middle of the day. And I assure you, she *is* the one responsible," he said, returning his gaze to Lucy who still hung in the air at the end of his arm.

It was a good thing vampires didn't need to breathe or the poor girl would have died by asphyxiation by now.

"Why are you so convinced Lucy's the one who took your precious jewel, brother?" The question had come from Vladislav and took everyone by surprise, not least his wife who darted him a venomous glance from across the room. Vladislav was the Eastern Covenant's third-in-command after Vulpe and Milena. A nice enough man, or at least less temperamental than his brother, but not someone one would expect to intercede on the behalf of a freshly turned novice.

"Because I saw her, brother."

"You saw me stealing from you?" Lucy's voice was deformed by the ruler's fingers pressing on her vocal cords, but bewilderment remained clearly perceivable in it.

"I suppose it would be more accurate to say that my slave saw you, but she was kind enough to share the memory of your encounter before she died. In your haste to exit my apartments you forgot to make sure she was dead. You didn't even take the time to drink her blood... By the time I woke up half of it had seeped through the floor—what a waste."

"And there can be no mistake, you are positive the woman you saw in your slave's memory was Lucy?" asked Vladislav.

This time the sigh of his wife was loud enough to fill the room, but

Irini ignored the woman. She was thinking about the slave's wasted blood. This was damning evidence against Lucy. Very few vampires possessed enough control to resist drinking blood oozing from a human, but Lucy was one of them. Lucy and Irini didn't require blood to live, they could feed off the menu of their werebeings' moiety and be perfectly satisfied with it. A good steak could keep Lucy going for a day, two if times were dire. Fortunately for Irini's pupil, the rest of the Covenant didn't know that.

"There are only two redheads in this castle, Vladislav, and I assure you I wouldn't mistake Peter for this ungrateful child," said Vulpe, throwing Lucy against the wall thirty feet away.

The impact made a dull sound but left no mark on the stones. Lucy landed on her feet, her terrified eyes darting in Irini's direction. She shook her head at Irini as if to say it wasn't her, that she hadn't done it, but at the same moment one of Cristos' men entered the room at a hurried pace.

"We found it," he said as he placed a crescent-shaped orange jewel in Vulpe's hand.

"Where?" asked Vulpe.

The man pointed at Lucy. "It was hidden among her belongings, in the crypt she shares with the other novices."

Vulpe turned towards Lucy. "What do you have to say in your defense?"

"I'm being set up. I swear I've never seen this artifact before."

"And yet, you know it's an artifact…"

Irini felt a knot in her throat as Vulpe turned his back on Lucy and walked towards the door. She'd known him long enough to guess what was coming.

The ruling fell as he exited the room. "I hereby sentence you to death. The sentence will be carried out at dawn."

Chapter 11

Patrolling the northern part of Yellowstone, the only section open to traffic during winter, Michael was pondering the mystery of the two thugs who'd been ransacking his cabin when he heard the call coming over the radio.

"Unit 9 to dispatch."

"Go ahead, Unit 9."

"I found an abandoned snowmobile four miles from Canyon on the road to Norris. It looked like it was heading west. I tried to start the engine, but it's dead. No trace of the owner either. Can you run the license plate?"

"10-4 Unit 9, read me the number," answered the dispatcher.

The ranger provided the requested information and the radio went silent for a while as the dispatcher looked for the bike's owner in the database. The park rangers' patrol cars were equipped with the same computers as other police cruisers, and during the summer months a ranger could access this type of information directly, but the snowmobiles they used in winter weren't equipped with the same technology.

"It's a rental. The sled's registered to Winter Sports Extravaganza in West Yellowstone," announced the dispatcher.

Michael sighed when he heard the news. This was precisely the answer he'd been dreading. Both Sheila and Bob had rented their snowmobiles in West Yellowstone, and since the bike had been found three and a half miles from his cabin, heading west, the chances it didn't belong to one of them were slim.

The dispatcher's voice came back through the radio a moment later. "I called the business. They say the bike was rented yesterday by a Robert Spencer."

"The name rings a bell," answered Unit 9.

"Chad, this is Unit 2," chimed in Michael. "Bob Spencer used to work with us before transferring to Denali. He came to visit me yesterday and left my cabin late last night. We need to call in search and rescue."

After spending the morning answering his boss's questions regarding the two men he'd killed in his cabin, Michael had spent most of the afternoon wading through several feet of snow searching for Bob. A dozen rangers had joined the search efforts, but they'd found absolutely nothing. It was pretty clear the sled had died on Bob on his way back to West Yellowstone, but what had happened to him after that was a mystery.

Unless Bob had grossly miscalculated the amount of ground the snowmobile had covered, he should have been heading back to Michael's cabin as soon as he'd realized he wouldn't be able to restart the bike. Which begged the question, had something happened to him on the way or had he managed to reach the cabin while Michael was out on his night stroll?

Yellowstone was a beautiful but dangerous place, especially in winter. A man could easily go into hypothermia in this weather if he weren't prepared, but Bob was a ranger himself and was perfectly familiar with the park's climate. He *would* have been prepared for something like that. There was always the possibility of a mountain lion getting to him, but it was unlikely. A lion would have to be positively starving to attack someone as big as Bob. A grizzly would have made a better culprit, but once again the odds were against such a scenario. The park's bears were hibernating in January and seldom got out of their dens in search of a snack, although it did happen.

It was more likely that Bob had managed to return to the cabin and had been attacked there. In addition to the two jerks he'd dispatched, Michael had clearly identified the odor of at least eight or nine more.

Why hadn't he found them in the cabin along with the other two? Maybe because they'd been escorting Bob somewhere after kidnapping him...

This was the most likely explanation, and the one with the best odds of finding Bob alive. Because one thing was certain, if Bob had disappeared on his way back to the cabin, he was dead by now.

Michael finally got back home around half past seven and had a quick bite while waiting for his visitors. He didn't have to wait long; they showed up at 8 PM on the dot.

He went to the door and let in Olivia, Daka, and three of the skinwalker's packmates.

"I brought some help," said Olivia as she sat down on the bench at the kitchen table. "Who are we looking for?"

Michael related the events of his day starting with his morning battle against the two intruders and ending with the unsuccessful search for Bob.

"And you're telling me that Jason Parish wants to handle the case himself?" asked Daka, referring to the home invasion that had cost the lives of the two invaders.

"I told him to call in the FBI, but he's reluctant. He says it's obviously a case of self-defense, and that for my own peace of mind we're better off letting it go."

"And what do you think?" sked Olivia.

"I would tend to agree. I'm not usually looking forward to interacting with the Feds, they tend to be much too nosy for my taste..."

"But?" asked Olivia who knew him far too well.

"But without their involvement, it will be hard to figure out who these two were and what they were doing here. And if their friends are detaining Bob, it may not hurt to have some help figuring out where they're keeping him."

"Did you tell that to Jason?" asked Olivia.

"Not in so many words, but yes. Whoever these assholes were, they're pros. They had top-of-the-line equipment and were well trained, too."

"And you have no idea what they were looking for?" said Daka.

"Not the slightest. I don't have anything that could be of interest to anyone. Nothing valuable either."

"And you think they have Bob?" asked Olivia.

"I hope so, but I want us to spend the night going through the area where he disappeared to see if we can find something. I couldn't morph this afternoon during the search with my colleagues and that drove me nuts. We need to get back out there and use our animal noses this time."

"But why would anyone want to capture Bob? And how did they know to find him here?" said Olivia.

This was a very good question and one Michael hadn't found a satisfying answer to. Why would they come on skis to the middle of the park at night to kidnap Bob? What had he managed to get himself into?

But suddenly the answer appeared in front of Michael's eyes, painful in its obviousness. They hadn't come to his cabin to pick up his friend. They'd come for him…

Chapter 12

Michael was asleep in bed when he woke to the sound of his cell phone ringing. He opened an eye to check the alarm clock: 5:42 AM. He'd roamed the woods in his bear form until late in the night and had barely gotten two hours of sleep.

With the help of Olivia, Daka, and the Shoshone's packmates, they'd covered quite a bit of ground. They'd found no trace of Bob, but Michael saw that as good news. It meant his friend might still be alive.

He got out of bed and fished the phone out of the pants he'd discarded on the bedroom floor before slipping into bed.

He was more than surprised when he saw Wawetseka's name appear on the screen. They hadn't talked in six months, not since Wawetseka—or Irini as she called herself now—had taken Lucy under her wing and the two of them had shipped out to Transylvania to introduce Lucy to the Eastern Covenant. What did she want with him this early in the morning?

"Hello?"

"Michael, it's Irini. I have some bad news."

What a surprise… People seldom called him at 5 AM with good news. "What's going on, Irini?" He had to make an effort to pronounce the vampire's adopted name: a name he despised more than any other.

"Lucy needs your help." The vampire sounded relatively calm, but Michael perceived the underlying worry in her voice. This was serious.

"What happened?"

"She was accused of stealing some kind of valuable artifact from Vulpe's safe and now she's been sentenced to death."

Serious didn't even start to describe the situation. "Are you joking? When will the sentence be carried out?"

"In a week from yesterday. She was supposed to die last night, but I managed to convince Vulpe to give me a week to prove her innocence. In six days, I'll need to present convincing evidence in front of the elders' council or she'll die."

"Did you find anything?"

"I'm afraid there is no proof to be found, Michael. I've spent most of the past twenty-four hours looking for something to exonerate her, but I've found absolutely nothing. Lucy claims to be innocent, but I'm not so sure. I think she might actually be guilty."

"Tell me what happened exactly."

The vampire recounted in detail everything that had taken place from the time Cristos and his men had come to pick up Lucy until a few minutes ago when Irini had finally given up on saving her pupil on her own and called Michael for help.

"And you say she's locked up in the castle's dungeon? Isn't there a way for her to escape?" asked Michael.

"The cell she's in was designed to detain creatures much stronger than Lucy. I'm not sure even you could bust out of it, Michael."

"How do you want me to help? Say the word and I'll be on the next flight to Transylvania."

"It's nice of you to offer, but we're in southern France right now. In the Covenant's summer quarters. A good thing because it will save you some time getting here. Vulpe gave me carte blanche for my investigation so I can bring you in as a law enforcement expert for a detailed analysis of the crime scene."

"I'm not a crime scene investigator, Irini."

"Who cares? Once you're inside the castle you can do your thing and look for clues. And if that doesn't work you can always do your other thing… kick some butts and break Lucy out of jail."

Irini's last statement comforted Michael in the belief that a large part of Wawetseka remained alive inside the tough shell the vampire flaunted to the world. She was taking a very big risk by bringing him in. If push came to shove and Michael had to resort to force against the Eastern Covenant, it didn't matter whether he succeeded in freeing Lucy or not… Irini would be held responsible regardless, and Vulpe Zamfir would have her head for it.

Chapter 13

Michael was finishing packing his backpack when his cellphone rang. "Hey, did you manage to get me a spot on the first flight to Paris?" he asked.

"It's already too late for today, but I got you a flight tomorrow, leaving from Bozeman early in the morning. You have a connection in Minneapolis and then it's direct to Paris where I reserved a car for you. It will still be a five-hour drive from there to the region you mentioned, though," replied Sheila.

"Thanks, Sheila, I owe you one. But please cancel the rental, Irini will pick me up at the airport."

"You don't owe me anything, Michael. I just wish you'd let me come with you, that's all."

"I wish I could, but it's going to be much too dangerous. This isn't a vacation."

"Because vacations with you are so relaxing…" she answered, clearly referring to their St Lucia trip where she'd been attacked by a werecougar.

"Anyway, I've got to go but I'll call you from Paris when I get there."

He knew Sheila wasn't duped but he didn't want to debate the matter with her.

"Alright, I'll let you go. Take care of yourself. I love you, Michael Biörn." She ended the call before Michael had a chance to respond. Apparently she'd decided to spare him the agony of having to say it back to her over the phone, and he loved her all the more for it.

Olivia arrived at his cabin a few minutes later as he was preparing himself a sandwich large enough to choke a rhino.

"What are you doing here?" he asked, immediately worrying that she had heard about her sister's fate. But his fear was unfounded; Olivia was simply here for a courtesy visit.

"Vivian from dispatch asked me to cover her shift this afternoon, and since I had a couple hours to kill until then, I thought I'd come and check on you. Did you manage to get some sleep?"

After her summer internship, Olivia had been hired by the park on a one-year contract for a position with a job description vague enough to cover just about every possible odd task under the sun.

"Not a whole lot," answered Michael. "I've decided to investigate Bob's disappearance more thoroughly and I'll be flying to Europe tomorrow."

"Europe? You think he's in Europe?"

Michael really had no clue where his friend might be, but he doubted he was anywhere close to Europe. However, he had no intention of telling Olivia he was actually going to free her sister. She'd demand to accompany him, and the last thing he needed was to have to worry about Olivia on top of rescuing Lucy. "Something about those guys' accents reminded me of Eastern Europe," he lied. "I need you to break the news to Jason whenever he finally notices I'm gone. Tell him I took Sheila on a week-long vacation to France if he asks."

"He's going to be pissed again."

Michael shook his head and sighed. "My heart bleeds for him."

"I can tell! It's pretty obvious... Anything else you'd have me do?"

"I don't want to burden you with this but if you don't mind keeping an eye open for any sign of Bob while I'm gone... I'm not asking you to spend your days searching the park for him, but if you hear anything about the investigation on the two jackasses I found in my cabin, let me know."

Olivia had been gone for an hour and Michael was taking a cat nap when he heard a knock on the door. Before he could even get to it, the door flew open and Ezekiel stepped inside. He slammed the door shut and took a few steps towards the kitchen before shaking vigorously in a manner that reminded Michael of a wet dog. The snow blanket he'd dragged in fell to the floor to reveal his eternal gray cloak and the pointy hat which, according to him, was a perfect disguise meant to fool humans.

When Michael had asked how dressing like a wizard straight out of a Walt Disney cartoon was supposed to help him blend in among humans, Ezekiel's answer had actually surprised him by its implacable truth: *"When humans see someone walking around dressed like me, the fact he might be a wizard never crosses their mind, they just assume I'm a lunatic… Perfect cover!"*

"Ez! To what do I owe the pleasure?"

The wizard gave him an irritated look and went to the stove where he started boiling water. "You can imagine, Michael Biörn, that if I come and visit you in this wonderful, godforsaken retreat of yours in the middle of winter it's not for pleasure!"

"I see. You came to discuss semantics…"

The wizard sat down at the kitchen table and invited his host to do the same. "I came to warn you to watch out for yourself and those misfit girls of yours, Michael."

"I assume you're referring to Olivia and Lucy?"

"Olivia, at least," answered the wizard who still had a hard time with the fact Michael was on friendly terms with a vampire. "You need to keep your eyes and ears open, my friend. A storm is brewing out there and it worries me down to my old bones."

"What in heaven are you talking about? You're even more cryptic than usual."

"That's because I don't understand it myself. I've never experienced such a thing in all the millennia I've roamed this earth. There is a disturbance in the magical field and I have no idea what it means."

"A disturbance in the magical field?" repeated Michael, uncomprehendingly.

"It's nearly impossible to explain to someone like you who possesses no magic. You don't know how it feels… But a witch, wizard or any other kind of creature with magical powers can perceive the energy surrounding them and tap into it. That's how I can tell when I'm in the presence of another magical being, for instance—it impacts the magical field. The more powerful the being, the greater the distortion of the field."

"And the field is distorted right now but you don't know why?"

"Exactly! It's distorted, but it shouldn't be. For a wizard to perceive the distortion someone like me exercises on the magical field, he would need to be relatively close, say within a few miles. A powerful wizard such as Tabitha or Methuselah could sense the distortion due to my presence from a few hundred miles away, but no more."

"Maybe whoever's responsible for the distortion is both a powerful magician and located within a few hundred miles, which is why you can sense him…" offered Michael.

"I can sense High King Dariel from here, Michael. The impact of the elvish ruler on the magical field is significant but still small in comparison to the distortion I'm talking about. Worse, I can sense this change in the field wherever I am located. From the tip of Patagonia to the frozen steps of Alaska, all the way to Eastern Europe. I can sense it nearly equally across the entire territory I oversee. It just doesn't make sense. There are no magical beings powerful enough to exercise such influence."

"I hope you didn't come to me for an answer because I really have nothing to offer."

"As I told you before, I only came to warn you to be on your guard, Michael."

"Why should I be on my guard?"

"Because that's not the whole story. There have been a number of werebeings suddenly vanishing over the past month and nobody seems to know where they've gone."

"What kind of weres?"

"A mountain lion in the southern Rockies, a couple of eagles in Alberta, but mostly wolves. At least thirty wolves have gone missing across the country in the past thirty days. And that includes four entire packs!"

"What could be getting to them? You think it has something to do with the disturbance in that magical field of yours?"

"It's more than likely, but I don't know how. Whatever is getting to these beasts, I'd hate for you to be next on that list."

"I find your concern touching, old friend. I mean it." Michael couldn't help but grin.

Ezekiel replied by shaking his head, sighing and raising his eyes at the same time.

Michael got up to fetch the water that had been boiling on the stove for a good minute and poured it into a teapot. "Since you're here, I have a question for you. What do you know about an artifact called the Eye of the Phoenix?"

"Why do you ask?" Ezekiel looked both perplexed and concerned.

Michael explained how Lucy was being accused of stealing a piece of it from Vulpe Zamfir, and how he was flying to France to try and get her out of her lethal predicament. Ez listened attentively until Michael finally concluded his retelling of the events.

"The Eye of the Phoenix is one of the most powerful magical artifacts ever created." Ez proceeded by telling Michael the story of the artifact and how it had been broken into three pieces to neutralize its power.

"And where are these three pieces?" asked Michael, pouring tea into two mugs and placing one in front of Ez.

"The exact location of two of the three fragments was unknown until now. But if your information is correct, it would seem Vulpe possesses one of the missing pieces. But that still doesn't tell us where the last piece might be."

"You said two of the fragments had been misplaced, but where is the third one?"

"The last time I checked, Lord Vaalt, the ruler of the faes on the entire European continent, is in possession of one of the fragments. But since I killed his son six months ago, I'm not in a position to go and ask him if he still has it!"

"You killed his son?" Michael heard the reproach in his own voice as he asked the question.

"To save your ass, youngster. Vaalt's son was the leader of the Fida'I organization that tried to kill you last year."

"Oh, I see…" Michael felt sheepish, not something he was used to. "And what does it do exactly… this artifact?"

"Finally, a question worth answering… The bearer of this artifact, my young friend, can use the powers of whichever fae he likes whenever he wants."

"Whichever fae?"

"That's what I said, which word are you struggling with? Would you like me to get you a dictionary for Christmas?"

Michael ignored the sarcasm. "So if I had the artifact in my possession and wanted to transform like a chameleon, I could?"

"Yep! You could also have the strength of a troll, the magical power of a high fae, and so forth and so on."

"But that would require having the three fragments, correct? If one only had one or two of the three, nothing would happen?"

"That was the intent when the artifact was broken, but it holds such power than two of the three will still give someone access to quite a bit of magic."

"How much exactly?" asked Michael, who thought the information might come handy during his trip.

"If you had two thirds of the artifact, you'd be able to use the power of any fae within your immediate vicinity, say a hundred feet or so."

Michael pondered his friend's statement for a moment. Why would Lucy want to possess this kind of power? He'd never thought of the young woman as the power-hungry kind, but he hadn't known her very well to start with and had no idea what turning into a vampire might have done to the poor thing's psyche.

How had she even learned about the artifact when he, a werebear who'd been around for a thousand years, had never even heard of it until today?

Chapter 14

Michael was running through the Minneapolis–Saint Paul International Airport, his backpack bouncing around on his shoulders. His flight from Bozeman had been delayed two hours, and he barely had ten minutes to catch his connection to Paris. He was still two hundred feet from the gate when he heard his name being called for the third and final time through the terminal's announcement speakers.

He picked up the pace and made it to the gate just as the attendant was getting ready to close it. He was sweaty and nearly out of breath. Bears were great sprinters but not so good on long distances.

He entered the plane and was shown to his seat as the aircraft doors were closing. Sheila, bless her heart, had reserved him a seat in first class, large enough for him to squeeze his 6'4" frame into. It wasn't a window seat, which he would have preferred, but his only neighbor was hidden behind a divider and was unlikely to bug him.

The plane had been in the air about twenty minutes and Michael was dozing off when the attendant came to offer him something to drink. He passed on the champagne and grabbed a glass of orange juice from the tray as another attendant was offering the same options to his neighbor.

"I'll have the champagne, thank you," he heard the woman reply and somehow the voice sounded very familiar—too familiar.

When he peeked around the divider, he found the pretty face of Sheila Wang sipping on champagne and staring back at him. "Good morning, Michael. I'm glad you caught the flight. You had me worried for a second there."

"What are you doing here, Sheila?" he asked in a tired voice, only now realizing she'd not only switched her perfume to throw him off but also applied an odor neutralizer to mask her natural scent: a cheap trick used by hunters to approach their prey.

"What do you think I'm doing, honey? Did you really think I would pass on a vacation to France?"

In retrospect, he should have known… Sheila had surrendered far too easily to his arguments when he'd explained how dangerous the mission would be. He'd managed to dodge the Olivia bullet, but now he had Sheila to worry about. How in heaven was he going to keep her safe?

Chapter 15

The lab was about three hundred square feet, windowless and furnished with stainless steel shelves, benches and cabinets that gave it a hospital-like atmosphere. Near the center of the room, Ike Brown was staring at the two diadem-like objects lying on the metallic bench in front of him.

"So, what you're telling me is that you don't know how they work," he said to the scientist in a white lab coat who stood on the other side of the bench.

"Not precisely, no. I didn't develop them."

"Who did?"

"I have no clue. You know how things are around here. Everything's on a need-to-know basis and I don't have the clearance level required to ask questions… All I can tell you is that they arrived this morning. Straight from the director."

"And she wants you to trial them on one of the beasts?" asked Ike.

"No! She wants your guys to put the blue one on one of the beasts. I'm just the messenger here. I'll quit long before I approach one of those monsters." The expression on the scientific face told Ike he wasn't joking.

"Why the blue one? They're not the same?"

"I guess not…"

"And she said to remove the collar… the only thing that prevents those freaks from turning into their beasts? You're sure of that?"

"That's what she said."

Ike was trying to understand the big idea here, but he simply couldn't. The collars they'd been using to restrain their captives had proven simple to use and reliable, so why would the director want to take chances with those diadems when there was nothing wrong with the collars in the first place? "Did she say anything else?"

The scientist's eyes went to the ceiling as he considered the question. "Oh yes, I was going to forget. She wants you to first try it on a mountain lion."

"I assume she didn't tell you why she wanted a cougar?"

"Why do you even ask?"

The pen hosting the mountain lions was located beside the wolves but was much smaller. Apparently weremountain lions were significantly rarer than werewolves, and if one were to believe the statistical distribution of the prison, the rumor was correct. They'd only captured two cougars so far, while nearly forty wolves already cohabited inside the facility's largest enclosure.

Just like the other detention pens, the cougars' cell was equipped with an airlock whose opposite gates couldn't be opened at the same time. This was only one of the many security features of the facility along with its stainless-steel-lined concrete walls and its thick Plexiglas dividers between the cells. And if things got out of hand, a gas lethal to the creatures could be pumped directly into their pens to regain a *permanent* control of the situation.

"You," said Ike, pointing at the woman inside the pen through the Plexiglas window. "Enter the airlock."

The woman gave a look to the male with whom she shared her cell but gave no indication she intended to obey the order. The two weren't a couple. They'd picked up the man in Utah and the woman hundreds of miles away in Arizona.

"Now!" yelled Ike, pointing a remote at the woman's collar, his voice resonating throughout the entire cell block.

The sight of the remote was enough to convince her to enter the airlock. The beasts were all well acquainted with the device by the time they reached the detention center.

Once she was in, the door closed heavily behind her and two-inch-thick steel bars slid back into their housings to secure it in place.

One of the guards activated the lock on the second door from inside the safety of his bunker located at the block's entrance, and the woman stepped out of the airlock to come stand directly in front of Ike. She stared him down from a distance of three feet but didn't push her luck any further; the four guards training their assault rifles towards her chest and the remote Ike still held in his hand presented convincing arguments for the value of good behavior.

"Follow me," he said, and reluctantly she obeyed.

Three minutes later, the mountain lion and her escort entered a room void of windows but equipped with a wide-screen TV mounted into the wall behind a protective armored glass cover. Ike led the woman to the center of the room before retreating to one of the corners to pull a cell phone out of his pocket. He dialed a number and, after a short conversation, the director appeared on the giant screen facing the cougar.

"I see you picked the female. Don't you trust the new device, Captain?" asked the director.

Ike was slightly surprised his motivation was so obvious, but he wasn't ashamed for it. If for some reason the diadem gizmo failed, and they found themselves facing a rabid werecougar, he'd reasoned that the smaller the cat the better off he and the guards would be. And since the male had a good seventy pounds on the female, the choice had been easy.

Before Ike could answer the director's rhetorical question, she said, "Place the blue diadem behind her head. The round piece should rest directly on top of her spinal cord at the base of the neck."

Ike handed the remote controlling the collar to one of the guards with the instruction to decapitate the cat if she even twitched a muscle. He then cautiously approached her from behind as she stood still in the center of the room. He placed the diadem behind her neck as instructed and immediately sensed the object moving of its own volition. At the same instant the woman emitted a brief moan of pain, or maybe surprise, Ike couldn't tell for sure.

The director answered the question for him. "Nothing to worry about, Captain. Our friend was just caught by surprise when the needles penetrated her spinal cord. Now place the red diadem on your forehead. Don't worry, yours doesn't have a needle."

Ike hesitated a second before walking back to the guard who was holding the other diadem. He grabbed the object from the man and placed it on his own head as instructed. Nothing happened at first, but within a few seconds, he started feeling like his mind was expanding: a strange sensation.

"You can remove her collar now," said the director.

Ike walked back to the guard who was holding the remote and after a slight hesitation pressed the button releasing the collar's locking mechanism.

"Now, Captain, ask our friend to take the collar off and throw it to you gently."

"Yes, Ma'am." Ike gave the order to the cougar and the woman obeyed, tossing him the object underhand as one would throw a pair of keys to someone across the room.

"And now tell her to morph," said the director.

"I'm not sure that's a good idea, Ma'am. What if she—"

"It's an order, Captain."

The director's order left Ike no choice. The tension in the room was palpable as he and the four guards started sweating in their uniforms. If something went the slightest bit wrong, none of them would be making it out of this room alive, except for the mountain lion of course.

Ike gave the order and the woman soon morphed into a two-hundred-pound beast with a jaw powerful enough to crush a grown man's skull.

"Don't be shy, Captain, give her another order. Anything you can think of."

"Lie down," said Ike and the cat dropped to the floor before he could finish his sentence. He then ordered the cat to ram into the wall and she did. The impact produced was powerful enough to shake the room.

"Now you see why I wanted you to try the device, don't you?" asked the director.

"I don't understand how this works…"

"You don't need to understand, Captain. All you need to know is that as long as she's wearing that thing, she'll do anything you order her to do."

"What about the other guards? Would she obey them as well?"

"Anyone wearing the red diadem can issue the orders, using his voice or, with a bit of practice, his mind."

"You mean I could control her with my thoughts?"

"That's precisely what I mean."

"And how can we be certain she's not faking obedience? What if she's just acting and waiting for an opening to turn on us?"

"I suppose we could sic her against a dozen of the werewolves we captured. Of course, that would be a suicide mission and we'd lose a valuable cougar, but that should convince you."

Ike was considering the offer when the director interrupted his train of thought. "Never mind. I think I have a better idea. A slightly less dramatic one, but one that will at least serve our cause."

Chapter 16

The three wizards stood facing each other in a small circle. January was the warmest month of the year in Antarctica, but the temperature at the South Pole where they stood was still well below freezing.

Without the spell they'd cast to protect themselves from the elements, the Second Circle of wizardry would have soon been turned into an ice statue.

"It's stronger here than it was at the North Pole," said Ezekiel.

"Quite a bit stronger," agreed Tabitha. The petite woman was draped in an Indian saree as bright as the sun: an outfit and an expanse of exposed milk-chocolate skin that had never before been seen on the frozen continent.

"Even if it means the source of the distortion is located somewhere in the Southern Hemisphere, it still makes no sense," said Methuselah. "How can it be felt all across the globe? Such power simply doesn't exist." He appeared as usual to his friends, a lean but strong figure cloaked in maroon and gold embroidered robes, holding a long mahogany cane with a beautiful multifaceted ivory handle erect at his side. His ever confident and serene charcoal face, however, showed a perplexity his companions had never witnessed before.

The three wizards stared at each other in silence for a minute until finally Ezekiel spoke. "Such power doesn't exist, and yet we can all feel it…"

There was no arguing with that fact and his fellow wizards didn't try.

"So what does it mean?" asked Tabitha.

"It can only mean one thing, my friends. Such power does exist now," answered Ezekiel. "Between the three of us, we have nearly twenty thousand years of combined experience on this earth and never have we seen such chaos in the magical field."

"The distortion triggered by the three of us standing in one location is minimal compared to that exercised by that force. Whatever it is, it can't be caused by a single practitioner. It's impossible," said Methuselah.

"You think we're dealing with someone channeling the magical powers of several entities, like Serafin did with the Voodoo witches in Louisiana?" asked Tabitha.

"Something like that, but on a much larger scale."

The three wizards pondered the idea for a moment as gusts of winds relentlessly assaulted the invisible walls they'd erected around themselves.

"What if it were a mage?" asked Tabitha. "How powerful could he be?"

Ezekiel didn't have an answer to her question, however. None of them had ever lived on the same plane as a wizard of the First Circle. The power of such a wizard would be significantly stronger than their own, but by how much was anyone's guess. Still, he doubted this was what they were dealing with. "A mage would have manifested him- or herself to us already. They wouldn't be waiting around for us to find them. Whatever is causing this, it's not one of our kind. Their intentions don't seem… pure."

"Are you saying that because of the werebeings that have gone missing? We have no way to know for certain that the two things are linked. They could be completely unrelated," said Methuselah.

"True," acknowledged Ezekiel. "And I hope you're right, old friend. Believe me… I hope you're right."

Chapter 17

Irini had borrowed one of the Covenant's Mercedes SUVs, and for once Michael found himself with enough room in the passenger seat. Behind him, Sheila was quietly observing the landscape passing by while trying to book a vacation rental. Per Michael's order, she wasn't to set foot within a fifteen-mile radius of the vampires' summer quarters.

Irini had picked them up at the airport in Paris and they were now on their way to the Périgord region where the Eastern Covenant's castle was located. A five-hour drive that Irini, who drove consistently fifty kilometers above the speed limit, clearly intended to do in less than four. The vampire had been surprised to see Sheila but thankfully had kept her questions to a minimum. Michael was still struggling with the idea that the journalist was part of the trip but at this point there wasn't much he could do about it other than keeping her as far as possible from the action.

"Now that we're on the freeway, maybe you could give me the lowdown on the Eastern Covenant? I'd like to know what I'm walking into," said Michael.

"Sure," answered Irini, discreetly nodding towards Sheila in the back seat with a questioning look.

"Sheila can be trusted. She won't say a word about any of this."

"Cross my heart," said the journalist without lifting her nose from her phone.

"Alright then. As you know, Vulpe Zamfir is the Covenant's leader. He's also not someone you should cross if you want to keep your head attached to your shoulders."

When it came to Vulpe, Michael was more concerned about Lucy and Irini's heads than his own. He'd fought a number of vampire elders over the years, and so far he'd always ended up on top. Granted, none of them had been as powerful as Vulpe Zamfir, but still.

"He's been ruling over the Eastern Covenant for nearly three centuries now, and the last time a vampire dared challenge his position was over a hundred years ago," continued Irini. "Needless to say, things didn't end well for the challenger."

"I can imagine." Michael had never met Vulpe, but if he showed as much empathy as Dragos or the original Irini—Wawetseka's maker—the challenger had probably ended with body parts scattered across the courtyard for the sun to consume.

"His wife, Milena, is a quiet woman with some degree of influence over her husband. She's actually Vulpe's second wife, but they've been married well over a half millennium and few are those who remember the first Mrs Zamfir."

Michal did some quick math and came to the conclusion that the ruling couple had been married for over two hundred years by the time Irini was born. "Do you know what happened to the first one? Was she a vampire?"

"She was, and no, I don't know. I tried to find out when I first learned about it, but I was made to understand it would be better for my health if I didn't ask questions on the subject."

"Do Milena and Vulpe have children?" asked Sheila from the back seat.

"No. They were both vampires already by the time they met and vampires can't reproduce."

There had been a subtle note of bitterness in Irini's answer. Did she regret not having children of her own? This was a point Michael had never considered before. In truth, he'd never imagined that bloodsuckers could have feelings of any kind... but Irini wasn't a true vampire anyway. "Any other relatives?" he asked, eager to change the topic.

"Vulpe has a brother, Vladislav."

"Tell me about him."

"He's about as old as Vulpe and therefore tremendously powerful, but he has a very different temperament. He's much less prone to anger and tends to think a bit longer than Vulpe before acting. He's one of the few elders who was always kind to me, even when I was a young vampire."

Michael gave Irini a look she interpreted correctly. "Nothing like that, Michael. Not that I would mind... But Vladislav is married, and it will be a cold day in hell before I cross his bitch of a wife. Anastasia is quite a piece of work."

"You're afraid of her?" Michael was surprised; he didn't think Irini feared anyone.

"Let's say that I have a healthy dose of respect for the bitch."

"She's that strong?"

"She is, but that's not what's worrying about her."

"Could you develop?" he asked, as a flash of light came from the side of the road.

"A radar," explained Irini. "For speed control. They're all over the country. You can't go twenty kilometers without passing one."

"That doesn't seem to deter you much," pointed Michael, nodding towards the speedometer.

"The Covenant can afford the fines."

"Anyway, you were explaining why Anastasia was so dangerous."

"Right, Anastasia... Anastasia's power comes from the fact she's the Eastern Covenant's best inducer."

"What's an inducer?" asked Sheila.

"Do you know thrall?"

"I'm vaguely familiar with the concept. Are they the same thing?"

"No, induction is another form of mind control. With thrall, vampires can control their victim's mind and body, with induction they can convince them of absolutely anything. They can drive them to insanity if they so wish. In many ways, induction is much more powerful than thrall. For one thing, vampires are immune to thrall but not to induction."

Michael gave Irini a perplexed look. "Could you give us an example?"

Irini thought about it for a moment before answering. "About ten years ago, Anastasia induced one of our new recruits to believe he was immune to UV light. The kid walked out of the castle one hour after dawn and would have died out there if one of our pet wolves hadn't dragged his sizzling ass back inside."

Michael had been around for over a thousand years and he'd never even heard of induction. But now that he had, the knowledge didn't alleviate his visceral dislike of bloodsuckers the slightest bit. "How does a vampire go about inducing someone?"

"It's very similar to enthralling. The vampire captures his victim's gaze and then enters his mind, but you need to be more subtle about it, especially if you're trying to induce another vampire. It takes tremendous skills. I, for one, would have great difficulties inducing the slightest thought into the mind of a vampire older than a few years. I simply don't have the skills, even though I mastered thrall centuries ago."

"What about Anastasia? How good is she? Could she implant a belief in an elder's mind, for instance?" asked Michael.

"I'm not sure about that. I've never heard of an elder being successfully induced with a foreign thought. Elders' minds are very powerful."

"And that Anastasia is Vladislav's wife, correct?" asked Sheila who had taken a notepad out of her bag and was jotting down some notes.

"Correct. Vladislav and the queen bitch have been married nearly four centuries, but don't ask me what he sees in her. She's never struck me as a particularly loving wife, but things have gotten a lot worse over the past few weeks. She's openly hostile to Vladislav these days, and in front of the other elders, too."

"What about him? How does he react?" The question was from Michael.

"He usually ignores her in public, but behind closed doors it's another story. There have been more than a few screaming matches coming from their chamber over the past month."

"Can vampires divorce each other?" asked Sheila.

"They can, but it's not very common, especially among elders. They tend to remain married while living separate lives."

"What do you mean by that?" asked Sheila.

"Vampires aren't a faithful lot to start with, so when a couple experiences tension, they tend to gravitate apart and towards other centers of interest quickly."

"But they remain married?" asked Michael.

"Most of the time, yes."

"And both parties are fine with that?" said Sheila

"I don't know if *fine* is the word. Appearances need to be maintained. It's one thing to screw a human here and there, it's even expected, but relationships with other vampires are frowned upon, especially if they live under the same roof. This generates tensions within the Covenant and that's not good."

"But it happens?" asked Sheila.

"Of course it does. But we keep it casual and try to be discreet about it. As long as nobody knows, it's not wrong…"

"What about Anastasia and Vladislav? Are they getting some action on the side?" asked Sheila.

Michael wasn't certain the question was relevant to the task at hand, but he didn't object. Understanding the Covenant's dynamic could prove useful in the long run.

"If they are, they're being very careful about it. It's not common knowledge. I've seen female slaves coming out of Vladislav's room before and I suspect they weren't there to clean, but that's all I ever saw on his part."

"What about Anastasia?" asked Sheila.

Irini seemed to hesitate for an instant.

"What is it?" asked Michael.

The vampire remained silent as she inserted the car into the flow of traffic of yet another freeway. "I overheard two of our slaves talking last month. A male and a female—a couple, I think. The female was one of Vulpe's regular playmates. Anyway, she was telling the man that she'd gone to Vulpe's apartments for their regular *playtime* but when she'd walked into the main room she'd glimpsed a naked woman disappearing into the bedroom. The slave didn't get a good look at her, but she recognized the clothes scattered on the floor—Anastasia's clothes."

"Vulpe is banging his brother's wife?" Sheila sounded amused. "If Vladislav found out about it, that could explain why his relationship with his wife took a turn for the worse."

"I don't know… The slave could have been wrong." Irini didn't sound particularly convinced.

"Could we maybe talk to that slave?" asked Michael, whose interest had been piqued by the revelation.

"That won't be possible. Vulpe sucked her dry the next day. Her boyfriend burned her body in a field beside the castle."

Chapter 18

Seemak was driving on a small road bordered by woods on either side. He was only a few miles from the Château de Chambord where he intended to spend the night and continue his scouting of Lord Vaalt's residence, when the car suddenly died on him. For decades, faes had been unable to use cars and other vehicles which were mostly made of iron, a substance extremely toxic to his kind. But over the past twenty years many vehicle manufacturers had switched from iron and steel to aluminum and this had changed the way faes moved around. Now most faes small enough to fit inside a car used them to get around. The largest faes such as trolls, ogres and spriggan could sometimes fit in the back of flatbed trucks and other eighteen-wheelers, but in many instances they still relied on their feet or the magic of high faes to move from point A to point B.

Seemak tried turning the specially ordered aluminum key a few times in the ignition, but no sound came from the engine block. He knew better than to look under the hood where cold iron would invariably be present in some of the parts composing the guts of the vehicle, so he got out of the car and started walking towards the castle whose spires were visible above the tree line in the distance.

He hadn't managed more than a dozen steps when a tall figure draped in a dark hooded cloak stepped out of the woods a few feet in front of him.

"Hello, Seemak. The master wants to know how things are progressing. Have you located the three fragments yet?" asked Demetra.

"I have located two of the three." Seemak didn't bother asking how she'd found him.

"Do you have them with you?"

Her tone was amiable enough, but Seemak wasn't fooled. The warlock meant business. The two of them were anything but friends. They were simply two tools in the hands of the master. And a blunt one at that, when it came to Seemak. "No. One of them is still in the vampires' stronghold and the other is still hidden in Lord Vaalt's private quarters in Chambord." Seemak had no doubt the warlocks would kill him as soon as he'd delivered the artifact to them, which was why he had no intention of doing so. He'd use the power of the artifact to kill the master and his acolytes and then move on to greater things.

"Do you know the precise location of those two fragments?"

"I do. And I also know how I will retrieve them."

Demetra took a few steps in his direction and stopped two feet from him. She was taller than the current body shape he was using, which forced him to look up to meet her gaze.

"This is good news, Seemak. Do you intend on carrying out the deeds yourself?"

"The room in which Lord Vaalt is keeping his fragment of the artifact is protected against my kind. Chameleons, I mean. I suspect to prevent the very thing we're trying to do."

"You mean to prevent a chameleon from impersonating him and fool whoever's in charge of guarding his treasures?"

"Precisely."

"So how do you propose to proceed?"

"With the help of a friend who will have no problem fooling the guards."

"And who might this friend be?" Demetra asked lightly.

"I'd rather not say."

To Seemak's relief, Demetra didn't insist. He had no desire to tell her that Victor would be the one robbing Lord Vaalt. The vampire had assured him that his magic would easily blindside the muscle keeping guard in front of Lord Vaalt's private quarters.

"And when do you expect to have these artifacts in your possession?"

"I cannot tell precisely. A week, two… Stealing from Lord Vaalt and the leader of the Eastern Covenant requires careful planning. I'm sure you'll understand."

Demetra gave him a smile void of any warmth before answering, "And I'm sure you understand that the master's patience is limited and shouldn't be abused… What about the third artifact, any leads?"

"I am still searching for it, but since your master assured me it was either in Chambord or in Zamfir's stronghold in Périgord, it will make the task of finding it easier."

Since the third fragment hadn't been in Vulpe's vault, it had to be in Lord Vaalt's possession, stashed away with the other fragment inside the high fae's chamber. And soon it would be in Seemak's pocket along with its two brothers. These warlocks had to be the dumbest representatives of their kind ever to walk the earth. Who would trust a fae with such a task?

Chapter 19

Olivia and Daka's wolves were out on an early-morning stroll in Yellowstone National Park. The sounds of their paws sinking into the fresh foot of snow that had fallen overnight were the only ones to disturb the absolute silence that had swallowed the park. Of course, a bird could be heard chirping from time to time and, on rarer occasions, the bugle of an elk would manage to disturb the surreal peace of the sleeping woods, but these musical intermissions were few and far between.

The beauty of the snow-covered wilderness, the absence of tourists and the perfect stillness of nature made winter Olivia's favorite season in the park—which made the young woman worried Michael was starting to rub off on her.

They were walking on the edge of one of the park's numerous thermal areas located between Canyon Village and Norris when Olivia caught a scent she didn't immediately recognize. The rotten-egg smell emanating from the steam vents to their left was overwhelming and mostly covered the other scent, but not entirely. The smell was still noticeable, a subtle fragrance of decomposition.

Olivia saw by the way Daka was sniffing the air that he'd noticed it, too. Their eyes met and a silent agreement was reached. They needed to identify the origin of the putrid smell that came and went with the shifting winds.

They started walking around the thermal area that lay somewhere between two and three football fields in size, being careful to stay in the zone closest to the snow where the ground, heated by the boiling water roaring underneath, wouldn't burn their paws.

The thermal features and the water coming out of them aside, the landscape was moonlike in nature. At least it was how Olivia imagined the surface of the moon. A yellowish powdery white surface, full of cracks and asperities. A small geyser erupted on their right, but the show lasted only a moment, and the scalding water it propelled into the air flowed away from the two wolves who knew where to step to avoid the traps laid by the treacherous landscape.

They found the origin of the smell an instant later. The body was face-down sixty feet or so in front of them. The steam surrounding it prevented them from having a good look, but it was definitely a man. This much was certain. The area where he lay was much too hot for the wolves' naked paws, unfortunately. They would be forced to retrieve their clothes and shoes hidden inside a hollow tree in the woods before they could return and try to ID the man, but it didn't matter much anyway. Olivia already knew who he was.

Chapter 20

Olivia, Daka and Jason Parrish all stood over the body in eerie silence. A light snow had started to fall again, but it didn't stick to the heated ground where the corpse lay. The corpse was facing up now, since Jason had rolled him to help with identification.

After recovering their clothes from their hiding spot, Olivia and Daka had jumped on the snowmobiles they'd parked in front of Michael's cabin and hurried back to the thermal area. The thick soles of their hiking boots had allowed them to reach the body without burning their feet, but the progression had been slow and steady. The mineral crust covering the thermal area could be particularly flimsy in places and with their body weight now spread over two feet instead of four paws, each step could send them through the ground and into a pool of water at nearly boiling temperature—a potentially fatal accident for Daka and a very painful one for Olivia.

"So this is the Robert Spencer we've been looking for?" said Jason, breaking the silence.

Daka had found the man's wallet in his jacket pocket and Olivia had immediately called dispatch from her mobile.

"How did you two manage to find him here? Were you still looking for him?" asked Jason.

"No. We were just enjoying a morning ride before heading to work when we spotted the body," lied Olivia, gesturing towards the snowmobiles parked on the side of the road a hundred feet away. Michael had asked her to keep an eye open for Bob, and she and Daka had done just that, though they'd never expected to find the man. Especially not here, surrounded by geysers and fumaroles.

"I suppose you've already told Michael? I'm surprised he's not here himself."

Olivia swallowed before answering, "Michael doesn't know yet."

Jason gave her a questioning look. "You called dispatch before calling him? I'm surprised. I thought the three of you were close."

"We couldn't reach him." The answer had come from Daka.

"He might have been in the shower, I suppose," reflected Jason.

"Actually, Michael's in France. He took his girlfriend to Paris for a vacation. It had been planned for months," Olivia lied again.

"I don't recall him mentioning anything to me, but of course this wouldn't be the first time." Jason was clearly upset now. "Do you have a way to contact him in France? Do you know which hotel he'll be staying at?"

"I don't know anything about his plans. You can try his cell phone, but I'm not sure he'll keep it on. I don't think he has an international plan so that would cost him a lot."

"Oh, that's going to cost him a lot. Believe you me." Jason was already heading back towards his snowmobile parked beside the other two.

"What about Bob's body, sir? What are we going to do about it?" asked Olivia.

Jason stopped and turned around to answer in a tired voice, "What is there to do about it? I'll send someone to pick it up and we'll arrange to send it back to his family."

"Shouldn't we ask a forensics team to have a look before we move it?" suggested Daka.

"What for? What happened to that poor man is pretty obvious. He was killed by a mountain lion, and a big one too. Didn't you see the bitemarks on the back of his neck? That's how they suffocate their prey. Same thing for the wounds on his stomach, right under the ribs. That's where mountain lions always start feeding."

Daka and Olivia were staring at the corpse's empty abdominal cavity. Jason hadn't said anything the two of them didn't already know but the ranger was missing some obvious points.

"What about his jacket?" said Olivia "It's wide open and doesn't have a tear in it. Bob left Michael's cabin in the middle of the night. It was freezing cold. He wouldn't have kept his jacket open like this. And a lion wouldn't have unzipped it before starting his meal."

"Maybe walking in the snow made him hot... Or maybe he opened it to take a whiz and that's when the cat attacked him... I don't know and I don't care. This man was killed by a mountain lion and there's nothing more to it. End of story."

Daka and Olivia stared at each other, silently seething with anger, while Jason got back on his snowmobile and took off.

"That man is either a complete idiot or he does it on purpose," Daka said finally.

"You're reading my mind."

There was little doubt Bob had been attacked and likely killed by a mountain lion; a child could have reached that conclusion. But one thing was equally certain. It wasn't a cougar that had brought the body where they'd found it. That was simply impossible.

A mile down the road from where the body had been found, Jason Parrish's snowmobile made a turn onto a small snow-packed dirt path. He progressed deep enough into the woods to make sure his bike wouldn't be visible from the road before killing the engine. He fumbled inside his pocket for his phone and hit number one on his speed dial.

The phone rang five times before going to voicemail. Jason was about to leave a message when the director called him back.

"Good morning, Ma'am. I'm sorry to bother you so early in the morning but there's a problem with the werebear," said Jason.

"Did he find his friend's body?"

"No. His werewolf protégée and her boyfriend found the body."

"So what's the problem? Why does it matter as long as someone found it?" The director sounded like she was quickly losing patience.

"That's not the problem, Ma'am. The werebear's gone; he skipped town. According to his protégée, he took his girlfriend on a vacation to Paris."

"Then let Captain Brown know when the bear's back in town and his men will grab him then. You've been working on this for over a year, another week or two makes no difference. We'll get him eventually, don't worry."

"I wouldn't worry if I were sure he'd be back, but I have a bad feeling about this. I'm pretty certain the wolf lied to me about where Biörn actually was. I don't think he's on vacation at all. I'm his boss and he's supposed to let me know when he's taking time off. Not only is this out of the blue, but why would his protégée tell me he's on vacation if he's not? I think she's covering for him."

"Covering what?"

"I don't know, Ma'am… What if he's onto me? What if he's suspecting something and went into hiding?"

The director remained silent a moment, but he could still hear her breathing on the other end of the line.

"We'll give him his week off, but in the meantime keep an eye on the wolf and don't lose her. If need be, we can always use her as bait to bring the bear back to us."

Chapter 21

The house Sheila had rented was thirty miles away from the fortified castle the Eastern Covenant called home half of the year. Michael instantly felt at home in the small renovated farm built in irregular off-white stone blocks, with its two spacious bedrooms and the rustic kitchen featuring a massive wood stove in addition to the more practical gas range. Had they come in summer, the thirty-foot-long swimming pool outside would have been great too…

The weather was nice for January, though, and the poolside lounge chairs appeared to appeal to Sheila who, with a light sweater on, intended to spend her vacation reading outdoors. At least, that was what the journalist had claimed, but Michael knew his girlfriend better than that. He would need to make sure Sheila wasn't hiding inside the trunk of Irini's car before he and the vampire headed to the Covenant's stronghold.

Aside from the large swimming pool, the house came with private woods and no neighbors within a mile radius: two features Michael particularly appreciated. Sheila had chosen well. He wondered how much the rental had cost her. She'd used her own credit card for the reservation, but he intended to pay her back one way or another. After several centuries of compounded interest, his finances could afford it.

"We should get moving soon, Michael," said Irini.

She hadn't mentioned anything about it, but it was pretty obvious the vampire hadn't approved of the detour they'd had to make to drop Sheila off. Michael didn't blame Irini either; Lucy's life was at stake and time was of the essence. They had only a few days left to prove the young woman's innocence or else Olivia would lose the only living relative she had left. Although when it came to Lucy, *living* was maybe not the best way to put it.

"Are you sure you'll be alright without a car for the rest of the day?" he asked Sheila.

"I'm sure. The Hertz guy said he'll have my rental here by nine tomorrow morning. With all the French pastries I got from that bakery, I could probably eat for three days without worrying about losing a pound. I'll be fine, Michael. Go get Lucy out of jail." She punctuated her sentence by a quick kiss on the lips before disappearing inside the house, suitcase in hand.

Michael was about to climb into Irini's car when his cell phone chimed in his pocket. The call was from Olivia. "Everything okay?"

"I'm fine, Michael."

Michael heard the strain in her voice. "What is it then, is Daka alright?"

"He's fine too, but I have some bad news. The two of us were strolling around the small geyser basin closest to your cabin on the Norris-Canyon road and we found Bob Spencer's body. It looked like he'd been killed by a mountain lion."

Michael felt his throat tighten at the announcement. Bob and he had been fairly close a few years back and his death, especially like that, was news he could have done without. "A lion? You're sure, Olivia? Daka agrees?" Michael knew the skinwalker's judgment could be trusted for this kind of things. Unlike Olivia, Daka had been living around the park his entire life, and as a member of the Shoshone tribe he knew his stuff when it came to identifying wildlife by their tracks on the ground or the bitemarks left in their prey.

"Daka agrees, but we also believe that something's not right."

That was for damn sure. A mountain lion attacking a man the size of Bob was probably unheard of in history. Lions seldom attacked humans and as far as Michael knew their victims were almost always women and children who were seen by the cats as less dangerous prey. "I know! A cat would have to be pretty desperate to go after Bob."

"That's not what I meant. We found his body in the middle of the basin between two geysers. We were in our wolf forms when we found it and the ground was too hot for our paws. We had to go retrieve our shoes and come back to get a closer look at the corpse. A mountain lion may have killed Bob, but it sure didn't happen where we found the body."

"I see what you mean," said Michael. Lions often dragged a body away from the kill site to hide it from other predators and scavengers while they sucked the carcass clean of all calories, a process that could take up to two days, but this wasn't what had happened here. Unlike bison and other hoofed animals, mountain lions, like wolves, had paws too sensitive to walk on the burning ground of Yellowstone's thermal areas. A mountain lion couldn't have been where the body was found without severely burning its paws. Someone had brought Bob's body to the geyser basin after his death. Which begged two questions. Who, and why?

"There is more," continued Olivia. "There's definitely a good chunk of Bob's abdominal cavity that's been eaten away, but the limbs are all intact and so is the rest of his body with the exception of the kill marks on the back of his neck."

"So the lion was disturbed while feeding…" concluded Michael.

"Are you going to come back early now that Bob's been found?"

"I still have a few things to settle here, but I'll come back as soon as possible. A week tops."

"Why not sooner? Weren't you going to Europe to investigate his disappearance?"

Michael had forgotten this was the excuse he'd given Olivia. The problem with never lying to anyone was that he had no practice whatsoever for the rare occasions when he had to. "I'm still investigating his disappearance. Now more than ever," he backpedaled. "Just because he's dead doesn't mean the case is closed. I want to find out who the bastards responsible for this are."

"Okay." Olivia sounded unconvinced. "But before you go, there's one more thing you should know. It's about Jason."

"Let me guess, he's having a hissy fit because I didn't file my paperwork in triplicate before skipping town?"

"Obviously, but that's not what I wanted to tell you. Jason was the first one to show up on the scene when we called in the news that we'd found Bob's body. And then he concluded that it was a predatory kill and saw nothing wrong with a lion dragging his kill to the middle of a geyser basin."

This was concerning. Jason had been a ranger in Yellowstone for nearly a year. He had to know better than this by now. The man could be thick at times, but this was really pushing it. That's when Michael remembered Ezekiel's warning. Weird things were happening to praeternaturals out there. Entire werewolf packs vanishing without a trace… Add to this Bob's suspicious demise and the death squad Michael had found at his cabin the same night his friend had gone missing, and things were starting to look a bit worrisome. "I want you to go into hiding, Olivia. At least until I get back. Go to Daka's reservation and make sure Jason Parrish doesn't know where you're going. You'll be safe there." At least that's what Michael hoped.

Chapter 22

As Michael and Irini drove up to the compound's main gate, Michael wondered if the ten-foot stone wall erected all around the property's perimeter had been the work of the castle's original builders back in the Middle Ages or a recent addition designed to improve the security of the world's oldest vampire covenant.

Like every vehicle in the Covenant's fleet, Irini's Mercedes was equipped with windows tinted so dark that UV light couldn't penetrate the protective glass, a precaution which allowed vampires to move about during the day without danger of turning into calcinated corpses. As such, the car was easy identifiable as belonging to the Covenant, but the four sentinels on duty at the gate still had a job to do. The guard who stood outside the perimeter approached to peek inside the car while the three others stood behind the gate, their FAMAS assault rifles at the ready.

When in Rome do as the Romans do, thought Michael, staring at the guns that had been the default weapons of the French Army since the late seventies. Despite the bulletproof windows, the stench was unmistakable. These men were werewolves. Most likely enthralled slaves protecting the bloodsuckers during the day, when the vamps were resting and therefore at their most vulnerable. Michael felt the hairs on the back of his neck prick up at the proximity of his ancestral enemies, but the reaction was tempered by a strange sensation. Pity… He actually felt pity for the enslaved praeternaturals.

"Who's with you, my lady?" asked the guard through the closed window. UV light had no effect on Irini, but beside Lucy, nobody at the Covenant knew that.

"A friend. Open the gate."

His nose nearly stuck to the window, the guard took a couple of deep breaths. "Your guest is no vampire—what is he?" His voice had an edge to it now. His wolf was sensing the presence of a praeternatural predator he couldn't identify, and it was making him nervous.

"Never mind what he is, wolf. He's with me, that's all you need to know."

"Get out of the car, sir," ordered the wolf. He was already going around the vehicle to the passenger side.

"Do you know who I am?" bellowed Irini. "Stand down and open the gate!"

But the wolf wasn't paying the slightest attention to her. His normal deference to a vamp was being overridden by his beast's instinct, which was currently focused on Michael with the intensity of a high-power laser.

"Don't worry, the car's bullet-proof," said Irini.

"Don't you guys use armor-piercing ammo? Besides, he can just rip the door straight off its hinges if he wants to. I'd better get out."

Michael opened the door and jumped out before Irini could answer. The wolf's gun, and by extension its knife-looking bayonet, were trained on Michael's heart.

"I'm a werebeing like you," said Michael, his hands raised in an appeasing gesture.

"What kind?" asked the wolf, his knuckles white around his gun.

From the corner of his eye, Michael saw the gate opening and the three other guards coming out for backup. Four against one, and they all had assault rifles… Michael had faced better odds, but he'd faced worse, too, and on more than one occasion.

"What kind? I asked you," repeated the wolf, more threatening than ever.

Michael waited for the other three to get within striking distance before finally answering the question, "A bear."

Before the guard could react, Michael stepped forward and ripped the FAMAS out of his hands. He then used it as a club and in a swinging motion broke the necks of two of the newcomers. The disarmed wolf was already morphing—probably involuntarily—which gave Michael just enough time to deal with the fourth one who was fumbling with the safety on his gun. He finally managed to thumb the safety off but received Michael's bayonet through the left eye before he could fire a single shot. The only guard still standing was halfway through his morphing by the time Michael broke his neck with his bare hands.

Michael had been careful not to permanently damage any of the wolves: a sign of good faith he hoped would appease Vulpe when the leader came to learn about the incident.

He picked up the guards' weapons and tossed them in the Mercedes' back seat. "Let's roll," he said, taking his place next to Irini.

"I'm sorry I didn't help, but I couldn't let them know I was immune to UV light. I still don't understand why they didn't obey my orders," said Irini as the car flew through the now opened gate.

"Don't worry about it, I didn't need any help."

As the car approached a fifty-foot-wide moat bordering the castle's ramparts, Irini pressed a key on the dashboard and the drawbridge slowly came down. Too slowly for Michael's tastes, given that Irini apparently had no intention of slowing down. But the woman knew what she was doing; the edge of the bridge had just made contact with the ground by the time the Mercedes reached it. The wolves patrolling the perimeter made no attempt to stop them; they had no idea yet about the little altercation at the gate.

The car reached the castle's courtyard where Irini drove directly to the entrance of a subterranean parking garage. The entrance had been designed to match the architectural style of the surrounding buildings but was clearly a recent addition to the overall edifice.

A moment later, Irini parked between two SUVs identical to the one she was driving and turned towards Michael. "The sun will go down in half an hour. We need to hurry and make you presentable before I introduce you to Vulpe."

"Is that really necessary?"

"You can't meet him wearing jeans and a tee shirt, Michael, even a long-sleeved one. There's an etiquette to follow if you want to be taken seriously."

"I meant meeting Vulpe."

"There's no way around it, I'm afraid. He needs to approve your presence on the grounds or else you won't last long among us."

Michael remembered his fight against Dragos and sighed. If he were to spend a few days surrounded by vampires even more powerful than that one had been, he needed to learn to play by their rules; his life and Lucy's depended on it. But there was one problem with that plan… he doubted he could stick with it.

Chapter 23

Dressed in a maroon robe that might have been fashionable in Transylvania sometimes before the French Revolution, Michael felt more than a bit awkward walking beside Irini along the castle's hallways. Finding something that fit him had been no easy task.

They reached their destination and Irini pushed open the French doors of the room she'd referred to as the reception hall.

The furnishing and paintings on the walls were exactly what Michael had expected and weren't unlike what he'd seen when he and his friend Leka had crashed a Western Covenant party in San Francisco a couple of years earlier. Armchairs and settees were scattered across the room, most of them occupied by vampires currently busy staring Michael down. As a matter of fact, everyone in the room, including the enslaved serving staff, was currently staring at him.

"What did you bring us," said a man from a comfortable-looking armchair near the center of the room. He held a crystal glass with patterns edged in gold that was probably worth three times the entire content of Michael's cabin. The glass contained the remnants of a thick, red liquid Michael had no difficulty identifying.

"This is Michael, a professional investigator. With your permission, my liege, he'll help me investigate the robbery and make sure the right person is punished for the crime."

Vulpe got up from his seat and walked towards them, his movements fluid and graceful, almost animal-like. The halfmoon jewel that dangled from a heavy brass chain around his neck caught the light from the multitude of candles scattered around the room.

Vulpe stopped a few feet from Michael, facing him. The elder was probably a good five or six inches shorter than the werebear, but he moved with such authority that his size seemed utterly irrelevant.

"Do you have a surname, Michael?" asked the vampire.

"Biörn." Michael saw a flash of recognition in Vulpe's eyes.

"That means bear in the old Norse tongue, doesn't it?"

"It does."

"It would seem your investigator has a sense of humor, Irini. I like that. But you should have introduced him properly, the council deserves to know who they're dealing with."

"What are you implying, brother? Who is this man?" asked an elder standing in front of a painting depicting a battle opposing vampires and skinwalkers, most of them of the wolf type. The man who Michael assumed to be Vladislav also wore a brass chain around his neck, but the pendant of this one was an emerald-green pyramid.

"You don't recognize the name, Vladislav? This is no other than the werebear who slayed Dragos."

At the revelation most of the vampires jumped to their feet, flashing fangs that had suddenly doubled in size.

"I admire your fearlessness, bear, but your judgement is significantly lacking. Did you truly think coming here was a good idea? Dragos had many friends in this room, very old friends…"

"Michael is my guest, my liege," intervened Irini. "And as such, he is under my protection. You gave me carte blanche to investigate the matter and Michael is the most suited person to do so."

Michael heard a sarcastic laugh coming from the direction of the fireplace, but with the crowd surrounding him it was difficult to identify precisely to whom it belonged.

"Forgive my wife, Irini. Lately her manners have been… lacking," said Vladislav as a petite woman appeared between two males, her eyes throwing daggers at Vladislav.

And that would be Anastasia, the queen bitch, thought Michael, trying to keep an eye on the throng of enemies closing in on him. But the presence of Anastasia was distracting. She was breathtakingly beautiful and yet the energy emanating from her was both toxic and repulsive. *She'd probably be more attractive asleep… or dead*, thought Michael as he averted his eyes and brushed away the thought, refocusing on the growing silence and hostility in the room.

The vamps all wore some sort of flashy jewelry around their necks, even Irini. Most of them were made of gold or other precious metals, but Anastasia wore an oval pendant the color of ruby.

Vulpe raised an open hand and the rumor that had enveloped the room an instant earlier died off. "Very well, Irini. I'm a man of my word. You still have three days to prove your little Lucy innocent and until then nothing will happen to your guest. But if he's still on the premises by the time the sun rises on the fourth day, he won't walk out of here alive."

A woman had come to stand close to Vulpe while he talked. Her skin was particularly pale, even for a vampire, and her crimson lipstick, dark eye shadow, and lustrous black hair only accentuated the effect. She was looking at Michael with curiosity while fingering the intricately carved sapphire dangling around her neck. Unlike the others in the room, Michael saw no malevolence in her sad eyes.

"Thank you, my liege," said Irini, bowing her head. "Would you be kind enough to inform Cristos that Michael isn't to be harmed? We ran into some difficulties with some of his wolves earlier today."

"So I've heard… Very well, Cristos will be notified."

"Thank you, my liege. Now, with your permission, we would like to get started."

The leader gave a dismissive gesture and Irini ushered Michael out of the room. Things had gone just about as well as Michael had expected, better even. A good thing too, because given the company Vulpe was keeping, there was very little chance Michael would have made it out of that room alive had things gotten out of hand. Now he just had to pray the elder wouldn't go back on his word.

Chapter 24

Jason Parrish entered the Mammoth ranger station and asked if anybody had seen Olivia today, but the answer was negative. He'd tried to reach her on her cell phone and had already left several messages, but she hadn't called him back. He needed to make sure the woman went along with his version of the facts and made no waves about Robert Spencer's death. The unzipped jacket had been a big mistake and he doubted the explanation he'd offered had convinced anyone.

"She was supposed to come in at 2 PM to help me sort out interns' applications for this summer, but she never showed," said a woman.

"Did she call to cancel?"

"No. I tried calling to check on her, but she never answered."

"Could you try again, please?" he asked the woman, whose name he'd never bothered learning. In his defense, he'd never expected to be stuck in this godforsaken park for so long. He'd been sent in on suspicion of praeternatural activity within the park and had confirmed relatively rapidly the presence of a werebeing among the employees: Michael. An added bonus, Jason had even uncovered two previously unknown werewolves, Olivia and Daka. But then things had slowed down to a crawl for him. The exact nature of Michael's beast had apparently been a surprise to everybody as his kind was unheard of before, and the special forces led by Captain Brown had requested a wealth of information Jason didn't have prior to tackling the big bad bear: information he'd spent another six months collecting.

Goddamn Biörn was as discreet as they came and Jason still wondered how the director had gotten onto him in the first place. As a matter of fact, he had no idea how any of those creatures were being spotted in the first place. Big data mining coupled with artificial intelligence algorithms was the official explanation provided by his boss, the program's director, but Jason suspected the woman had a few spies up her sleeve as well.

"Still no answer," announced the interpretive ranger, replacing the phone's handset in its cradle. "I hope everything's okay. It's not like Olivia to bail like that, without warning."

"Let's hope so," answered Jason, who was starting to feel queasy about the situation. The director had told him to keep an eye on Olivia and he'd managed to lose her in less than a day. "Does she still live in the dorms?"

"No, there was a small vacant house and the superintendent told her she could use it until someone higher ranking needed it."

"Do you have the address?"

The woman pulled a map from her drawer and unfolded it on her crowded desk. She stared at it a minute before pointing at a spot. "That one. That's where she's staying."

Jason thanked her and took his leave.

The majority of staff housings were located at Mammoth and a two-minute walk later, Jason was knocking at Olivia's door. He knocked a second time, and then a third, before finally letting himself in using the master key issued to every law-enforcement personnel inside the park.

He found the house empty. No surprise there. But so were the closets, and that was more concerning. He found no clothes, suitcase or backpack in the entire house. No toothbrush or toothpaste in the bathroom either. The bitch was gone.

He swore under his breath as he picked up his mobile and dialed the director's number for the second time that day. She didn't answer and he was glad of it. Explaining the situation to her answering machine would be easier than in person.

He exited the house and locked it back up. He was walking towards his snowmobile when his phone rang in his pocket.

"I got your message. How did you manage to lose her so quickly?" The woman sounded pissed.

Jason apologized profusely while conjuring a few excuses that sounded made-up even to his ears.

"I've heard enough! I don't care about that wolf of yours. What I want is the bear. So only spend energy finding her if you think she can lead us to him. Understood?"

"Absolutely, Ma'am."

"In the meantime, I'll have someone check on his Paris trip story. If he flew anywhere under his name, we'll be able to track him down."

Chapter 25

Ezekiel was back in the US, walking along a Santa Barbara beach in a wet suit. He'd also adopted a much more youthful body for the occasion and was even equipped with a surfboard to complete the disguise. Michael would have probably found his outfit hilarious, but Ez wasn't in a joking mood. He couldn't recall the last time he'd felt so uneasy as a matter of fact. Whatever was going on, and whoever was behind it, it wasn't good news. And after weeks of looking into the matter, he still had no idea what the whole thing was about.

Wizards didn't need much sleep to function at peak capacity, but it had been over five days since his last nap, and he was starting to feel the effects of sleep deprivation. His thoughts were slower, his powers fainter. Nothing strikingly obvious, but obvious enough for him to notice.

It had only been a day and a half since he'd met with Methuselah and Tabitha, but he'd done so much since that it felt much longer. Since his companions had been equally unable to come up with an explanation for the strange phenomenon impacting the magical field, he'd decided to look in depth into the only tangible thing they had. Ezekiel had therefore spent the past thirty hours investigating the last known locations of all the werewolves that had gone missing, and what he'd found so far wasn't very encouraging.

He reached the remnants of a bonfire a few minutes later and planted his surfboard upright into the wet sand. Whoever had snatched the Santa Barbara pack had made a mistake. They'd missed one of the wolves and Ezekiel had found him.

The wolf had been on a date with a girl he'd just met while his buddies were getting snatched. He hadn't been able to reach any of his packmates since.

It was unclear whether the kidnappers were even aware they'd missed a wolf since one of his packmates had brought her human boyfriend to the bonfire and he, too, was missing.

His senses wide open, Ezekiel slowly walked around the pile of ashes and charred logs and felt the same thing he had at every other location he'd visited recently: absolutely nothing. Not a speck of residual magic in the air. Whatever had happened to those wolves, magic had nothing to do with it.

This observation was both reassuring and worrisome at the same time. Reassuring because whoever was responsible for the current massive distortion in the magical field was apparently not behind the werewolves' kidnapping. A good thing, because if a magical entity as powerful as the one they were dealing with had a werebeing army at their disposal, stopping them would be just about impossible. But it was also troubling because it meant there were two mysteries to solve instead of one, and the Second Circle still had absolutely no useful lead for either of them.

Whoever was snatching the werewolves was being extremely careful to leave no trace behind. Ez had been carefully looking at all the crime scenes and had so far found nothing at all. Of course, identifying the locations from which the praeternaturals had been abducted was far from an exact science and there was an above average chance that some of the places he'd been investigating were plain wrong. But this time around, he was fairly confident he was at the right spot.

The only footsteps around him were his own and those of a couple of joggers he'd seen a few minutes earlier, but the wizard wasn't without resources. He chanted an incantation in a language resembling high elvish and started walking in expanding circles around the site. As he did so, a multitude of footprints recently erased by the wind and the rain started appearing in the dry sand.

There were far too many to count, but he didn't have to. What he was looking for was a pattern. Something that would tell him the story of the abduction.

In addition to the prints, the spell revealed several deep circular holes in the sand, each roughly the diameter of a dime. Ezekiel placed his opened palm on top of one of the holes and soon a deformed bullet rose from the ground.

He continued his inspection of the site and found a few more bullets along with the tracks of those who'd most likely fired them. Tracks left by boots of different sizes, but which all had the same pattern, military boots. Of course, they could belong to mercenaries, but that wasn't relevant at the moment. What was relevant was the nature of the kidnappers. Those behind the attacks were humans. And although conflicts between humans and werebeings weren't unheard of, Ezekiel had never heard of any instance where the humans had come out on top. Until now…

Chapter 26

Nearly bent double, Michael was following Irini along a narrow hallway that had been built eight centuries earlier for men of a much smaller stature. The walls of the underground tunnel were wet to the touch and the smell of mold saturated the air they breathed.

The guard they found sitting on an aluminum chair in front of Lucy's cell was of the bloodsucking kind. Michael wondered which short straw the vamp had drawn to be forced to spend his nights on babysitting duty in this hole, but he wasn't curious enough to enquire.

"Open the door," ordered Irini, while they were still twenty feet from the cell.

"I cannot do that. I have strict orders. You'll need to talk to Cristos."

"I have Vulpe's benediction, I'm sure it will do."

"I'm sorry but I need—"

Before the man could complete his sentence, Irini, who'd closed the distance between them in a flash, hissed wildly at him. Her face couldn't be more than an inch or two from his. The guard got the message and backed down in front of the elder. He was smarter than he looked. He unlocked the gate and left the premises in a hurry, no doubt to report to Cristos.

It was pretty clear that the role of the guard was to prevent anyone from entering the cell from the outside rather than preventing Lucy's escape. The cell itself did a great job with this last point. The walls of her underground jail were made of a three-foot-thick layer of stones and the original wooden door had been replaced by a two-inch-wide metallic one. The door was too light to be made of steel and Michael suspected titanium had been used instead. A lighter, nearly equally resistant material that had the advantage of not corroding, a plus given the permanent humidity drowning the premises.

"It's me, Lucy, and I brought Michael with me," said Irini as they entered the pitch-black cell.

"Who's Michael?" Lucy's tentative question had come from a corner of the narrow room.

Michael turned on the electrical lantern Irini had given him for this purpose and put it down on the stone floor at the center of the cell.

"Michael!" exclaimed Lucy, who'd finally recognized him. "What are you doing here? You came to get me out?" The joy and hope in her voice nearly broke Michael's heart.

"I'm going to do my very best, Lucy. I can promise you that."

Irini told the prisoner about their arrangement with Vulpe, and that they'd come to ask her a few questions in order to help build her defense.

They sat on the ground in a circle centered around the lantern and Michael finally managed to get a good look at Lucy. Her clothes were stained with dirt and so was her face. Her normally gorgeous red hair looked oily and fell in clumps over her shoulder. She had the faint vampire scent typical to the newly-turned members of the race, but she didn't smell unclean. The fact vampires didn't sweat or secrete any other bodily fluid or solid had no doubt a lot to do with it.

"I need to know the truth, Lucy. Did you steal Vulpe's jewel?" asked Michael.

"I didn't! I swear it! On Olivia's head... I had absolutely nothing to do with this. I saw the pendant for the first time when Cristos' man brought it to Vulpe, claiming he'd found it hidden in my stuff." Lucy's voice was strained by fear and stress, but he was pretty sure the woman was sincere.

"Who had access to your sleeping quarters? Who could have planted the pendant there in order to frame you?"

It was Irini who answered the question. "Just about anyone. Lucy shares her room with a dozen vampires her age, I mean freshly-turned ones. There's no lock on the door, anyone already inside the castle could come in and out of the room as they please."

"Do you have any enemies here? Someone who's threatened you before, or simply dislikes you? Someone you may have rubbed up the wrong way?"

Lucy shook her head. "Not that I can think of."

"I haven't noticed anything either," concurred Irini.

"You said you'd never seen the pendant, but had you heard of its power? Had you ever heard of the Eye of the Phoenix before?"

"The Eye of the Phoenix? That's what that moon-looking thing is called? It doesn't look like an eye to me."

"It's only a third of it," explained Michael. "But you say it's moon-shaped? Was it the pendant Vulpe was wearing tonight?" He'd asked the last question of Irini.

"It was. He always wears it at night and only places it in his vault during the day."

"Why's that? Wouldn't it be safer around his neck at all times?"

"Vampires can sleep very deeply during the day. Depending on which phase of sleep he's in, Vulpe might not even notice if someone took it from around his neck. Plus, his vault was supposed to be as safe as it gets. Nobody but him has the combination, and the castle is better guarded than Fort Knox."

"His wife doesn't know the combination?" asked Michael.

"Actually, she does. I asked Vulpe that before you got here. But she's the only one," said Irini.

"Okay. Let me resume. Number one, Vulpe, and potentially his wife, are the only ones with the vault's combination. Number two, the vault wasn't forced. And number three, Vulpe is convinced Lucy's the one who stole the artifact." Michael paused and looked in turn at Lucy and Irini who both nodded. "Then how does Vulpe explain the fact Lucy knew the vault's combination?"

"I've been wondering the same thing ever since they locked me up in here. It makes no sense," said Lucy.

"I agree, but it's immaterial," said Irini. "Vulpe saw someone looking like Lucy when he read his slave's mind and that's good enough evidence for him."

Michael filed the information somewhere in his brain and moved on to the next subject. The question was for Irini this time. "Who in the castle knew that Vulpe's pendant was a fragment from the Eye of the Phoenix?"

"I don't know, Michael. I had no clue, which means it's not common knowledge even among the elders."

"What about the other pendants I saw tonight? Most of the vamps in the room wore some type of jewelry around their neck. Are any of those magical in nature?"

"Not that I know of. Vampires like to showcase their wealth. Clothes, jewelry, you name it. Every gathering is an excuse to show off how much money you have. Money is a sign of power for our kind."

"Just like for humans…" The concept disgusted Michael.

"Not quite," corrected Irini. "With humans, money gives them power. While with vampires it's usually the other way around. You can only be rich if you are physically powerful enough to hold on to your wealth. In other words, the wealth we flaunt around is indicative of the pecking order. You may have noticed that only four of the elders wore precious stones around their necks. The others wore gold, platinum, rhodium even, but no jewels."

Michael thought back to what he'd observed that afternoon. Vulpe's crescent moon had looked like it was made of citrine. Citrine wasn't a precious stone but as a fragment from one of the most powerful artifacts known to the world, its value far exceeded anything else he'd seen in the room. Michael had also noticed a pyramidal emerald around Vladislav's neck, a large ruby resting on Anastasia's chest and, of course, Milena had worn a huge sapphire. "The jewels are reserved for the ruling family," he concluded.

"Correct. Only the Zamfirs wear them. If someone else were to show up at a social gathering wearing one, it would be seen as a challenge. That doesn't happen very often…"

"And where do the others keep their pendants during the day? In their own vaults? Or would they put them inside Vulpe's?"

"I doubt they'd bother. They probably keep theirs around their necks. They may be of great financial value but unlike Vulpe's, they're all replaceable. And the Zamfirs have enough money to buy themselves truckloads of them."

No surprise there; Michael had enough money himself to own a few pounds of diamonds if the fancy struck him.

"We're digressing here. Let's get back to the task at hand," he said. "There's one thing I just don't get in this business. Something that makes absolutely no sense."

"What is it?" asked Irini.

Michael looked Lucy in the eyes as he said, "Anyone getting caught stealing from Vulpe would no doubt be executed, so why would someone risk their lives just to frame you? You're a newcomer here, a nobody… It would be one thing for someone to take such chances if they wanted to steal the artifact for themselves, but to go and hide it in your room so you would get caught with it, to go through the trouble of finding a Lucy lookalike to carry out the deed… I'm sorry, but that simply makes no sense at all. Are you sure you can't think of a reason someone would want to do this to you, Lucy?"

"I can't." She sounded defeated.

The darkness in the room could have played tricks on his eyes, but Michael could have sworn that a shadow had fallen on Lucy's face for a brief moment. Was she hiding something? "Is there anything else you can tell us that would help your case? Anything at all?"

The young woman looked hesitant, as if she wanted to say something but wasn't sure she should.

"What is it, Lucy?" asked Michael. "What do you have in mind? Now is really not a time for secrets."

"Nothing. I'm sorry, but I really can't think of anything," she said finally, shaking her head.

This time Michael was convinced she was lying.

Chapter 27

The two visitors stood a few feet inside the Parisian airport's video surveillance room, looking blasé. This was their first time conducting this kind of investigation, but their attitude was designed to convince their hosts otherwise.

"Detective Inspectors McDowell and Clark are with the Interpol's US office. They're looking for a man called Michael Biörn who landed here two days ago. We've been asked to fully cooperate with their investigations," said the cop in accented but otherwise perfect English before translating in French for those of his colleagues who weren't fluent in Shakespeare's tongue.

"What do you need from us detectives?" asked Pierrot, the man in charge of the video surveillance room where three men and one woman spent their days staring at banks of monitors showing live feeds of every corner of Paris-Charles de Gaulle, the French capital's massive airport. With nearly ninety million tourists visiting the country every year, France was the most visited country in the world. And the vast majority of the tourists who flew into the country landed at Charles de Gaulle.

Without further information, trying to identify a specific person among the thousands of travelers' ever-changing faces would have been a real nightmare, but the two Americans knew on which flight Biörn had been and this would make things significantly easier.

They gave instructions and then watched the fingers of the only woman in the room fly over her keyboard as she isolated footage corresponding to the exact time and location of interest.

Standing behind the woman's back, McDowell gave a discreet nod to his colleague. Things were going more smoothly than they'd hoped for. Nobody had questioned the legitimacy of their mandate or their identities: a mistake since they were equally fake.

The two had been sent by the director to locate a werebear named Biörn who'd managed to skip town under the nose of the agent in charge of bringing him in. They'd been assured that their fake credentials would withstand scrutiny and, apparently, they had. The director sure knew how to get things done.

"Here, that's him," said Clark, pointing at the monitor that showed a mountain of a man exiting a jetway and entering a terminal. Next to him was a pretty little thing of Asian descent, his girlfriend, apparently. Maybe the two of them truly were on a vacation. In which case the assignment would be pure pleasure. There were worse things in life than spending a week in Paris tailing a couple of tourists.

"Can you follow him through the airport?" asked McDowell.

"I can try," answered the woman with an accent so thick it would have made Inspector Clouseau proud.

Finding the booking Wang had made for their flight had been fairly easy, but the tech team had found no car rental or hotel reservations under either of their names. Consequently, they had no idea where the two were heading from the airport.

"Here again," said the woman, pointing at her own monitor where Biörn and Wang could be seen retrieving their luggage from the conveyor belt. After another twenty minutes of video screening, they found the two standing on the curb in front of the terminal waiting for someone. Biörn was talking on the phone.

The woman fast-forwarded the recording fifteen minutes and they saw a black Mercedes SUV stop in front of the two. Biörn threw their luggage into the trunk and they climbed into the car.

"Can we zoom in on the license plate?" asked Clark.

"Only in the movies," answered the woman.

Both the angle and the resolution of the camera made it impossible to read the only thing that would allow them to find the vehicle's owner. They could distinguish a seven and what looked like the letter A, but that was it, and it wasn't nearly enough.

The two fake Interpol agents were starting to despair when the woman pulled a shot taken from another camera down the road. One in which the Mercedes' license plate was crystal-clear.

Chapter 28

The half dozen patrons drinking their glasses of blush and red wine around the bar were the only other occupants of the small café in which Seemak sat awaiting Victor's arrival. The chameleon had driven all the way to Périgord from the Chambord castle where he served the Vaalt family. The fae had found the four-hour drive through the countryside more pleasant than he'd expected.

Périgord was famous for its idyllic scenery made up of beautiful castles and troglodytic villages carved into the mountains and overlooking meandering rivers. Outside the tourist season that started in May and ended in September, however, the region was nearly deserted, and most villages turned into ghost towns. In the middle of January, finding an open drinking establishment not too far from the vamps' stronghold had been a real challenge.

Seemak was sipping on a hot chocolate—the only thing drinkable on the menu—when Victor walked in and spotted the fae sitting in the most remote corner of the room.

The vampire seemed to hesitate a second, but then walked to Seemak's table and sat in front of him. The bartender enquired about the vamp's drinking preference from behind the counter, but Victor gave him a dismissive gesture and the man didn't insist.

"How's your night going, friend?" asked Seemak.

"I didn't come here for chit-chat, *friend*. Let's get to the point so I don't have to spend a minute longer than necessary smelling those wine bags over there."

Seemak smiled at the reference. Alcohol tainted the blood of humans, a taste that often repulsed vampires. "Do you have Vulpe's artifact?"

"You know I do," answered Victor.

"I meant did you bring it here with you, as I requested?"

"No. That I didn't. On the account that you cannot be trusted, my dear Seemak. I'll show you mine once you show me yours, if you know what I mean."

Taking another sip of cocoa, Seemak considered the new

information for a moment. "Very well. Since you don't trust me, how about we steal Lord Vaalt's fragments together?"

"Fragments? So you think Vaalt has the two missing pieces?"

"I suspect so, yes." It was the most logical conclusion based on the master's revelations, but Seemak wasn't about to tell Victor how he'd reached it.

"And you need my help to steal them, don't you?"

"We need each other, friend. Vaalt's apartment are protected against intrusions by the likes of me, but your invisibility mind trick should easily fool the mountain troll and the minotaur keeping guard."

"It sounds to me like I'm doing all the work in this little association," said the vamp with a twisted smile.

"Let's not forget you're the one with a debt towards me. And you'd never be able to enter Chambord let alone reach Lord Vaalt's apartments without my help. Teamwork *is* required here."

The vampire remained silent a moment while considering the fae's offer. "Fine, you do need help, but it doesn't have to be mine. I already retrieved one third of the artifact, that's enough to erase my de—"

"Without you, we'll never retrieve the other two pieces," interrupted Seemak. "Your mind trick is needed to fool the guards."

"You didn't let me finish. I'm not willing to take the risk, but I can provide a substitute. A vampire with skills equal to mine, but more... expendable."

What was Victor trying to pull? The offer was more than a bit suspicious, but in the end did it really matter? "I assume your substitute can be trusted?"

"That goes without saying."

"Very well. Tell your substitute to meet me at this location at sundown two days from now," said the fae, sliding a napkin across the table where GPS coordinates had been jotted down.

"Why two days?"

"Because Lord Vaalt is hosting a reception in two days and this will give us the window we need to retrieve the fragments from his quarter."

"Very well, my substitute will meet you in two days," said Victor, pocketing the coordinates.

"And make sure he brings the artifact along with him, we'll need it to escape if we were to get caught."

Victor eyed him suspiciously before giving a nod. The vampire then got up and exited the café.

Alone once again at his table, Seemak thought back on their discussion. What was this substitute business about? Victor's explanation had been less than convincing.

Chapter 29

Irini and Michael were looking for clues inside Vulpe's private quarters under the watchful eye of Cristos. The presence of the Covenant's head of security had been mandated by Vulpe himself in exchange for his consent to allow them to enter his apartments. Michael had been surprised that Vulpe had agreed at all. Maybe the vamp was less of a hard ass than he wanted his people to believe.

The first thing Michael had done after entering the room was to go straight to the vault dissimulated behind the frame of a massive painting. He'd stared a long moment at the steel behemoth and its digital keypad used to enter the eight-digit combination required to unlock the safe.

An eight-digit code implied a hundred million possible combinations in the first place. If one added to this the fact that the safe was programmed to go into alarm if the wrong digits were entered three times in a row, there was little chance that anyone could have gotten into Vulpe's secret stash by sheer luck.

Michael was currently staring at the dark stain left on the stone floor by the blood of the slave who had been killed by the thief. "What was the slave doing in this room? Coming to clean up?" he asked Irini.

"No. Cleaning service in Vulpe's quarters is done by three servants an hour after sunrise. According to the slave's memory she was struck about two hours before sunset."

"So what was she doing here?"

"I haven't figured this out yet. She was the girl in charge of fireplaces. Her main job was to clean the hearths of their ashes and stock them with firewood. An hour before dusk, she would go around the rooms and light the fires so that the temperature would be comfortable by the time the elders got out of bed."

"But apparently she entered the room two hours before dusk. Why? I doubt she would come into Vulpe's room unless she had a particularly good reason."

"I agree, but I've no idea. Maybe we can interrogate the other slaves," suggested Irini.

"She came to light the fire," said Cristos.

Michael and Irini both turned towards the man who'd stood statue-like in absolute silence ever since they'd entered the room.

"An hour ahead of schedule? How do you know that?" asked Irini.

"Because I heard Anastasia talk to the girl about it the night before. Vulpe had complained that his room was too cold early in the night, apparently. I suppose Anastasia wanted our liege to be more comfortable when he gets out of bed."

Cristos' answer had been matter-of-fact, but Michael couldn't help wondering if there hadn't been a hint of innuendo in the vamp's statement. Assuming Anastasia had indeed been Vulpe's mistress, had she planned on visiting him early in the night and wanted the room to be nice and warm for whatever activity she had in mind?

"Thank you for the information, Cristos. I appreciate it," said Irini.

The vampire didn't reply, and Michael resumed his search. On the wall opposite the safe was a gigantic library nearly filled with ancient books, all in perfect condition. "Vulpe likes to read, it seems."

"He does, but he loves collecting rare volumes even more than reading them. All the books you see are first editions, and most of them are signed by the authors. The shelves are temperature-controlled and the room's humidity is maintained within a range optimal for book preservation."

Michael went to stand in front of the bookshelves, right at the center of the library, and turned around. Directly in front of him, on the opposite wall, was the frame hiding the vault. He considered his position for an instant and shook his head. That couldn't work. Since the hinges of the painting were located on the right side of the frame, Michael scooted down a few feet to the left and started carefully studying the bookshelf and its volumes with a pen light.

He spent about ten minutes without finding anything useful and scooted down a couple feet more before resuming his search. This time he found something of interest: behind a row of books, a small rectangular space where the dust layer was thinner than on the surrounding area. Something had been sitting behind these books not long ago. This at least shed some light on one of the questions that had been bugging him.

The quarters Lucy had shared with her fellow novices weren't nearly as luxurious as Vulpe's apartments, but they were still a few orders of magnitude nicer than her current accommodations in the guts of the castle when it came to comfort. Equipped with nearly a dozen bunkbeds, the windowless room reminded Michael of a military dorm. The narrow dressers marked with the names of the new recruits to whom they'd been assigned standing between the beds only accentuated the impression.

Only a third of the room looked like it was being used and at the moment the novices' quarters were empty with the exception of a male and a female. The male, who was combing his hair in front of a mirror, looked to be in his early forties. Contrary to popular belief, a vampire reflection did appear in mirrors and the bloodsuckers weren't afraid or harmed by the reflective surface in any way.

The female was lying on her bed reading a magazine. She looked younger than the man, twenty-five maybe, but looks could be deceiving among vampires.

Michael started examining the contents of Lucy's dresser but found nothing unusual among the young woman's clothes and other personal items. Irini and he then turned their attention towards the man who'd finished dressing and was about to go grab a bite, as he so humorously put it. Unfortunately he had absolutely no useful information to reveal. He was rapidly dismissed, and the two investigators moved on to the solitary female who was now openly staring at them.

"What's your name?" asked Irini.

"Claudia, my lady." The vamp had gotten to her feet as she answered in a low-pitched voice Michael hadn't expected.

"Do you know Lucy well?" he asked.

"We aren't close friends, but we talk from time to time."

"Did you ever see her in possession of the artifact she's accused of stealing?" continued Michael.

"No."

"And did you notice anyone who didn't belong in this dorm the day the artifact was taken?" This time the question had come from Irini.

"I didn't, my lady."

Michael thought he'd detected a split second of hesitation before Claudia's answer. "Are you certain of that?" His voice wasn't openly threatening, but it conveyed enough authority to make the vampire stand a bit straighter.

"I'm quite positive." She answered looking Michael straight in the eyes—a provocation she'd never dare with Irini. The vamp had accurately ruled out Michael as one of her kind, but she was too inexperienced to realize the man standing in front of her could have ripped her head off her shoulders faster than she could say her name.

"What is it, then? You look like someone who has something to say."

The woman looked from Michael to Irini and back to Michael before answering, "Actually, I think Lucy did it."

"What makes you say that?" asked Irini.

"She wasn't in her bed the day the artifact was stolen. I woke up in the middle of the day and Lucy's bed was empty, she was nowhere to be seen."

"Do you often wake up in the middle of the day?" asked Irini, and Michael could tell by her tone that this wasn't normal vampire behavior.

"I'm not a great student, my lady. And when my performance isn't to his satisfaction, my maker punishes me by withholding blood from me. At the time, I hadn't fed in three days and it was the pangs of hunger that woke me."

Irini accepted the explanation without further question and Michael decided to do the same. "Had this happened before? Had you ever caught Lucy out of bed in the middle of the day in the past?"

"No. This was the first time."

Things weren't looking good for Lucy. Why hadn't she mentioned anything about it when they'd met with her earlier? Already then, he'd had the feeling the girl was hiding something. Had she been the one stealing the artifact after all? Michael had a hard time believing it, but it was becoming increasingly obvious that Lucy wasn't being truthful with them. Whatever she was hiding, she needed to come clean in a hurry because one thing was certain: time was running out for her.

Chapter 30

Jason Parrish's snowmobile had been spotted the minute it had entered the Wind River Shoshone Reservation located southwest of Yellowstone National Park, and Daka had been informed immediately. The skinwalker had then related the information to Olivia and his packmates, and measures had been taken in preparation for the ranger's arrival.

When Jason finally made it to the not-so-small log cabin Daka had built with his own hands, with help from his packmates, the ranger found only Cameahwait sitting in a rocking chair on the porch. Wrapped in a tightly woven blanket made of colorful strings assembled in intricate patterns, the old man was smoking a pipe, eyes nearly closed. But the Shoshone elder was far from asleep; the leader of Daka's pack was patiently waiting for the intruder to state the reason for his presence on their land.

"Hi there, I'm looking for Daka. Is he in?" asked Jason.

Cameahwait didn't bother opening his eyes to welcome the newcomer. He shook his head slowly in answer to the question and took a long draw from his pipe.

"Do you know where he is?"

Cameahwait shook his head once more and started humming in a low voice.

"Any idea when he'll be back?" The ranger's voice was starting to betray his growing impatience with the old man. His latest question was met with exactly the same answer as the previous ones, however.

"What about his girlfriend, Olivia—any idea where I could find her?"

After more shaking of the head from the elder, Jason got back on his snowmobile and took off in a hurry. He would probably try to ask the same questions of others on the reservations, but he would obtain nothing useful from the Shoshones who'd all been warned about the man.

Ten minutes after Jason's departure, Cameahwait finished his pipe and entered the house. "He's gone," he said in English for Olivia's benefit.

A moment later Daka and Olivia came down the stairs to meet the elder who was already surrounded by three of Daka's packmates who'd been hiding in various rooms on the first floor, ready for action.

"Be careful, child. This man has a dark aura. You shouldn't return to Yellowstone as long as Michael isn't around."

Olivia nodded. "Thank you, Cameahwait."

"She'll stay here with me for now," said Daka.

"I'm afraid he might be back," said Cameahwait. "And if he is, he won't be alone. The two of you need to take a vacation. I would suggest a camping trip in the heart of the Shoshone National Forest. No one will find you there."

Chapter 31

The next interview on Michael and Irini's list was going to be a much tougher one than those they'd had with Lucy's roommates. Whereas Irini's authority and reputation alone had sufficed to coerce the novices into talking to them, the same authority wouldn't be nearly enough to convince Vladislav Zamfir to do the same. The elder was third in the Covenant's hierarchy and owed respect only to the ruling couple.

Irini seemed confident, however, that Vladislav would probably grant them an interview out of the kindness of his heart, if he happened to be alone. She gave a vigorous knock on the door but, unfortunately for the two investigators, it was the queen bitch in person who answered.

"What do you want?" Anastasia made no effort to hide her disgust towards Michael, wrinkling her nose as she spoke.

"I wish you a good night, Anastasia. I was wondering if we could have a word with Vladislav. It would only take a minute or two of his time," answered Irini.

The bitch gave her a dirty look before calling for her husband as she slammed the door in their faces.

Vladislav came to the door an instant later. "What is it, Irini?"

Over the vamp's shoulder, Michael saw Anastasia rummaging through a wall safe half the size of Vulpe's. She pulled out a ruby necklace and clasped it around her neck.

"As you know, we're investigating the robbery in Vulpe's chamber and we'd like to ask your opinion on a point or two. It will only take a moment."

"Very well. Let me put on something warmer. I'll meet you outside in a minute."

Vladislav retreated inside the apartments he shared with his wife but didn't shut the door behind himself.

From where he stood, Michael had a clear line of sight to Anastasia who'd retired to one of the two wide armchairs placed on either side of the room's fireplace. The vamp was reading a book, and it took Michael only an instant to recognize the cover. He'd seen that gold and teal jacket before. This book was part of a series he had spotted earlier that day in Vulpe's library.

According to Irini, Vulpe was very protective of his books and didn't let others borrow them, so why was Anastasia reading one of them at this very moment? She could, of course, have taken the volume without Vulpe's knowledge, but Michael doubted this was the explanation. He found it much more likely that Vulpe had loaned her the volume: another indication that the relationship between the ruler and his sister-in-law might not be as platonic as it should.

Michael and Irini walked alongside Vladislav on the outer edge of the moat circling the castle. Since vampires saw perfectly well in the dark, and since werewolves were only on guard duty during the day, the property hadn't been equipped with electric lighting and the only light was that percolating from the moon and the stars in the mostly cloudy sky.

"My apologies for dragging you out here, but this will at least save us from Anastasia's spiteful tongue. What was it you wanted to ask me?" said Vladislav.

Michael wasn't used to hear vampires apologizing, especially not one as high ranking as Vladislav.

"Thank you for giving us a few minutes of your time, Vladislav. We wanted to talk to you because we need your help."

"And how can I help you?" The vampire sounded a bit surprised.

"We haven't found much evidence proving Lucy's innocence so far," started Irini. "And I'm afraid things are looking pretty grim for her if we don't find something more substantial to present to Vulpe during her trial tomorrow."

"I fail to see how I can help." The elder's voice had taken a slightly defensive edge, something Michael didn't fail to notice.

"You were the only one who questioned her guilt the day she was arrested and brought in front of the council. I was hoping you had reasons to believe in her innocence. Some information that might help her case, maybe," pleaded Irini.

But Vladislav shook his head. "I'm afraid I have nothing to offer you. Lucy seems like a nice kid and I wanted to make sure my brother had valid proof of her guilt before he decided to take her life. But if she was seen committing the deed through the slave's eyes… then she must have done it."

There was something that sounded odd in the man's reply, an obvious lack of conviction in his own words.

"But Lucy had no way of knowing that Vulpe's jewel was a fragment from the Eye of the Phoenix, no way to know the combination of his safe… She's just a novice, you know that."

"I do, Irini. And I suggest you find a way to prove that to Vulpe tomorrow. I wish I could help you, but there's nothing I can do. Now if you'll excuse me, I must get back to my lovely wife."

The vampire turned around and retraced his steps all the way to the drawbridge while Irini and Michael stood there at a loss for words.

"I think we need to start thinking about plan B, Michael. We're going to need to break Lucy out of jail."

"We cannot do that."

"I know what you're going to say. Even if we succeed, I'll never be able to go back to the Covenant. I'll be marked a traitor and I'll need to watch over my shoulder for the rest of my life. But I don't care, Lucy doesn't deserve this. I know she's innocent."

Michael wished he could share Irini's conviction, but he simply couldn't. He had seen no proof of the girl's innocence, and he found her behavior more than a bit suspect.

"We need to get her out of here tomorrow morning, Michael, as soon as the werewolves' shift has started. They'll be easier to fight than the vampires."

Michael wasn't entirely certain of this, but it was irrelevant anyway. "I'm worried about what would happen to you if we managed to get Lucy away from this place, but that's not why I don't want to try, Irini."

"Why then?"

"Because it's simply not doable. I've been studying the security in this place ever since I got here. There's absolutely no way we can get Lucy out of here alive. Not as long as she's in that cell of hers."

"So that's it, we're going to let her die?" Irini looked more pissed off than defeated.

"I didn't say that… I believe we may have a sliver of a chance to escape tomorrow during the trial."

"But the room will be packed with vampire elders and Cristos' men… we won't even make it to the door."

"You're going to have to trust me, Irini. If I tell you it's our best chance, it's because it is." Michael tried to put as much confidence as he could muster in his voice, but he couldn't kid himself. Whichever way he looked at it, the odds were most definitely against them. Unless, of course…

He carefully considered the idea for a moment before turning to Irini. "I may have a solution to our problem. It's a long shot but worth trying."

Chapter 32

Nearly thirty hours had passed since McDowell and Clark had landed in Paris to follow Biörn's trail, but the trail had grown cold. Very cold.

The license plate of the Mercedes that had picked up Biörn and Wang in front of the terminal belonged to a corporation headquartered in Gibraltar, which was itself owned by an LLC in the Bahamas, and so on and so forth. With a dozen shell corporations between the vehicle and its owner, it would be nearly impossible to find the owner of the car and therefore obtain an address.

They'd hoped to be able to pick up the car's location as it traveled through the French capital—assuming it was even heading to Paris—but their hopes had been in vain. Contrary to London where CCTV cameras watched every building and street corner, the video surveillance in Paris wasn't very developed. Apparently, the French government still valued the privacy of its citizens, or at least feared them enough to think twice before provoking their wrath in this way: a wise decision in a country where people infamously took to the streets at the drop of a hat.

The two fake Interpol agents had spent the morning going from one Parisian hotel to another, showing Biörn and Wang's pictures to staff in the hope they'd checked in under fake names and that someone might recognize them. But so far, they'd had no luck. Since the two *fugitives* had flown in first class, the detectives had started showing their pictures in the fanciest hotels of the capital. The reasoning had some merits but had led nowhere.

They were walking down the Champs-Elysées with rumbling stomachs when they spotted a three-story McDonald's. Forgoing French delicacies, they pushed open the door of the franchise and ordered something they could at least pronounce. The fast food joint was packed with students and tourists in equal proportion and when McDowell felt his cellphone vibrating inside his pocket, he had to step outside to take the call.

"McDowell," he said.

"Hello, my name is Laure Pelletier. I work for Interpol's National Central Bureau in Paris and I was told you were looking for a Mercedes." The woman's French accent was one of the most subtle he'd heard since he'd landed.

"That's right. You found it?"

"Not exactly, but it was caught speeding by an automatic radar in Dordogne yesterday afternoon."

"Dordogne? Never heard of the city. Is it close to Paris?"

"Dordogne is a region, sir. And it's nowhere close to Paris. It's in the southwest of France. It's a tourist area also known under its old name of Périgord."

"I assume that region has many hotels?" said McDowell, thinking about the daunting task ahead of them.

"Yes, many. But this time of the year they will all be closed save for maybe a few in Périgueux and Bergerac. In January Dordogne is nearly deserted."

"Good. Could you give me the exact location of that radar?"

It took a few minutes for the woman to locate the information. When she finally did, McDowell wrote it down in his notepad, thanked her for her precious assistance and returned inside to grab his colleague. They needed to hurry; they had a four-hundred-mile drive ahead of them.

Chapter 33

The furniture inside the reception hall had been rearranged to host Lucy's trial. The room had been divided in two by a central aisle and seats had been arranged on either side. At the very front, aligned with the center aisle, Vulpe sat in an armchair facing the audience.

Michael and Irini sat alone in the front row on the right side of the aisle. As a matter of fact, they were the only ones sitting on this side of the aisle at all.

Sitting in the front row on the opposite side were Milena, Vladislav and Anastasia. Two dozen elders sat behind the ruling family, chatting as if they were in a theater. A proper analogy, for Michael doubted strongly that this trial would be anything other than a production. A parody of justice designed to distract Vulpe's court. Lucy's fate had been sealed long before Michael even set foot inside the Eastern Covenant's fortress.

Since the vampires wanted a show, Michael would give them one, but he doubted the audience would appreciate the performance.

Lucy hadn't been brought to the room yet, but Cristo's men were already posted at every window and three of them stood at the door. Michael had also noticed wolves patrolling the outside perimeter of the castle, something they weren't supposed to be doing at night according to Irini, but there they were. Michael's reputation was probably the cause of what seemed like an overabundance of security.

Lucy entered the room escorted by two vampires who walked her up the aisle. She winked at Michael as she passed by his chair, but he didn't wink back. The guards dropped her off ten feet in front of Vulpe's armchair before taking a few steps back to stand at the ready on either side of the aisle.

"The day of your trial has come," said Vulpe from his seat, as he poured himself a glass of fresh blood from a pitcher sitting on an end table beside him. "Your defense team has had a week to uncover new evidence in your favor. Evidence aimed at convincing me of your innocence. Let's hope for you they found something."

The leader took a sip from his glass before turning to Irini. "What do you have for us, *counselor*?"

Irini stood up and took a few steps towards Vulpe. "My liege, I am ready to make the case for Lucy's innocence, but before I start, I beg you to consider the evidence I'll present in the same light as the evidence against her."

"What do you mean by that?"

"I mean that the evidence we have in her defense is circumstantial, but so is the evidence at charge. Your slave saw a red-headed woman who resembled Lucy, that is all."

"I know what she saw, Irini, having read her mind myself... So I hope for your protégée that your evidence isn't too *circumstantial*. Now on with it."

"Yes, my liege," said Irini, her voice deferential. "To start with, Lucy has only been among us a few months. She is by all accounts a novice in this Covenant. How could she have learned that you were in possession of such a valuable artifact? I myself ignored it and our interviews revealed that it was also the case for the vast majority of the audience. We knew your pendant was valuable, but nobody here knew what it was until you revealed it to us the day it disappeared."

Vulpe gave Irini an utterly unconvinced look before gesturing for her to continue.

"There is also the matter of your vault. How could Lucy have found out where you kept your artifact during the day? How could she have learned the safe's combination?"

"The same argument goes for everyone in here, Irini. Only Milena and I knew the combination and my wife is above suspicion in this matter. That means that whoever stole the artifact figured out the combination one way or another. This doesn't exonerate your pet in any way."

Irini took a deep breath, a purely instinctual reflex since vampires didn't need to breath. "And now I'd like to bring your attention to a much more likely suspect than Lucy."

The remark generated commotion in the audience, but it quickly died when Vulpe slammed his fist on the table beside him. "Continue."

"The Eye of the Phoenix is a fae artifact. There's no one better suited than the faes to locate it. Faes are also well equipped to impersonate others. They could have used glamour to introduce themselves inside the castle."

"Glamour wouldn't have fooled the noses of our wolves, Irini." Vulpe sounded amused by the idea.

"But a chameleon could have," interjected Michael.

These were the first words out of the shifter's mouth and Vulpe, who'd acted as if Michael didn't exist up to that point, turned his attention towards him. "Who gave you the right to speak, bear?"

"Please forgive Michael's lack of manners, my liege. He's not familiar with our rules. But he raises a valid point. A chameleon could easily have fooled the werewolves and the slave. He could have seen Lucy in a hallway and adopted her distinctive appearance to commit the deed. This to deflect suspicions away from the faes."

Vulpe was now drumming his fingers on the chair's armrest, looking bored. "Are you done?"

"For now," answered Irini, tentatively.

"Then tell me why your chameleon would have hidden the jewel in Lucy's dresser instead of disappearing with it."

Irini had no plausible explanation to offer, however.

"That's what I thought," declared Vulpe triumphantly. "And now let me produce a witness for the prosecution."

The announcement took Michael and Irini by surprise. Vulpe clapped his fingers and a female was ushered into the room by one of the guards. Michael recognized the young woman immediately. It was Claudia, Lucy's roommate. He knew full well what she had to say, and it wasn't good news for Lucy.

As expected, Claudia testified that Lucy hadn't been in her bed the day of the robbery. She was then excused and sent out of the room as Vulpe turned his attention to Lucy who was still standing transfixed in front of him. "What do you have to say in your defense, child? What were you doing out of bed in the middle of the day? I'd suggest you choose your words wisely as they will likely be your last."

Lucy seemed taken aback by the question. She turned towards Michael with a questioning look.

"You have nothing to answer, child? Very well, in this case your original sentence is confirmed. You will be exe—"

"Lucy didn't steal your artifact, brother." Vladislav was standing up in the front row on the left side of the aisle. All eyes were on him. "Lucy wasn't in her bed at the time the crime was committed because she was in mine. She spent that whole day with me and left my bedroom shortly before dusk."

A loud ruckus engulfed the room as the audience reeled at the implications of Vladislav's revelation. The vampire had admitted to adultery in front of his wife and the entire council. This definitely wasn't part of the etiquette, and Anastasia was unlikely to take the affront philosophically.

Vulpe banged his fist on the table a few times and the clamor died down inside the reception hall. "In view of my brother's testimony, the charges against you are dismissed, Lucy. You may reintegrate with the ranks of the novices." The leader looked both surprised and disappointed with the turn of events.

Before he could pronounce another word, Anastasia rose from her seat and violently slapped her husband in the face before leaving the room, quickly followed by Milena and a dozen members of the audience, mostly women.

"And now that this trial is over, your safe conduct has expired, bear," said Vulpe, standing up and looking at Michael threateningly.

"My liege, my guest will be leaving the premises immediately," interceded Irini. "You must grant him safe passage until he exits the grounds. He has no quarrel with us."

"He killed Dragos, I'd say that qualifies as quarrel."

"I beg you, my liege." Irini's voice sounded imploring.

"Very well. I will once again grant your request, Irini. Your *guest* will be given a brief respite. He has precisely two minutes to leave the property, after which he'll be hunted down by every vampire and wolf on the premises."

"Stay out of this, Irini," yelled Michael who was already running towards the closest window. The vamp guarding it didn't step aside, but he didn't make a move to stop Michael, either, as the ranger dove through the stained glass.

After a twenty-foot drop, he landed on his feet in the castle's inner courtyard where a half dozen novices were practicing their combat skills. He sprinted towards the gate of the fortress, but the drawbridge was up.

Michael had located the lever operating the bridge the previous day during a recon walk around the compound and now he made a beeline for it. He reached it a moment later under the questioning eyes of the novices and pulled the lever down.

The bridge started going down ever so slowly and Michael took this opportunity to morph into his bear, a much faster and fiercer opponent for Cristos' vamps who were now pouring into the courtyard from all wings of the castle.

The drawbridge wasn't all the way down, but the bear could no longer afford to wait. He took off at full gallop on the inclined bridge that was still a good eight feet from the ground and jumped over the gap. The ground trembled under the impact of the eight-hundred-pound animal, but Michael didn't break stride. He needed to reach the outer bailey's gate as soon as possible.

It was already too late, however. As he raced toward the property's main portal, he could see Cristos' vamps converging on him from all directions. Over a dozen werewolves in their beast form were with them.

Michael didn't like his odds. Unlike Serafin's daywalkers, these vamps knew what they were doing, and he suspected the wolves to be equally well-trained. The gate was still two hundred feet ahead of him when the four werewolves guarding it dropped their guns and started morphing into their beasts.

Michael was sprinting at nearly forty miles per hour, but the vamps were still faster than him and the first one reached the bear an instant later. The bloodsucker punched him on the side of the head and although his bear registered the blow, it didn't even twitch. The vamps went for another punch and this time Michael grabbed his arm in his powerful jaws and chopped it off above the elbow. The vampire screamed in pain, but the bear wasn't done with it. Still running, he kicked the injured vamp in the chest with both back paws and sent him colliding into two bloodsuckers that had been closing in on him. The impact sent the two vamps flying while the one-armed bloodsucker hit the floor and stayed there.

Michael was able to dispatch another vampire before he noticed two wolves coming at him from his right side on an interception course. The gate was only a hundred feet or so away now, but it might as well have been a mile. Michael also doubted his enemies would magically cease the pursuit if he miraculously managed to reach the portal.

When the two wolves were only fifteen feet away, Michael abruptly changed course and headed for the first of the two. The move surprised the wolf, which didn't get a chance to correct its trajectory before Michael careened into him and grabbed him by the neck. He felt his enemy's spine give under his jaws and the wolf's head soon rolled to the ground as Michael redirected his attention towards the other beast. But this one avoided the confrontation and retreated to a distance, probably awaiting back-up. The behavior surprised Michael who thought an enthralled wolf would have lost all instinct for self-preservation. But before he had time to wonder about it, the four guards from the gate fell on him in a hurricane of fangs and claws that sent his bear tumbling to the ground.

He quickly got back on his paws and took on the four werewolves as an army of fifty vamps was closing in. He had no time to be subtle. Using his four-inch claws as spears, he simultaneously perforated the heart of two of the wolves using his front paws, before grabbing the tail of the third one between his teeth and using it as a flail against the fourth one. The two wolves collided with such velocity that it effectively knocked them out.

Michael wished he had time to finish them off but he truly didn't. The nearest enemy was the wolf who'd already cowered away from him once, so Michael decided to make a dash for the gate. He crossed its threshold an instant later as the vanguard of Cristos' army was closing the distance. The coward werewolf was still on his tail, however. Michael had managed to exit the castle, but the enemy wouldn't give up the fight.

He could sense the wolf right behind him but couldn't afford to turn around to check how close the rest of his foes were.

Michael ran fifty feet along the main road before dashing into the woods; the rumble of the mob chasing him wasn't as loud anymore and he risked slowing down a second to have a peek. He found the werewolf ten feet behind him, but the animal was alone.

Michael stopped running and turned to face the beast which stopped dead in its tracks. Through the trees, the bear could still see the main gate. It was wide open and jampacked with his enemies, but none of them stood outside. It was as if they were all stuck inside unable to cross the domain's property line.

Michael had a good idea of what was going on, but he was still caught by surprise when the lone wolf turned into Ezekiel in front of his very eyes.

Chapter 34

It was nearly one in the morning by the time Michael reached the house Sheila had rented to find the lights on. The front door was unlocked, and he let himself in. He wasn't particularly surprised to find Sheila sitting in the living room laughing at something witty Ezekiel had just said, no doubt at Michael's expense.

"Good evening, honey. Are you hungry? I cooked you three T-bones but I'm afraid they must be cold by now. I was expecting you earlier; Ezekiel's been here for over two hours already."

"Three hours to cover thirty measly miles?" said Ez, checking an imaginary watch on his wrist. "What an athlete."

"I was forced to stick to the woods and the fields to avoid attracting attention. People around here aren't used to seeing grizzlies roaming the countryside. The closest bears are in the Pyrenees two hundred miles south of here and they don't look anything like me."

"If you're done making excuses, maybe you can answer Sheila's question."

"Sorry, Sheila. Yes, I'm hungry, but no need to warm anything up. Cold will do just fine."

"I don't know how you put up with him, my dear. How a lovely woman like you doesn't find it unbearable to be around an oaf such as that one will always be a mystery to me."

Ignoring both his friend's provocation and the silverware Sheila had brought with his plate, Michael grabbed one of the steaks from the tray in front of him and sank his teeth into it. It was barely cooked, just the way he liked it.

After walking along beside Michael for three or four miles, the wizard had decided he didn't need the exercise and had opted for more expedient means of transportation to reach Sheila's rental. Means that weren't accessible to the likes of Michael.

"Ez tells me he had to save your life once again," said Sheila in a reproachful voice, a stern look in her eyes. He knew she was mostly joking, but he also knew a part of her was serious. She worried about his wellbeing the same way he worried about hers.

"I've no doubt he told you all about it. But did he also mention that before saving my life he spent the evening playing drag queen? Again…"

Amused, Sheila turned to the wizard. "You forgot to mention that part, Ez."

"I'm starting to think there might be some type of repressed Freudian need behind this hobby of yours," teased Michael.

The wizard shook his head in disbelief. "Your boyfriend omitted to mention a small but important detail. It's at his request that I impersonated Lucy for the evening. And I had to do this because he was unable to come up with a way to rescue the poor girl on his own. Big surprise!"

"Where's Lucy now?" asked Sheila.

"She's still at the Covenant. Her trial went better than I'd expected; she was exonerated of all charges."

"What happened exactly? Where was Lucy during the trial if Ez was impersonating her?" Sheila still looked perplexed.

"She was hiding in Irini's car in the Covenant's underground parking garage. Ezekiel snuck into her cell a few minutes before Lucy's jailers came to get her for the trial. As soon as the guards got the fake Lucy out of the dungeon, the real one went to hide in the garage. By now, Irini has no doubt told Lucy the good news and the two of them are likely back among the vamps as if nothing had happened."

Michael took a bite out of his steak the size of a fist and barely chewed it before swallowing. "When did you change into a wolf? I didn't see you doing that."

"If you'd seen me doing it, I wouldn't be much of a wizard, would I? All eyes were on you, so I took advantage of this opportunity to take a shortcut from the courtyard to a grove of trees near the portal and change into a wolf away from prying eyes."

"And you also erected a force field around the vamps' property as soon as I passed through the gate, I suppose?"

"And they say you're not very smart... Anyway, you were lucky I was there. Lucy would have been just fine without me, but your ass would have been vampire fodder."

Michael didn't doubt it for a moment. "But since you were going to help, why didn't you do it earlier? Why did you wait for me to cross the portal's threshold?"

"Because I play fair. Vulpe gave you an ultimatum and I stayed out of it as long as he honored his own terms. His terms, however, were exceeded when his men tried to chase you after you'd escaped the domain."

Michael found the explanation less than convincing but didn't push the issue. Supernatural beings like Ez weren't supposed to get involved in praeternatural matters in the first place, and he was grateful the wizard kept breaking the rules on his behalf. Michael was also convinced that, had he been in a truly dire situation, the wizard would have intervened earlier. "Once again, thank you for your help, Ez."

"In this instance, you're truly welcome, Michael. Not only did I find the spectacle of you being chased by those bloodsuckers highly entertaining, I also learned something very interesting. Something I don't quite understand at the moment."

"Would you care to share your discovery with us?" asked Michael.

Ezekiel gave them a suspicious look before finally answering, "Nah. I don't think so."

"Why not?" Sheila looked genuinely surprised.

"I'm just kidding, sweetie. What I found out concerns the Eye of the Phoenix. A fragment of it was in that room during the trial..." announced Ezekiel as if he'd just found a cure for human stupidity.

"Of course, it was the crescent moon Vulpe wore around his neck. I told you that yesterday already."

"And that's where you're wrong, young insolent. The pendant around Vulpe's neck carries as much magical energy as a piece of coal. I sensed the artifact fragment as soon as I stepped into the room, but the flow of energy emanated from somewhere behind me to my left."

This was surprising information, but it wasn't narrowing things down a whole lot. With the exception of Vulpe who'd sat in front of Ezekiel, and Irini who'd been on his right, every other vampire in the room had been sitting behind Ez on the left side of the aisle. "Are you certain of this?"

"How do you dare ask such questions of me? Have I ever been wrong about anything, ever?"

Michael was pretty certain such a thing had happened on more than one occasion, but he refrained from pointing it out to the wizard. "So you're saying one of the other vampires had the artifact with them?"

"Precisely. I can even narrow it down a bit further for you. It was one of the vamps who left the room after Anastasia's little scene."

Michael thought back on the faces of those who'd followed the queen bitch out of the reception hall. There had been a number of females and a couple of males, most of them unfamiliar to Michael.

Ezekiel's revelation had at least solved part of the puzzle. Michael now knew why the thief had gone through the trouble of stealing the artifact only to hide it amongst Lucy's belongings. He hadn't... The piece of glass used to frame Lucy was a decoy.

According to Ez, the artifact was still inside the castle, however, hidden on one of Vulpe's loyal subjects. All Michael needed to do now was figure out which one. And for this, he needed to return to Vulpe's castle.

Chapter 35

The woods teemed with nocturnal animals but Seemak didn't mind. Unlike humans, faes had always been at one with nature. Sitting on a fallen tree a hundred feet from the edge of the forest and the road beyond, he was waiting for Victor's *substitute*. He'd been sitting there fifteen minutes when the vampire appeared without a sound from behind a tree as if she'd been there all along.

"Seemak, I assume?"

The fae nodded. "And what is your name?"

"You may call me L if you wish," answered the gorgeous woman.

Seemak had never encountered a vampire with red hair before, but this one had the fieriest mane he'd ever seen. She looked to be in her twenties, but she'd likely been in her twenties for a few decades. Victor wouldn't have sent a novice on such a delicate mission. "Do you have the artifact with you?"

She pulled a pendant in the form of a crescent moon from under her clothes and showed it to him.

"I'll take it for now. As insurance, I'm sure you'll understand. We wouldn't want you to have all the pieces at once, that wouldn't be fair."

The woman handed him the pendant without protest. "Victor had warned me you'd be requesting it."

Of course he had... "Have you mastered thrall? Can you play mind tricks to make yourself invisible to the guards? This won't be an easy job. Rest assured that were we to get caught, the consequences for the two of us would be most unpleasant."

"Have no fear, Seemak. We won't get caught."

Seemak appreciated the vampire's assurance, but he didn't share it.

The minotaur standing guard in front of the door leading to Lord Vaalt's apartments was eleven-foot-tall without the horns. After factoring in the thick and pointy appendage that sat atop the creature's bull-like head, he was closer to twelve. Fortunately for him, the vaulted ceilings of the Chateau de Chambord could easily accommodate his stature, just as the width of the hallways was more than enough to accommodate the six-foot-wide shoulders of the mountain troll that kept him company.

Aside from his animal head and gigantic proportions, the minotaur looked human enough. This wasn't the case for his companion that seemed to be coming straight out of a kindergartener's worst nightmare. The troll's yellowish-gray skin was as thick as the bark of a tree and his hairless head as large as a boulder. His stout legs were remarkably short for his thirteen-foot-tall body, but his orangutan arms easily made up the difference.

Peeking at the scene from around a corner, Seemak saw the door of the apartments slowly swing open and then close without the two energumens being the wiser. The vampire was in. So far the bloodsucking hottie hadn't disappointed him, but the night was still young.

Seemak had given her very precise instructions regarding the artifact's location inside Lord Vaalt's quarters. Unlike the fragment that had, until recently, been in Vulpe's possession, Vaalt's artifacts weren't kept inside a safe or behind bars but were protected by enchantments against faes—all types of faes. But Lord Vaalt had never foreseen that a non-fae could get inside his chamber and this would be his downfall. In theory it couldn't have happened. Without Seemak's assistance, the vamp would have never been able to enter Chambord… and now she was going to have a very hard time leaving. The time for betrayal had come. In a few minutes, he'd be in possession of the three fragments and then his time as a powerless chameleon would be over. He'd soon be as powerful as the most powerful faes. The equal to Lord Vaalt in person. And the warlocks would be in for a surprise if they dared show their faces to him ever again.

He finally saw the door of Lord Vaalt's quarters swing open and shut once again and he knew that the vampire was on her way back to him with the two fragments, for he was certain Vaalt had the two in his possession—he had to.

Seemak wasn't too worried that the vampire would try and sneak out of the castle with her loot without saying goodbye. Even with two fragments, she still had no experience with fae magic. It was highly unlikely she'd be able to fool the guards in charge of watching the outside perimeter. They weren't as easily deceived as trolls and minotaurs.

Seemak was starting to wonder where the vampire had gone when he heard her voice whisper in his ear. "I'm going to need the fragment I gave you earlier back now. It's a fake, of course, but I wouldn't want Lord Vaalt to discover it on your corpse."

She was behind him. Before he had a chance to turn around, he felt a cold blade pierce his back all the way to the guard, the burn of the iron so overwhelming he collapsed to the ground without uttering a sound.

Chapter 36

With Lucy out of trouble and three days of their vacation left, Michael and Sheila had decided to spend some time relaxing at the rental.

Looking at Sheila running from the house to the pool in her bikini, Michael couldn't help but smile. The air temperature didn't exceed fifty degrees, but the sun was out and since pool was heated, Sheila was adamant they should use it at least once. Michael hadn't packed bathing shorts so he followed her into the water wearing boxers.

They'd cranked the pool's heater all the way to eighty degrees, the maximum temperature it would go to, but Sheila still shivered comically, her arms covering her chest and shoulders.

"It's freezing," she said, her teeth chattering with cold.

The pool was only four feet deep and Michael waded to the journalist who stood in the middle of the pool. He came to stand behind her and gently wrapped his giant arms around her, drawing her towards him.

Her back against his chest, Sheila warmed up enough for her teeth to stop rattling in her mouth. "You're not cold? How do you do it?"

"I'm used to the cold, and the water's temperature isn't bad at all," he answered, sweeping her feet from under her and gently immersing their two bodies up to the neck. For Michael, the conditions were almost balmy. Hot springs aside, eighty-degree water was unheard of in Yellowstone where the lake's temperature seldom rose above forty.

He gently kissed her neck before moving on to her earlobe. Sheila didn't protest, but it was clear that she wasn't in a mood for more. The pool had had the effect of a cold shower on the woman's libido.

Tea was brewing on the kitchen table when Michael's cell phone started vibrating on the countertop. Seeing Olivia's name on the screen, he answered, "Olivia? Is everything okay?"

"I'm fine, Michael, but I'm not sure everything's okay. Jason Parrish came all the way down to Daka's house in Wind River to look for me. I don't even work for the guy…"

"Did he see you there?"

Olivia related the events and her growing suspicions about the man to Michael. He listened carefully and had to agree that his boss's behavior was rather unusual. "Where are you now? No, don't tell me."

"You're worried the line might be tapped?" asked Olivia.

"It wouldn't be the first time… Go buy a disposable phone, I'll do the same and I'll find a way to send you my number."

Michael hung up and poured himself a cup of tea before sitting down at the kitchen table. Sitting across from him, Sheila sipped on a mug of coffee, a questioning look on her face. He was about to relate Olivia's half of the conversation when a loud knock came from the kitchen door and Ezekiel walked in.

"I hope I'm not interrupting anything," said the wizard, who hadn't bothered waiting for them to come answer the door.

"Twice in two days… To what do we owe the honor?" asked Michael lightly, but he could tell that Ezekiel meant business. This wasn't a courtesy visit.

"Lord Vaalt's fragment of the Eye of the Phoenix was stolen last night," said Ezekiel, sinking into the empty chair beside Sheila.

"By whom? How do you know?" asked Michael.

"How I know is irrelevant, let's just say I have my spies. By whom is a much better question, however. It looks like an inside job right now, but first impressions are often deceiving…"

"An inside job?" Sheila's curiosity had been piqued. Michael could see the wheels starting to turn inside the journalist's head.

"One of Lord Vaalt's chameleons was found stabbed in the back not too far from where the artifact was stolen. The blade should have gone straight through the heart, but whoever stabbed him apparently ignored an important fact about chameleons: their heart isn't where you'd expect it to be."

The information didn't shock Michael. Chameleons could shift into whichever shape they wanted, but no matter what they looked like on the outside, they remained chameleons, and who knew what the internal plumbing of these creatures looked like. "I take it the chameleon's still alive?"

"Obviously… Why would I bother mentioning it otherwise, Michael Biörn? He's not only alive, but quite healthy. He'd lost a lot of blood by the time he was found, but he regained consciousness after a transfusion. He was still very much out of it, though, and he started talking about a stolen artifact. That's when the thievery was discovered. After that, Lord Vaalt wasted no time getting the chameleon back in tiptop shape. Apparently, his healing abilities, at least for his own kind, far exceed what I'd been led to believe."

"So the chameleon stole the artifact?"

"If he did, he had an accomplice. The fae didn't stab himself in the back… But the details are still fuzzy. Rumor has it that Lord Vaalt's interrogating him at this very moment. If that's the case, it won't be long before the chameleon reveals everything he knows. Vaalt has a talent for interrogation."

"That's two pieces of the same artifact stolen within a week. I doubt it's a coincidence," said Michael reflectively.

"As soon as you're done stating the obvious, I'll get to the point of my visit." Ez's banter sounded less playful than usual. "I'm afraid there is a link between the Eye of the Phoenix and the distortion I've been sensing in the magical field. Whoever's responsible for this distortion has untold power at their disposal. And now two of the three fragments from one of the most powerful magical objects on the planet have been stolen.

This can't be a fluke."

Michael got up from his chair and started slowly pacing the kitchen. "But why would such a powerful *entity* need the Eye of the Phoenix? From what you're saying, they seem to be plenty powerful enough without it."

"I don't know, Michael, but I don't believe in coincidence. I still don't know what this *entity*, as you put it, may be. It has yet to reveal itself, which is plenty worrisome enough."

"You don't think it could be a benevolent *entity*, do you, Ez?" Sheila sounded concerned.

"I don't. Benevolent entities don't usually hide. They tend to make themselves known to the likes of me."

"But if their intentions are less than amicable, why haven't they made a move yet?" asked Sheila.

"Maybe they have," suggested Michael. "You told me that were-beings have been disappearing, Ez. Maybe the *entity*'s building an army like Serafin did with his daywalkers."

"I thought about it, but I don't think so. I've been looking into this as well, and it seems humans are behind those abductions."

"Humans? Are you sure of that?" Michael was more than surprised. What kind of humans could go after a pack of werewolves and come out on top?

"I'm pretty sure. I sensed no residual magic at any of the locations I visited, and I found evidence of a military or paramilitary operation in at least two of those locations."

Michael's mind went to the two men he'd killed in his cabin a week earlier, and then to Bob. He hadn't thought much about Bob these past couple of days, but now that Lucy was out of danger, he needed to get back to the States and figure out what had happened to his friend. And if Jason Parrish had anything to do with that military outfit, the prick would answer for it.

"Are you still with us, Michael?" The wizard was pointedly looking at him.

"Sorry, Ez, I was just thinking."

"Good, keep doing that. That's why I'm here. I need you to help me figure out who's after the Eye of the Phoenix. We need to find out who stole those two fragments and make sure the artifact doesn't fall into the hands of the *entity*."

The framing of Lucy had left a bad taste in Michael's mouth and this was all the motivation he needed. "I'll do what I can, but getting back inside Vulpe's stronghold won't be easy."

"I realize that and I'll help as I can."

"You still have no idea where the third fragment might be?" asked Michael.

Ezekiel looked somber as he shook his head.

"I suppose you can't cast a spell to find out?" Sheila sounded almost apologetic for asking.

"No, my dear. Locating artifacts of such power through spell casting isn't part of my skill set, unfortunately. At least as long as the three pieces are kept apart. If the Eye of the Phoenix were to be reassembled, I'd be able to feel its power from a hundred miles away."

In all the centuries he'd known him, Michael had never seen his friend sounding less confident, and Ezekiel's worry was contagious. All warmth had drained from the room. Whoever or whatever their enemy might be, they had the most powerful circle of wizardry on the planet running scared and that wasn't something to take lightly. What was Michael to do against such a foe? He caught Sheila staring at him and managed a forced smile, which she returned. Why did she have to come on this trip with him? How was he supposed to protect her this time?

Chapter 37

The atmosphere was more than tense in the Eastern Covenant's reception hall where nine faes stood surrounded by roughly two dozen vampire elders. As one of the Covenant's enforcers, Irini was positioned a few feet to the left of Vulpe who was facing Lord Vaalt at the center of the room.

The fae delegation was composed of four high faes, four bodyguards, and what looked like a prisoner dangling in the hands of one of the guards. Although the high faes and the prisoner could have easily blended in among humans, their escort looked anything but human.

Irini was no type of fae scholar, but she was pretty certain the five-foot-tall monstrosity slithering back and forth in front of her was nothing other than a six-headed hydra. Behind Vaalt stood a minotaur holding a four-foot-long broad sword, while the two giants standing on either side of their lord were a troll of a type unfamiliar to Irini and a swamp ogre recognizable by the fishy smell that emanated from the bearded giant.

Irini wasn't fooled, however; the muscles had been brought over for show. Each bodyguard was extremely dangerous in his own right, but the real danger came from the high faes whose magical powers outmatched those of the most powerful vampires by several orders of magnitude. And the delegation standing in front of them was only the tip of the iceberg. At least a hundred more faes of all shapes and sizes were currently surrounding the domain, waiting for a signal to begin the assault.

"This is all very moving, Lord Vaalt, but what makes you think we have anything to do with this robbery?" said Vulpe. "How would one of us manage to sneak inside your residence? I imagine the security measures you have in place would prevent such things, wouldn't they? You know as well as I do that vampire magic is much more restricted than your own."

Vaalt snapped his fingers and the ogre propelled the prisoner forward with a powerful tug. The man collapsed at his lord's feet, head bowed.

"This is Seemak, a traitor of the worst kind who conspired with no less than two members of your Covenant in order to steal from me." The high fae sounded disgusted.

"And why should I believe the words of a traitor who'd say anything to save his skin?" asked Vulpe.

"Because faes can't lie."

Vulpe seemed taken aback by the reply as if he'd forgotten this most basic principle.

The ogre sneezed at this instant and the whole room vibrated as Irini felt her hands tensing around her assault rifle. She wasn't certain how much their bullets would actually hurt the faes if it came to that. Had the Covenant expected the visit, their guns would have been loaded with cold iron ammo specially designed for this type of situation, but the faes had caught them by surprise at dusk.

The vampire elders had gathered in a hurry in the reception hall without taking the time to make themselves presentable. Irini couldn't recall the last time she'd seen Vladislav's hair in such disarray.

"Repeat what you told me, Seemak," ordered Vaalt.

Seemak started telling how he and Victor had conspired to steal the fragment of the Eye of the Phoenix Vaalt kept in his chamber. Irini saw that Vulpe was itching to ask him if they'd also tried to steal his own fragment, but he couldn't do so without revealing to the faes that he was in possession of such fragment—something Vaalt wouldn't be seeing kindly.

"Who's that Victor you're referring to? And when did you supposedly meet him?" asked Vulpe.

Vaalt gestured for his underling to answer. "I've met with him several times over the past ten days. The last time was two nights ago."

"Do you see him in this room?" Vulpe sounded less than convinced.

Seemak looked around before answering negatively.

"Show him his picture," demanded Vaalt.

Seemak fished out a color picture bent at the corner. It had been taken at night and from a distance, but the quality of the print was good and the vampire in its center clearly recognizable.

Vulpe took a look at the print before turning towards his brother. "Isn't it one of yours?"

Vladislav grabbed the picture and nodded. "Yes. I'm his maker and his name's indeed Victor. He's been with us for about twenty years."

"A scumbag," chimed in Anastasia. "He'd have been out on his own years ago if it were up to me. But Vlad—"

"Enough!" interrupted Vulpe, turning to Cristos. "Fetch me this Victor."

"Let me save you a trip," said Vaalt, before Cristos could take his leave. "There's someone else you need to bring back. Tell him, Seemak."

"Victor put me in contact with another vampire. A woman. She's the one who stole the artifact and stabbed me aft—"

"No one cares about your stabbing, traitor," interrupted Vaalt. "Tell him what she looks like."

"She looks to be in her twenties. Very pretty. Long red hair."

Irini felt the blood freeze in her veins at the description.

"Very well. Cristos, get Lucy while you're at it." Vulpe looked like he was about to explode.

The next few minutes were spent in uncomfortable silence until Cristos came back holding a bewildered Lucy by the arm.

"It's her. I never forget a face," confirmed Seemak.

"My men are still looking for Victor, my liege. Apparently, he hasn't been seen in days. We'll bring him to you as soon as we put our hands on him."

"What do you have to say in your defense this time, child?" Vulpe asked Lucy.

"I didn't do anything. I was here all night. I never left the premises. You can ask the guards."

"Don't take me for a fool, child. There are ways to leave the castle without being noticed. Especially if the wolves are on duty."

"But it's true! I was in the castle. Some of the other novices saw me, they can confirm it."

"Your roommates or someone else?" Vulpe was now looking at his brother who almost imperceptibly shook his head to deny the unspoken accusation.

"I want my property back, Vulpe. I want the artifact returned to me now! And we're taking this one with us, too," said Vaalt, pointing at Lucy.

"Where's the jewel?" Vulpe was staring Lucy down like a rabid pitbull would a chihuahua.

"I don't know, my liege. I'm telling the truth. You have to believe me!"

Irini knew that there was nothing she could say to help Lucy now. In the current situation, not even Michael would have been able to save the poor girl.

"We'll hunt down this Victor and look for your artifact, Lord Vaalt. If we find it, it will be returned to you promptly."

"The word of a vampire. That will do me much good," mocked Vaalt.

The remark brought laughter from his entourage, but Vulpe wasn't amused. He seemed to hesitate an instant before gesturing toward Lucy. "In the meantime, I'm keeping that one."

The high fae raised his hand towards Vulpe and all the guns in the room turned towards him.

"You're not in a position of strength, Lord Vaalt. A war between us would hurt both sides."

Vaalt gave an ice-cold smile to the vampire before heading for the exit with the other faes. At the door he paused an instant and turned towards Vulpe. "You have twenty-four hours to bring the artifact back to me. Not a minute more."

Chapter 38

It was the middle of the night in Australia when the master erupted in the living room of the small shack where the two warlocks were trying to get some sleep in particularly uncomfortable armchairs.

"Your chameleon failed us, Demetra," announced the master, flipping on the light switch.

The master's reproachful tone immediately put Demetra on guard. "What happened, Master?" she asked, as her eyes tried adjusting to the sudden brightness in the room.

"I had placed a mark on your Seemak to make sure he wouldn't vanish with the artifact. The trace just disappeared. It can only mean one thing: your pet is dead."

"Where was he when he died?" asked Demetra, more to say something than because she thought the information might be useful.

"He was inside Lord Vaalt's castle in Chambord." The master appeared surprisingly calm, but Demetra knew better.

"He probably got caught stealing the fragment and was executed," suggested Lotar, who'd jumped to his feet as soon as the master had entered the room. "He probably wasn't able to retrieve Vulpe's artifact either," he added patronizingly, no doubt for Demetra's benefit.

"Only one way to know. Get me a witch. Now!" The master pronounced the words looking at Lotar and the warlock instantly vanished.

"You disappointed me, Demetra." This was all the master said before leaving the room, but the warning was clear.

Lotar returned a few hours later dragging a haggard Aboriginal man in his sixties. This time the warlock had come through the door, however. Like Demetra, Lotar could travel instantly without the use of his feet, but the witch didn't have this kind of power and the warlock had been forced to take the long way back with his package in tow.

Without a word, the master grabbed the witch by the hair and forced him to bend over the room's only table before slashing his throat with a knife entirely carved in bone. The paralyzed witch couldn't even scream as he watched his vital fluid escape his body and collect in a large wooden bowl placed under his neck.

The corpse was left where it fell, and the master wasted no time using the fresh blood to draw the necessary glyph on the dusty floor, followed by the incantation pronounced in the same chanting voice as the time before. The master was once again trying to locate the artifacts. Just like the first time, a misty fortified castle appeared out of thin air in front of them, but this time the Renaissance castle didn't manifest itself, nor did anything else.

"The three artifacts are now in Vulpe's lair," announced the master. "It looks like your theory was wrong, Lotar."

Eyes turned to the floor, Lotar felt no need to reply.

"Go to France, both of you, and bring me back the artifact pieces! The Eastern Covenant will be no match for you."

Before the two warlocks had time to vanish the master turned towards them and added, "Betray me, and you'll know a fate worse than death."

Chapter 39

Irini had been in Vulpe's chamber arguing once again in favor of Lucy's innocence when Cristos knocked on the door and let himself in. He saw Irini and hesitated an instant before walking towards them with long strides. "Still no sign of Vaalt's artifact, but we've found Victor, my liege. The traitor is dead, however."

"Dead? Who killed him?" Clearly Vulpe wasn't pleased by the news.

"We don't know, my liege. He was found dead in his sarcophagus. His head was detached from his neck and his heart is missing."

"How convenient," commented Irini.

Vulpe gave her an annoyed look. "What's convenient about it?"

"It's convenient because he cannot be questioned. All we have pointing towards our Covenant involvement in this affair is the word of a chameleon."

"A chameleon who cannot lie, Irini!"

She decided to drop the issue for the moment. Alienating Vulpe wouldn't get Lucy out of the cell which she'd been sent back to.

"How long has Victor been dead?" asked Vulpe.

"At least four days, maybe five or six."

Slimy Seemak had declared the night before that he'd been in contact with Victor two days earlier. An impossibility, since Victor had been dead by then. Irini pointed out the fact to Vulpe in the most tactful way she could manage.

"That's right. How's this possible?" said Vulpe, apparently pleased with her observation.

"Since Seemak can't lie, that implies he truly believes that he met with Victor while Victor was already dead. Which means someone's impersonated Victor, and very likely Lucy too."

Vulpe wasn't ready to exonerate Lucy just yet, however.

"Who could do an impersonation convincing enough to fool a

chameleon?" asked Cristos.

"Probably another chameleon. This story is just about faes backstabbing each other and trying to frame the Covenant for their misdeeds, my liege."

Vulpe appeared to be considering the value of Irini's argument when a voice came through the small two-way radio Cristos carried at his belt. "Cristos, do you copy?"

There was a sense of urgency in the voice and Vulpe gestured for the head of security to answer.

"I copy."

"We caught someone you'll want to see. Man, it's freaky."

Whoever it was that the guards had captured, Vulpe's curiosity had been piqued. "Tell him to bring his catch over right away."

As Cristos transmitted the message to his man, Irini was trying to figure out who the mysterious prisoner might be. She was hoping Lucy hadn't escaped from her dungeon cell only to get caught by the guards. But it was unlikely, Lucy had no way to get out of her jail. Could Victor have faked his own death and been caught trying to escape the castle?

When two of Cristos' men dragged their find through Vulpe's door five minutes later, Irini wasn't sure what she was looking at, and neither was anyone else in the room. The man looked like Cristos himself, down to the last detail. And he wasn't only a perfect twin, he also wore the same clothes and carried the same radio at his belt.

"I'd just talked to you in the hallway when I saw this one outside, he was hurrying towards the main gate," said one of the guards to the Cristos standing beside Vulpe.

"Let me go, imbeciles! I'm the real Cristos! This is the impostor," vociferated the prisoner, pointing at the other Cristos. His act was pretty convincing and for a split second Irini almost believed him, but then she realized it couldn't be the case. Cristos was an elder who'd been head of Vulpe's security for over two centuries. The two guards could never have overpowered him.

"Who are you and what are you doing in my home?" The ice in Vulpe's voice could have frozen the blood in the veins of a human, but the impostor clearly wasn't human. In an instant he turned into a fifteen-foot-tall moving tree with arms too thick for the guards to hold on to. Irini had heard of spriggans—a type of fae that lived deep in the forests and protected the trees—but she'd never actually seen one.

Shocked by the transformation, the guards stood staring at the thorny tree who was bending down to fit through the doors. But Vulpe crossed the room in a flash and used his momentum to deliver a powerful blow through the tree's midsection before he could escape. The elder's fist went through the tree entirely and came out the other side.

What followed was the most bizarre thing Irini and probably everyone else in the room had ever witnessed. The tree turned back into Cristos before morphing into Irini herself and finally liquifying into a gooey mess spreading across the stone floor.

"This was a fae?" Cristos sounded as puzzled as Irini felt.

"It sure looked like it," answered Vulpe, removing his robe soiled with what was left of the fae.

"I believe it was a chameleon," said Irini. "Chameleons only take the appearance of others, they don't inherit any of their strength or magic. A real spriggan would have been much tougher to deal with."

"Now we need to figure out what this thing was up to and how long it's been hiding among us."

Irini was about to ask Vulpe if he still believed Lucy was guilty when a thought crossed her mind. "Cristos, do you still have one of your men watching Lucy's cell?"

The vampire gave her a questioning look before answering, "I do."

"Call him and ask him to go check on Lucy."

Cristos turned to Vulpe, awaiting his approval.

"Do it, goddammit!" yelled Irini who was reaching the end of her tether.

"Do as she asks," said Vulpe.

Irini was already picturing Lucy dead in her cell. She was convinced the puddle currently seeping through the cracks of Vulpe's floor had been part of a commando sent by Lord Vaalt to assassinate the girl.

"Tarek, do you copy."

The guard's answer came almost immediately. "I copy, Cristos. What's going on?"

"Do you have eyes on Lucy? Is she in her cell?"

"I thought she was still with you."

"What do you mean, still with me?"

"I mean nobody brought her back since you came to get her." Tarek sounded particularly confused.

"And when did I come to get her?" asked Cristos, who'd understood the situation by now.

"It's been about twenty minutes, I guess," answered Tarek tentatively.

"Put the whole compound on lockdown and organize the search. We must find her," ordered Vulpe.

But Irini had little hope Lucy would be found. She was long gone. The faes had her now.

Chapter 40

Twenty miles from Michael and Sheila's vacation rental, Ezekiel was walking along the streets of La Roque-Gageac. The medieval village had been built against a steep cliff along the Dordogne river, and in the middle of January, none of its four hundred inhabitants appeared to be home. This wasn't surprising—like the rest of the region, the village was virtually deserted during fall and winter—but spring would soon bring its population back so the village could prepare to receive the many tourists who would invade it over the summer months. These considerations were far from Ezekiel's thoughts at the moment, however.

Ez had come here to think, and the peace and quiet suited him perfectly for his reflective stroll past the quaint stone houses that had been built directly against the cliff. These homes had been standing here, holding the mountain, for nearly a thousand years and there was little doubt they'd still be here in another thousand. At least he hoped so. Of late, he'd been uncharacteristically worried about what the future held.

He'd been in nearly constant contact with Tabitha and Methuselah over the past few days, but the two other members of the very restricted Second Circle didn't have a better grasp on the situation than he did. They still had no clue who the enemy was—assuming there even was an enemy—or where they might be hiding. The Southern Hemisphere was a vast place to search...

Ezekiel was more and more convinced that what Michael had creatively named the *entity* was somehow linked to the attention the Eye of the Phoenix had been receiving lately. And since the *entity* was proving problematic to locate, the wizard had elected to stay close to the artifact itself. He'd sensed the presence of at least one of its fragments inside the Eastern Covenant's stronghold and had no intention of leaving the region until he had a better place to be.

The wizard was halfway down a flight of stairs leading to the riverbank when he felt a wave of magical energy ripple through his body. He spun around but found nothing behind him. The wave had passed, and he now only sensed a subtle shift in the already distorted magical field. A powerful magical being had passed through the village, or at least close enough for Ezekiel to sense their presence, but it was gone now, though not completely. The slight vibration he still perceived wasn't due to residual energy; it was real. This much was certain. Whoever had been at the origin of the ripple hadn't left the region. They were nearby. But not near enough for Ezekiel to locate them. He had a pretty good idea of where he should start looking, though.

Chapter 41

Michael and Sheila had been in bed nearly two hours when Michael woke up to the characteristic sound of gravel shifting under tires. He immediately roused Sheila and told her to remain silent by placing a finger over his own mouth. He then walked to the window and peeked through the gap between the wall and the shutters. He didn't recognize the vehicle parked in front of the house, but the instant the driver's door opened, his nose told him it was Irini. She hadn't come alone, though; another vampire's smell even more potent than hers was assaulting

Michael's nostrils. The scent was familiar, but it took him a second to place it, not because his olfactive memory was betraying him, but because the answer was so unlikely. What was Vladislav Zamfir doing here?

Michael told Sheila to get dressed but to remain in the bedroom for now. With some luck, maybe the journalist would listen to him for once. He then walked downstairs and opened the door to find Irini on the other side, fist raised and about to knock.

"What's going on, Irini? A bit late for a courtesy visit, isn't it?"

"Vampires seldom visit during the day, Michael," she replied with a knowing look.

Michael got the message. Vladislav didn't know she was a daywalker and she wanted to keep it that way.

"I came to tell you that Lucy's disappeared."

Michael didn't like the way Vladislav's eyes followed Sheila as the cute brunette moved around the kitchen, busying herself brewing both coffee and tea. They had no blood to offer their visitors, but somehow Michael didn't feel bad about it.

"If the faes have Lucy, we need to get her back as soon as possible. Their kind isn't known for their clemency. If she stole from them, they'll make her confess. Trust me! And it won't be pretty," he said.

"And if she's innocent?' asked Sheila, placing a mug in front of him.

Michael hesitated an instant before answering, "She'll confess anyway. Just to be done with it."

"We must find out where they are," said Vladislav. The vamp had been pretty quiet up to that point, but he looked wound-up now.

"I've already contacted someone to help with that, but until he calls me back, there's not much we can do," replied Michael.

"Who's this friend of yours and how can he find out such things?" asked Vladislav.

"It doesn't matter. The important point is that he can be trusted."

The innuendo in Michael's answer was clearly understood by Vladislav who gave him a dirty look. The vampire elder was used to people treating him with respect and deference, but Michael wasn't in the habit of showing deference to bloodsuckers. The fact this particular specimen was screwing Lucy behind his wife's back didn't play in his favor either. Whatever Olivia's sister had seen in the elder, Michael sure didn't see it.

"If Michael trusts his friend, Vladislav, then he can be trusted," said Irini to defuse the tension.

Michael's phone rang a moment later and he answered right away.

"Yes. On which road? You're sure? Yes, I know… Sorry," he said, gesturing for Sheila to give him something to write on.

The journalist handed him a notepad and a felt pen that had been hanging on the wall beside the landline phone, and he started jotting things down, his back turned to the others. He then ended the call and placed the note in his pocket.

"They're heading to Chambord. We need to go now. They already have two hours on us."

The two vampires got up and Sheila grabbed her purse, but Michael stopped them. "I meant Irini and me. I'm sorry, Vladislav, but you can't come. We'll drop you off on the way."

"I don't need your permission, bear." The vampire had lost all friendliness.

"If you care about Lucy, let us handle it alone. If we want to have a chance to succeed, we need my friend's help, and he doesn't play nice with vampires. Irini will be fine, but I can't guarantee your safety."

"I think you underestimate my powers, bear."

The look on Irini's face suggested she agreed with Vladislav, but she kept silent.

"I'm sure I do, but you could be ten times stronger than Vulpe himself, it wouldn't change a thing. My friend could still beat you to a pulp with both hands tied behind his back while dancing a jig."

Chapter 42

The chains binding Lucy's ankles to a stone pillar near the room's fireplace looked flimsy enough, but their appearance was deceiving. Despite her unusual strength, the vampire-werewolf hybrid couldn't bend a single link of the golden chains. There was little doubt they were enchanted.

The room had probably been designed as a bedroom back in the day, but now it was mostly empty. The noticeable exception was the massive armchair in the center of the room, and the two ogres keeping guard at the door who were staring at her with the eyes of cows overdosing on Valium. The armchair was empty, but Lucy doubted it'd been brought here by chance. She expected a visit any moment.

She'd been told that faes were deceitful before, but now she'd experienced firsthand the extent of their treachery. She hadn't suspected a thing when Cristos had grabbed her out of her musty cell to supposedly take her to Vulpe. She'd been a bit surprised when he'd led her outside instead of directly to Vulpe's apartments, but she'd been so worried about what the leader was going to do to her that the late-night stroll through the domain's gardens had come as a welcome distraction.

They'd found Vulpe sitting on a bench in front of a massive boxwood shrub pruned in the shape of a red deer. He'd given her a strange smile and before Lucy had a chance to wonder why, she'd felt massive hands closing around her torso, effectively pinning her arms to her side. A woman had appeared right in front of her at the same instant and placed a sticky substance on her mouth. Lucy had tried to fight her aggressors off but the troll was much too strong for her, and the gooey mess on her mouth absorbed every scream she tried to project.

Before she knew it, she'd been thrown into a large leather bag and carried away bouncing on the troll's shoulder. She had no idea how the faes had managed to evade the castle's security and sneak her out of the vampires' fortified compound, but she suspected the high fae who'd silenced her had something to do with it. She and the troll had appeared out of thin air, and since trolls didn't have this type of power as far as Lucy knew, it implied the high fae had cast an invisibility spell over them.

She'd then been thrown into a car and had spent the entire drive inside the bag, trapped by the suspiciously strong leather. They'd driven for hours and she suspected the bag had been as much designed to protect her from the rising sun as to restrain her. Her kidnappers had no way to know that UV light had no effect on their prisoner.

Lucy heard steps approaching and tried to mentally prepare for the newcomer, but she still felt a knot at the pit of her stomach when Lord Vaalt walked into the room, accompanied by two high faes Lucy had never seen before and a minotaur carrying a large hunting knife in one hand and a medieval flail in the other. The flail had a single brass striking head hanging from a chain of the same metal attached to its wooden handle, but the striking head was twice as large as Lucy's fists and covered in thick two-inch spikes.

Such a weapon in the hands of a minotaur could easily take her head off with one blow. At least it could have back in the days when Lucy still had a pulse. She was a lot tougher now, but she doubted her strength would be a match for the eleven-foot monster standing in front of her.

Lord Vaalt sat down in the armchair while the other high faes stood a tad further back to his left and right.

"I don't believe introductions are required, so let's get straight to the point. You have something of mine and I want it back. I assure you that you'll eventually tell me what I want to know, so I suggest you save your pretty bloodsucking face a lot of pain and suffering and tell me where my artifact is before Tyrok gets started on you. Seemak confessed that the initial idea came from him, so I might even show more leniency towards you than I did towards him… as long as you don't keep me waiting."

Lucy's eyes were trained on the minotaur. At that instant, she'd have loved to tell Vaalt all he wanted to know, but she didn't have anything to reveal. "I don't know where your artifact is. I never took it. That's the truth."

But Lord Vaalt wasn't swayed. He simply looked at her disappointingly, as a parent would a lying child. "Tyrok…"

The flail came at her head in a circular motion she easily avoided by ducking. But the minotaur quickly corrected his mistake and the spiked ball came back with a fury to land in her left ribs. Lucy fell to the ground under the impact as blood oozed out of the wound. The quickly spreading stain was nearly invisible on her black outfit, but she could feel the crimson fluid leaving her body.

Lord Vaalt's humorless laugh filled the room. "Seemak was only able to withstand two of Tyrok's attacks before leaving this world," he said. "Let's hope you can do better."

Chapter 43

Despite Irini's maniacal driving, they'd only managed to shave thirty minutes off the four-hour drive to Chambord, and the sun had been up for an hour and a half by the time they parked their car on the edge of the woods and Michael got out to finally stretch his legs. He went to the trunk and unzipped the duffle bag he'd brought with him to retrieve a thick leather harness through which he passed his arms before tying the leather straps over his chest with a complicated knot. He then pulled his battle axes out of the trunk and placed them on his back inside the harness' holster. He was glad airport security had raised no objection when he'd checked the weapons with his luggage.

They crossed the woods in about twenty minutes and arrived at the rendezvous point Ezekiel had given Michael to find it wizardless.

"Where's your friend?" whispered Irini.

"He'll be here, don't worry." Michael was surveying the castle in front of him. Chambord, Lord Vaalt's stronghold, was in all points identical to the original castle of the same name located twenty miles upstream on the Loire river—one of the most famous and visited castles in the country. The faes' replica, however, was hidden at the heart of a heavily forested area and saw absolutely no tourists. Thanks to the magic of the high faes, it was also undetectable from the sky and, miracle of miracles, didn't appear on Google Earth.

The guards patrolling the ground were more subtle than the military-style patrols of Cristos' men, but Michael knew better than to trust his eyes. He knew that the human appearance of the men guarding each door was nothing other than glamour designed to fool visitors who might stumble upon the castle by chance. Michael didn't know what kind of muscle-bound giants were hiding behind those flimsy bodies, but he was sure they'd soon find out. He was reflecting on the best way to get inside without dying in the process when Ezekiel appeared beside Irini, startling both Michael and the vampire.

"A bit jumpy, are we?" The wizard spoke in a low voice but was clearly satisfied with his entrance.

Ez had spent a good part of the night as a peregrine falcon searching the main freeways heading from Périgord to Chambord. With a top speed of well over two hundred miles per hour, it had taken the raptor about forty-five minutes to locate the faes' vehicle heading north on the A20.

"Where were you?" asked Michael, ignoring the comment.

"I was having a closer look at the security measures they have in place. I hope you don't mind?"

"I'm sure you remember Irini?"

"I remember," said Ez coldly.

Even though Irini wasn't a true vampire and hadn't killed a human to feed on in six months, clearly this made little difference to the wizard. Michael couldn't blame him. For centuries he himself had despised the thing the woman had become and had only recently come to peace with it.

"Walk exactly in my footsteps if you don't want to be blown to pieces... or worse," announced the wizard as he headed towards one of the gates. "I can cast an invisibility spell over you, Michael, and your friend can use her own magic to do the same. But the spell will only fool the most thick-headed guards around here. The magic of those protecting the doors will see through those spells, have no illusions."

They made it to one of the side doors without problem, but by the time they were ready to enter they were surrounded by a dozen faes of all sorts who no longer bothered using glamour to maintain a human appearance.

"Well, well, well, look what the gargoyle dragged home." The remark had come from the fae standing at the top of the short flight of stairs leading to the entrance door. It had the hooves, legs and horns of a goat, but its upper body and face were otherwise human. The faun wasn't much to look at, but he nevertheless seemed to be the one in charge. Michael had no idea where fauns stood on the magical scale, but apparently they were above the trolls, ogres, and other goblins surrounding them.

"I am Ezekiel, wizard of the Second Circle, and I have come to talk to Lord Vaalt. If you could be kind enough to announce us to your master."

Ezekiel's name had erased much of the faun's bravado, but he wasn't ready to let them through quite yet. "Let me see what I can do," he announced, before disappearing inside.

He came back in under a minute accompanied by a female high fae who confirmed that the wizard wasn't an impostor.

"What is your business with Lord Vaalt?" asked the woman whose beauty rivaled Lucy's.

"I'd rather expose it to Lord Vaalt himself," replied Ez amiably.

"I'm afraid this isn't a good time. Lord Vaalt is busy at the moment. You and your pets will need to make an appointment."

The woman's reply caused laughter among the goblins, and the faun soon joined in—the other faes were apparently too stupid to get the joke.

"I'm sorry, my lady," replied Ezekiel to Michael's surprise. "I blame it on my secretary. She assured me she'd made the necessary arrangements... Oh, what a pickle! What to do, what to do?" Ez was now stroking his chin as if absorbed in deep thought. "I'll tell you what, why don't you show us to the drawing room or the library, and we'll wait there for Lord Vaalt to be done with his current affairs." As he spoke, he had started to move towards the door, but the high fae snapped her fingers and the guards got the message. They all converged towards the visitors only to bounce on the force field that the wizard had erected around the trio.

Ez was at the door now, followed closely by Michael and Irini. The high fae seemed to hesitate an instant, but finally stepped away. Michael knew that the woman wasn't without power, but apparently she'd decided Ez was an adversary too tough to tackle on her own. Smart decision.

They were shown to the library and asked to wait there. They didn't have to wait very long. Within ten minutes Lord Vaalt in person entered the room, accompanied by six other high faes and two minotaurs. Michael was glad he'd brought his battle axes with him. It looked like they were going to come handy.

"So it's true. Ezekiel of the Second Circle is standing in my library," said Vaalt as the other faes fanned out around their leaders. "So that's what the murderer of my son looks like."

That small detail had skipped Michael's mind up to now. In retrospect, he was starting to wonder if Vladislav wouldn't have been more welcome than Ez.

"Murder is a bit of an exaggeration, Lord Vaalt. Your son ran a praeternatural assassins-for-hire business. This line of work comes with a certain amount of risk…"

"I didn't approve of my son's career choice, but what can a father do? Boys will be boys…"

"I'm also sorry to say that your son started the fight and had no intention of sparing my life had I not prevailed." Ezekiel spoke in a conciliatory tone Michael wasn't used to.

"Be that as it may, you killed him, wizard. He wasn't my favorite offspring, not by a long shot, but he was still my son. So you'll understand that when his killer willingly walks into my house, it's only natural for a father to want to avenge his child." Lord Vaalt sounded dispassionate, pragmatic, as if he were discussing a simple business transaction.

"You may try to avenge your son and perish as he did, or you can listen to what we came to discuss. The choice is yours, Lord Vaalt."

Ezekiel was truly a powerful wizard, but despite his bravado, they were dealing with six high faes and Michael doubted even Ez could come out on top of such a fight. And that was without counting the two literally bull-headed killing machines who made Michael's three hundred pounds of muscles look puny in comparison.

"And what is it you came to discuss, wizard?"

"But the Eye of the Phoenix, of course."

Recognition appeared in the fae's eyes. "I knew this one looked familiar," he said, nodding towards Irini. "I saw you yesterday. You stood beside Vulpe when we dropped by for a visit."

"That's right. I was there."

"Are you bringing back what was stolen from me?"

"Not quite yet," intervened Ez. "For now, we just came to retrieve what you took from us?"

Vaalt acted confused, but his acting skills weren't very good. He knew perfectly what Ezekiel was referring to. He finally dropped the act and smiled widely. "You can have her back as soon as I'm done with her. But I must warn you, she'll be in pieces…"

That's when Michael saw the woman appear behind the faes. Where had she come from, and what was she doing here?

Chapter 44

The sun had been up a few minutes inside the fake Interpol agents' hotel room when McDowell's phone rang. The two had arrived in Périgord four days earlier and had still not found any trace of Biörn. Though mostly deserted during the off season, the region was three times the size of Rhode Island and locating Biörn without further indication was equivalent to finding the proverbial needle in a haystack…

And this was assuming the bear was even *in* the region. The car he'd been seen getting into at the airport had been flashed by a local radar, but they had no way of knowing if he'd still been in it by then.

But the director's order had been clear: the two agents were to stay in Périgord and go from town to town showing the pictures of Biörn and his girlfriend to the population. A fruitless endeavor which, despite the assistance of the local authorities, had borne as little fruit as one would expect.

McDowell answered his cell as Clark was getting out of the bathroom, his face full of shaving cream and holding a razor.

The phone conversation didn't last very long. "Very well, we're on our way," concluded McDowell before terminating the call. "That was Ike," he said, turning to Clark who was already wiping the cream off his face with a towel. "The techies found a house rented for the week by Sheila Wang. Short of a monumental coincidence, we're talking about Biörn's girlfriend."

"What's the plan?"

"The director wants us to go check it out ourselves, but we're to keep our distance. We'll request back-up once we've confirmed Biörn's in the house."

Chapter 45

The puncture marks left by the minotaur's flail were starting to close up on Lucy's side and face, but the throbbing pain assaulting her ribs and jaw was still highly unpleasant. Thanks to the superior clotting abilities of her vampire blood, she hadn't lost too much of the precious fluid yet, but she had no doubt she soon would. Whatever emergency had pulled Lord Vaalt away from the interrogation chamber, he'd be back sooner or later, and the torture would resume.

She was already coming up with lies she could feed the fae to try and escape this ordeal with her life. What if she told them the artifact was hidden in Vulpe's castle and that she would retrieve it for them? But with her luck, faes would possess an inherent ability to detect lies and she would only bring herself more pain at the hands of the minotaur.

The beast's eyes were trained on her at the moment, void of any expression, human or animal. A totally blank stare. The two high faes had followed Vaalt out of the room, but the ogres still stood guard at the door. The expression on their faces made the minotaur look smart in comparison.

The woman appeared in the middle of the room as if she'd materialized from thin air. She looked vaguely familiar, but Lucy couldn't have placed the face and petite body in a context if her life had depended on it.

An ally or a foe? The woman winked at her and Lucy felt reassured. If the ogres' reaction was any indication, she had to be an ally. The two giants had rushed towards her as soon as she'd appeared in the middle of the room a few feet behind the minotaur.

The vibration of the floor under the ogres' feet alerted the minotaur who spun around to face the newcomer. As the flail's handle started rotating in the beast's giant hand, its brass ball described large vertical circles. Had the weapon hit Lucy with such momentum, her head would have been pulverized.

The petite woman appeared less than impressed, however. As the two ogres were closing in behind her, she projected her hands towards the ground and the tiled floor turned into a pool of liquid that rapidly swallowed the two guards up to their neck. The floor then returned to its normal solid self, enclosing the ogres' body in thousands of cubic feet of stone and mortar.

The tops of their heads were still visible above the ground, however. Their eyes darted left and right in a silent scream their buried mouths couldn't produce. The beasts wouldn't die of asphyxiation, though, as the woman had been kind enough to leave their noses above ground.

The minotaur's arm extended suddenly towards his opponent, but the spiky ball missed the woman's head by a good foot. The second attack came an instant later and would have been devastating if the ball hadn't suddenly changed trajectory in midflight to forcefully return towards its sender.

As the ball struck the minotaur on the forehead right between the eyes, he emitted a low guttural sound that was neither human nor bull. But the message was clear: the beast had been hurt. Apparently not enough, however, for he ripped the spikes out of his flesh and bones and charged the woman with his thick but terribly pointy horns.

He was about to impale his opponent when the woman vanished and reappeared right behind him. She then shoved a palm forward as if giving the beast a push and even though she never actually touched him, the minotaur went flying headfirst towards the nearest wall. The horns speared through the wall's plaster veneer but whatever material was underneath did not agree with the beast as its head passed through it. The minotaur was out cold.

The woman then went to Lucy and took a long look at the chain binding the prisoner's feet as she introduced herself. "My name's Tabitha. I'm a friend of Ezekiel."

Now Lucy's memory came back, jolted to a part of her life she'd done her best to forget. Though the two women had never been properly introduced, this was the second time the wizard had saved Lucy's hide.

Chapter 46

Michael was still trying to figure out why Tabitha had suddenly appeared behind Lord Vaalt and his entourage. If Ezekiel had recruited her help to rescue Lucy, why hadn't he mentioned it? When Michael finally noticed Lucy standing a few feet behind Tabitha in the wizard's shadow, his theory was confirmed. The woman had rescued Lucy while Ez distracted Lord Vaalt. Michael felt slightly annoyed that Ez hadn't bothered exposing his plan to him, but he soon understood the wizard's reason: Irini. Ez simply didn't trust the vampire.

"Actually, Lord Vaalt, I'd rather Lucy remains in one piece, which is why we didn't wait for you to be done with her before getting her back," said Ez, gesturing towards Lucy.

Fearing a trick from the wizard, Vaalt didn't turn around. The high fae knew better than to turn his back to his enemy, but another fae did and confirmed that Lucy was indeed standing by the door along with another woman.

This time, Vaalt lost his dispassionate composure. "Who do you think you are, wizard, to invade my house and steal from me?"

"May I remind you that you yourself invaded Vulpe's castle last night to kidnap this young woman, Lord Vaalt? We haven't done anything you haven't done yourself in the past few hours."

Anger perspired through Vaalt's every pore. The tension of his muscles and the murderous lights dancing in his black eyes constituted unmistakable signs of the brewing storm.

"Before you do something you'll regret, Lord Vaalt, let me introduce my friend and colleague standing behind you," started Ez amicably. "This is Tabitha of the Second Circle. Tabitha's every bit as powerful as I am, and the odds are now even less in your favor than they were a moment earlier."

"You will pay for this treachery, wizards, both of you. Mark my words." The high fae was still simmering with rage.

A part of Michael was preparing for the fight, all senses tuned to the mood of the room and ready to pounce at the first sign of trouble, but another part couldn't help but marvel at the fae's reaction. He'd been calm and moderate when referring to his son's death at the hands of Ez, treating the occurrence like a simple business transaction, but the trick Tabitha had pulled had put Vaalt beside himself. Faes, the masters of deception, truly loathed to be tricked.

"This is no treachery. I came to talk to you about the Eye of the Phoenix and still intend to do so. You had a friend of ours in our custody and it was *only natural* to attempt to free her while we were here. Believe you me, Lord Vaalt, it's better for everyone that way. You really didn't want us to have to fight to get Lucy back."

Vaalt sneered at the suggestion that he might be outgunned in his own castle, and Michael tended to agree with him. The eight faes present in the room were but a fraction of the forces at the lord's disposal.

"You want to talk about the Eye of the Phoenix? Let's talk then." Vaalt had regained some of his calm.

"As you know, your fragment of the artifact is missing, but what you may not know is that it's not the only one," said Ez. "A second fragment has been stolen over the past few days and this can't be a coincidence."

"A second fragment... Who had it and who stole it?"

"Who had it is perfectly irrelevant." Obviously Ez had no intent to reveal that Vulpe had been in possession of one of the fragments for centuries. "The question *who* stole it, however, is most relevant. Because it is most likely the same person who stole your piece of the jewel."

"This one stole my fragment." Vaalt was pointing an accusatory index finger towards Lucy who was smart enough to let Ez do the talking.

"It's highly unlikely, Lord Vaalt. We have it on good authority that Lucy spent that night at her Covenant's castle. Numerous eyewitnesses corroborate her story."

Michael thought *numerous* was a bit overstating the facts, but Irini had indeed found two novices who'd been with Lucy at the time the artifact had been stolen.

"Whoever's after these artifacts is a lot more dangerous than Lucy," started Tabitha, forcing Vaalt to turn towards her. "I'm sure you sensed the shift in the magical field."

"What about it?" The fae sounded ticked off but curious.

"The Second Circle finds the coincidence of all those events to be more than suspicious. We strongly suspect that whoever's responsible for the perturbations we are sensing is trying to restore the power of the Eye of the Phoenix for himself."

"For which purpose?" asked the fae.

"Global extinction, world domination, your guess is as good as ours." Ezekiel's tone had been light, but the implications were eminently serious.

"And why are you talking to me about this? Why should I care?"

"Because your kind is an integral part of this world, Lord Vaalt. And because there may come a time when your people will need to fight alongside ours to save this planet."

"I find your doomsday predictions a bit pessimistic, wizard. All I want is what is rightfully mine—the artifact."

"I give you my word that if found, *your* fragment will be returned to you," said Tabitha. "The Second Circle has no interest in seeing the power of the reunited artifact in *your* hands or any other. When found, each fragment will be returned to its latest owner."

"I will hold you to your word, wizard. You can be sure of it." Lord Vaalt seemed strangely appeased, his anger vanished. He appeared almost pleased.

Michael didn't like the sudden change in the fae's behavior. What was he up to? When Vaalt's reinforcement showed up an instant later, Michael wasn't even slightly surprised. Four high faes, five trolls, a hydra and a spriggan had showed up behind Lucy. Added to the two minotaurs and six high faes—including Vaalt—already in the room, the balance of power had no doubt tilted back in the fae's favor. And it was only the beginning; Michael suspected more troops were already on their way.

"I'd warned you your treachery wouldn't go unpunished, wizards. And neither will the death of my son."

Michael knew that Ez and Tabitha could simply teleport out of the room if needed, but he also knew they wouldn't. The two wizards would never abandon Michael and Lucy. He wasn't too sure about Irini, though...

"May I suggest a compromise." The first words out of Michael's mouth caught everyone by surprise. All eyes were on him now. "You need to avenge your son's death and you need to get back at us for rescuing Lucy behind your back, I get it. But from what I understood of this magical field mumbo jumbo, the world can't really afford to lose you, any of your high faes or any wizards right now."

"What are you suggesting, Michael?" Ez looked worried.

"I suggest you name your champion, Ez, and Lord Vaalt names his. One fight to the death between the two champions to settle the score."

"Intriguing offer," said Vaalt. "I accept, but on one condition. If my champion wins, not one but two of the missing fragments will be returned to me, once found. After all, the faes are the Eye of the Phoenix's rightful owners."

Michael looked at Ezekiel. There was anxiety in the eyes of the wizard, but Michael suspected Ez was more worried about what would happen to his champion than about returning two fragments to Vaalt.

"We accept your terms," said Ezekiel, "but if our champion wins, Lucy will come back with us and all grudges you hold against this group will be forgotten."

Vaalt nodded his approval. "You have a deal, wizard. Who will be your champion?"

Ezekiel, of course, selected Michael and the group then turned to Lord Vaalt who was taking his time to make his selection. Michael was hoping for a troll. These creatures were as stupid as they were powerful, and outsmarting them wouldn't be a big challenge. A minotaur would be a much tougher opponent, but Michael's battle axes had already defeated one in the past and he was confident he could do it again. On the other hand, the spriggan would be a problem; the wooded creature wouldn't be much impacted by his bear's bite and he would likely have to rely once again on his battle axes. Same thing held true for the hydra, but for entirely different reasons. The hydra's bites were notoriously toxic and his bear would never be able to keep track of the creature's six heads. His axes should be able to slice through its necks quite efficiently, though…

"Clarissa will be my champion," announced Vaalt finally, pointing at the hydra.

Michael took a deep breath and reached for his battle axes as the fae added, "Naturally, weapons of all kinds are forbidden during the fight. Each champion must prevail using the strengths given to them by nature alone."

Michael glanced at Ezekiel. They were completely screwed.

Chapter 47

Olivia rolled in her sleeping bag, unable to find sleep. Beside her, Daka was snoring softly. They'd been camping in the Wind River Forest for five days now and although she enjoyed the one on one time with him, she felt like a coward. This wasn't a vacation; they were effectively hiding from Jason Parrish.

Cameahwait had warned them that the ranger had shown up three more times at the reservation since they'd left, each time asking about Daka and Olivia. If nothing else, the prick was tenacious.

There was little doubt the man was up to no good, but Olivia hated to have to hide from the likes of him, especially since they had no clue who he actually was. He was human, this was certain enough—Olivia vividly remembered Jason's encounter with a weretiger who had knocked him out for the count with a single blow—but they had no idea who he was working for or what he was up to, beside actively partaking in the cover-up of Bob Spencer's murder.

"You can't sleep?" asked Daka.

Absorbed in her thoughts, Olivia hadn't even noticed that her boyfriend had woken up.

"No. Too many things going through my mind. I feel useless hiding in here while Jason's out there up to no good."

"I feel the same way, but that's what Cameahwait and Michael want us to do and it's good advice. If Jason has anything to do with Bob's death, if he's in league with the guys Michael killed in his cabin, it's safer for us to stay away for a while. At least until Michael comes back."

"Where the hell is he anyway? I don't understand why he's not back yet. He supposedly went to Europe to investigate Bob's disappearance. God only knows why Europe… Now, it's been six days since we've found Bob's body and Michael still hasn't returned. Tell me you don't find that suspicious!"

Daka kept silent which Olivia interpreted as an admission. "Before he left," she went on, "Michael asked us to keep an eye open for Bob, didn't he?"

"Yes…" answered Daka cautiously.

"It's not because Bob's dead that the mission Michael gave us is over. We still owe it to Bob to find out what happened to him."

"I doubt that's what Michael had in mind, Olivia."

"Who knows him better? You or me?"

"You do, but—"

"Listen to what I have to say first, you can object later," she interrupted. "I'm not suggesting I go back to work in Yellowstone or anything like that, but it wouldn't hurt to keep an eye on Jason to try and find out what he's up to."

"And how do you suggest we do that?"

"We could go incognito to the park and hide a couple of microphones in his house and patrol car. Maybe even one on his snowmobile. That way we can keep close tabs on most of his conversations and figure out what he's hiding."

Daka was nodding, but he looked more skeptical than convinced. "I suppose we should wear baseball caps and fake beards to blend in among the rangers in a park that's all but closed to the public at the moment?"

Olivia sat up inside the tent and looked down on him, smiling. "Actually, I was thinking about a furrier disguise…"

Chapter 48

Michael was observing his opponent slithering her way to the center of the room. She moved slowly, but he suspected this was a trick designed to hide her true speed. He'd never seen a hydra fight before. But now he was about to witness the creature's fighting skills firsthand, and the idea didn't fill him with confidence.

Lord Vaalt's library having been judged inadequate for the combat, the party had moved to the dining room. Vaalt had ordered the room to be cleared and within minutes the gigantic table, the chairs and the rugs had been moved to an adjacent room to free the space for the two champions.

Ezekiel had argued for Michael to be allowed to use his battle axes, but Vaalt hadn't budged. In the end they'd been forced to accept the fae's terms. Lord Vaalt had known full well that Ezekiel's champion would expect to fight with his weapons, and he'd picked the hydra because she presented the greatest challenge to an unarmed man. But Michael wasn't a man and he had a couple tricks up his sleeve yet.

He took his position facing Clarissa, his opponent, in the improvised ring but at a distance of twenty feet.

"Is your champion ready?" Lord Vaalt was gleeful with anticipation.

"Not quite," replied Ezekiel, nodding to Michael who proceeded to strip in front of the audience.

Once he was down to his boxers, he picked up his clothes and threw them in a corner of the room. The move didn't appear to surprise Vaalt or any of the other faes who'd expected Michael to shift into his furry alter ego. Surprise clearly registered on Vaalt's face, however, when the alter ego in question turned out to be a gigantic bear. They'd clearly never encountered his type before: nothing surprising about that since Michael was, more than likely, the last surviving member of his kind.

Walking on four paws, the bear cautiously approached the hydra who stood at the center of the room, being careful to remain out of striking distance of the creature. The part of the fae's body that rested on the floor resembled a gigantic snake. Easily three feet in diameter, it made the widest anaconda on record look skinny. The tail end was surprisingly short, though: no more than seven or eight feet. But Michael was most concerned with the other half of the monster, the six almost dragon-like heads, each supported by a five-foot neck thicker than Sheila's waist. Equipped with razor-sharp fangs, each pair of jaws was plenty impressive on its own and Clarissa had six of them. The icing on the cake, each bite carried enough venom to paralyze an average prey within seconds. Michael wasn't an average prey, and the poison probably wouldn't act as fast on him, but Clarissa's bite would still prove devastating to his reflexes.

The first attack came from the hydra, but her jaws sprang shut a good three feet from Michael's head. The monster's mephitic breath was motivation enough to stay away from the biting ends.

Michael started pacing slowly around the hydra, who managed to keep two or three pairs of eyes on him regardless of where he stood. Thankfully for the bear, there was plenty of space in the room to circle his opponent while remaining out of reach. Having completed a first circle around the beast, Michael turned and completed another one in the opposite direction, looking for a chink in Clarissa's scaly armor. The beast struck a couple more times, but he was too far away to be worried about her attempts.

When he reached the tip of her tail he sprang forward and sank his fangs into the cold appendage, retreating just in time to avoid the incoming strike of one of the heads. The end of her tail was the only part of Clarissa's body far enough from her torso to safely attack, and even then he had to be quick about it. Unfortunately, the tail was unlikely to host any vital organ.

Clarissa shifted at a speed much greater than she'd demonstrated up to now and Michael found himself facing the dragon heads once more. How did one kill a hydra? He had no idea, but he suspected chopping the heads one by one would do the trick. Now he just needed to do that six times, without his battle axes, while avoiding being struck a single time by the monster which weighed at least twice his bear.

Two heads flew at him at once in a lightning-fast attack that he miraculously avoided by getting up on his back legs. With two or three feet on his opponent, he now possessed an offensive advantage, but it was easily balanced by a reduced mobility which could prove fatal if the hydra rushed him. Clarissa did just that an instant later, her body sliding on the floor at a speed she shouldn't have been able to achieve. Three heads came at him at once. He was able to deflect two of them using his front paws, but the third one got him on the side just above the hip joint.

The beast hissed in pain as Michael's four-inch claws sliced through its necks with the devastating precision of a scalpel in the hands of a surgeon. Clarissa retreated promptly. Two of her heads hung limply at the end of their necks, blood oozing through the severed arteries, but still attached to the rest of the body by thick lumps of torn flesh.

Michael was also licking his wounds, however. His thick fur had partially protected him from the bite, but a couple of the hydra's teeth had still found their way deep into his flesh, and he was praying they hadn't been the ones bearing venom. He felt no ill effect from the poison so far, just the searing pain of being stabbed by spear-like fangs. His wounds soon closed up and he was back on all fours and ready for round two by the time Clarissa returned with a vengeance.

After her first semi-successful attack, the snake-like creature had retreated to the end of the room to assess the damage to her body, but now she was coming back towards him at full speed. She'd be on him in a second and there wasn't enough space in the room to outrun her.

Reacting on instinct, Michael waited until the hydra was a mere ten feet away and then rushed her. The move caught Clarissa off guard and the bear's powerful jaws closed on one of her necks at the base of the skull, while the claws of his right paw skewered one of the remaining heads through the brain. He managed to slice through another neck with his left paw, but the monster's last remaining head sunk its fangs deep at the junction of his neck and shoulder. This time the effect of the venom was almost instantaneous. The monster's last head had triumphed over the bear.

As the poison flowed through his veins, Michael started losing control of his upper body, and his uncoordinated attempts at slicing through her remaining neck with his front paws proved futile. He still had control of his lower half, however. In a desperate move, he bearhugged the hydra and crouched to the ground until his rump hit the floor. He then put all his remaining strength in thrusting the claws of his back paws through the hydra's thick torso just below the junction of her necks with the rest of the body. The monster released the bear and hissed in agony as his razor-sharp claws pierced her heart.

Michael had just enough time to roll around to avoid being trapped under the collapsing body of his slain enemy before complete paralysis set in.

Chapter 49

Michael made it back to the rental in the middle of the afternoon accompanied by Irini and Lucy. As they parked the car near the house, Sheila came out to welcome them.

It had taken over thirty minutes for Michael's body to fight the hydra's venom off and recover the use of his muscles. Lord Vaalt had tried to argue that the fight had been a draw, since both champions had been neutralized, but Ez had brushed away the absurd concept. When Michael had finally recovered the use of his muscles, not a scratch was left on him. Clarissa, on the other hand, still lay lifeless in a puddle of her own blood, and Lord Vaalt was forced to concede his defeat.

As Michael got out of the car, a whiff of a scent that shouldn't have been here reached his nostrils, carried by a gentle breeze. He immediately felt his hair rise on the back of his neck as he surveyed his surroundings, but the breeze was gone and so was the scent, erased by the cooking aroma emanating from the kitchen. Had he imagined it?

He kissed Sheila on the lips and said he needed to stretch his legs before disappearing around the corner of the house in search of the unwelcome scent. But he found nothing and after five minutes of sniffing the air in all possible directions, he started wondering if the hydra's poison wasn't still playing tricks on his body.

He joined the women in the living room as Sheila announced that the food wouldn't be ready for another thirty minutes.

"You should have warned me earlier that you were bringing guests over. A one-hour heads up isn't enough, Michael…" she said reproachfully. But Michael knew she was joking.

Ezekiel and Tabitha hadn't made the journey back with them; they had other urgent matters to attend to. Ezekiel was under the impression that something was going on around Vulpe's castle. Apparently he'd sensed some sort of powerful energy in the area and wanted to go back to check it out. Tabitha for her part had returned to the Southern Hemisphere, still trying to locate the *entity*.

"I've baked a strawberry pie and bilberry muffins for Irini, and there's eight pounds of lamb roasting in the oven for Lucy and you," announced Sheila as Michael settled down in an armchair with a mug of black tea with honey.

Both their guests thanked Sheila for accommodating their dietary peculiarities and the hostess answered that it was nothing. Michael knew she was just glad the two vampires weren't on a strict blood diet. As hybrids, Lucy and Irini were able to live on the diet of their respective werebeings. This meant meat for Lucy, who'd inherited some of Olivia's werewolf genes, and pretty much anything for Irini, who had some bear blood running through her veins. The elder showed a marked preference for berries of all kind, though.

"You've now been framed not once but twice, Lucy," said Michael. "And we need to figure out who's behind this. Ezekiel suspects the *entity* of trying to collect the three fragments of the Eye of the Phoenix. If he's correct, finding out who framed you may lead us to the *entity*."

"Seemak's involvement suggests the faes are behind it. Even if Lord Vaalt isn't involved, another fae could be pulling the strings from behind the scenes," said Irini.

The argument had merit and was worth considering, but Michael had his doubts. "Ezekiel doesn't seem to think that a fae could display the type of powers showcased by the *entity*. It would have to be a group of faes who somehow managed to pull their powers together into a unified force. I don't know faes very well, but Ez and Tabitha didn't think such a thing was likely to happen."

"Whoever framed me was able to change their appearance to look just like me. It had to be a chameleon…"

Michael had already spent hours thinking about it. What else indeed would have be able to fool Seemak himself?

Simple glamour wouldn't have fooled the chameleon. It had to be a polymorphic shape shifter, which seriously reduced the number of options. "A wizard of some sort could have done it too," he suggested finally. "I don't know how strong of a wizard it would require, but I've seen Ez make some very convincing impersonations on more than one occasion…"

"But why would a wizard single out Lucy?" The question had come from Sheila, who'd just returned from the kitchen. "Why would he want to frame her, and not once but twice?"

Nobody had a good answer to offer and the journalist continued, "I think it's more likely Lucy's being framed by someone she knows, someone who holds a grudge against her."

"Maybe Anastasia found out about you and Vladislav…" suggested Irini. "If she knew, she'd be more than capable of framing you. That would be just her style."

"How long have you been... seeing Vladislav?" Lucy's sex life was the last thing Michael wanted to talk about, but the information was too relevant to ignore.

Lucy didn't look particularly happy about discussing the subject either, but she answered all the same. "It started about a week before Vulpe's artifact was stolen. I would sneak into Vladislav's bedroom during the day while his wife was asleep in her sarcophagus. We were very discreet."

"Maybe not discreet enough," said Irini. "How many times did it happen?"

"Seven, I think. As I told you it started exactly a week before the robbery and I saw him every single day during that week."

"Every single day? When?" Irini sounded surprised.

"We would meet a couple of hours after sunrise, and I would leave him about eighty minutes before sunset, to avoid getting caught by the servant in charge of lighting the fireplace in his room."

"You can't have seen him every day; we spent the whole Wednesday of that week together, Lucy. We took one of the cars and went to visit the area. I showed you those hanging gardens, remember?"

"The gardens were the week before."

"No! It was that week."

Lucy looked confused. "I guess you're right. Okay, then I only saw him six times instead of seven. What does it change, anyway?"

Michael considered the question carefully. As Lucy had pointed out, it was unlikely to be of any significance, yet he felt the detail was strangely relevant. He had no idea why, however. Something he'd heard earlier, perhaps? Whatever the reason might be, it was currently locked somewhere inside his brain. A critical piece of information lost in the folds of his memory.

As Sheila announced that the food was ready, they all rose from their seats and Michael turned to Irini. "I need you to do me a favor, Irini."

"Sure, what do you need?"

"There is a book in Vulpe's library. A book of great interest to me. I need you to ask him if you can borrow it. Tell him that *you* want to read it."

Chapter 50

Demetra and Lotar had spent the whole day and a good part of the previous night observing the vampires' compound, both from a distance and up close. The fact they could transport instantly inside the walls of the domain and the fact invisibility spells were well within their skills made things a lot easier than they could have been, but they still needed to be careful. The enthralled werewolves guarding the property didn't need their eyes to locate intruders; their noses did the trick just as well and possibly better.

"I'd say we're dealing with two hundred vampires, possibly more. And over fifty werewolves," said Demetra.

They both stood invisible against the ten-foot wall delineating the property. In the distance, two wolves disappeared around one of the corners of the castle.

"Maybe retrieving the artifacts won't be as easy as the master suggested," said Lotar.

For once the two warlocks were in agreement. With powers such as theirs, they had little to fear from the likes of Vulpe, but Vulpe wasn't alone. He had hundreds of vampires at his disposal, an arsenal large enough to wage war on a small country and plenty of brain-washed werewolves ready to tear apart anything that didn't belong inside the compound.

"How do you suggest we find out where the three pieces are located? We can't even sense them from here," said Lotar.

Demetra wasn't used to him asking for advice; usually he was busy trying to outshine her to impress the master. The current situation was different, though, and neither of them knew where to start. Regardless, one thing was clear: they needed to come up with a plan and fast, as patience had never been the master's strong suit.

"We need to search the castle room by room until we pick up the fragments' energetic signature. Then we follow the energy threads until they lead us to what we're looking for," suggested Demetra.

Lotar nodded. "There's something strange about this; the fragments are still apart at the moment. We would sense the united artifact from here otherwise."

"Why is it strange?"

"If the three fragments are in the hands of the same individual, why haven't they rebuilt the artifact to enjoy its power for themselves?" replied Lotar.

It was actually a really good question. Why would one go through the trouble of stealing from Lord Vaalt and not reassemble the artifact? There was one possible explanation: maybe the three artifacts weren't yet under one roof. But this would imply that the master was mistaken, and Demetra wasn't about to suggest such a thing in front of Lotar.

Suddenly Demetra felt a powerful wave of energy washing over her. For a split second she thought the Eye of the Phoenix had been reassembled, but she quickly discarded the thought. This was different. This was the signature of a wizard, and a powerful one.

By the way Lotar was looking at her, she knew he'd sensed it too. What was a wizard doing here? This was going to complicate things a bit.

"What do we do?" whispered Lotar.

"We can't start a fight here with all these wolves around. We can't afford to betray our presence at this point."

"The wizard's getting closer…"

"I know. I feel it too. Let's see who we're dealing with. I'll go stand over there." Demetra was pointing at the castle wall a hundred yards in front of them. "We'll be able to attack on two fronts if need be."

The two warlocks pulled their wands out of their sleeves and Demetra vanished.

Chapter 51

Their early dinner was over and Sheila was serving coffee to Michael and their guests at the dining-room table when a booming voice came from outside the house. "Michael Biörn, this is the police. The house is surrounded. You have no way out. Come out through the front door with your hands up in the air."

The order had been given in English, but despite the distortion caused by the bullhorn, the heavy French accent was obvious.

Before Michael had a chance to stop her, Sheila ran to one of the windows and confirmed that the house was indeed surrounded with what looked like police officers. "It's written Gendarmerie on the vehicles, though, not Police."

Michael wasn't surprised by the announcement. Small towns and villages didn't have their own police force, and it was usually the Gendarmerie who was in charge of police matters for these areas—just like small US towns relied on the county sheriff for matters of law and order.

France actually had two police forces, the Police Nationale and the Gendarmerie. But the latter was actually a branch of the French armed forces and, unlike the Police Nationale, the Gendarmerie operated both within the borders of the country and abroad in zones of armed conflicts requiring a police force.

"What do they want?" asked Sheila, but Michael had absolutely no idea.

"We can take them," said Irini, who wasn't above attacking humans.

"I'm not hurting these people unless they start shooting at me. And the two of you will do the same, understood?" Michael's remark was directed to Lucy and her mentor. "There's got to be a misunderstanding. I'll do as they ask and clear things up. But just in case, I'd suggest the two of you don't show yourselves."

An instant later, he was stepping outside, arms raised above his head.

The first thing he noticed were the dozen gendarmes pointing their guns at him from behind their cars and around the corners of the three stone outbuildings that had once respectively been a barn, a bread oven and a rabbit hutch. The second thing he noticed was the smell he'd thought he'd recognized a couple hours earlier when he'd returned to the rental with the two vampires. There was no longer any mistake possible. The same odor had lingered in his cabin the day Bob had disappeared.

Michael had no idea what the man was doing here six thousand miles and an ocean away from Yellowstone, but he was absolutely convinced that, whatever this was about, the asshole was behind it. The whole thing stunk to high heaven.

Michael hadn't done anything wrong, he didn't need to let these people arrest him, but things could only go down one of three ways. He could run, hoping that their shots wouldn't take him down, but then he would have several dozen sworn-in officers testifying to whoever wanted to hear it that he was bullet-proof, a type of publicity he couldn't afford.

The second option was to kill them all. It was easily doable, especially with Irini's help. The vampire was wound up like a spring, hoping for an excuse to unleash her wrath on the unfortunate officers. But these gendarmes had kids and wives waiting for them at home. They'd come to arrest someone they no doubt believed was a dangerous criminal. They'd been deceived and didn't deserve to die for it. So... Michael opted for option number three.

"What's going on? Why am I being arrested?" he asked in perfect French to the man holding the bullhorn.

"You'll need to ask these gentlemen, sir," answered the man, gesturing towards two men in plain clothes while one of the gendarmes was placing handcuffs around Michael's wrists. The flimsy bracelets had less chance of restraining him than a string of yarn would a rottweiler, but he decided to play nice and not damage the metallic restraints, at least for the time being.

Once the handcuffs were on, the two plain-clothes officers approached Michael holding Interpol IDs reading Detective Inspector McDowell and Detective Inspector Clark. Americans... Before either could say a word, Sheila stormed out of the house, holding her phone in front of her like a tape recorder. She walked straight up to Michael and the two men. "Sheila Wang with the Houston Post. For the record, detectives, what is this man accused of?"

"That's none of your business, Ma'am. Go back inside. We'll come and interview you in a minute," answered McDowell.

"Maybe you could tell *me* then? I believe it is my business," said Michael. He was doing his best to appear relaxed about the arrest, but the presence of the two Americans was more than concerning. These men were in all likelihood linked to Bob's disappearance and therefore his death, and Michael still had no idea what they wanted with him.

"You're correct," answered McDowell. "You have the right to know why we're taking your ass straight to jail. Michael Biörn, you are under arrest for the murder of Robert Spencer."

Chapter 52

Michael had been taken into custody and Sheila wasn't too sure what to do about it. Usually she had no problem making split-second decisions and, as a journalist, following her instinct had served her well on numerous occasions, but in this instance her instinct told her nothing. The man she loved had just been arrested by Interpol for the murder of one of his friends. A ludicrous accusation, but Michael was nonetheless facing these serious charges.

How was it even possible? What kind of evidence could have led Interpol to issue an international arrest warrant less than a week after Bob's body had been discovered? According to Olivia, a mere two days earlier Jason Parrish had seemed convinced the death had been caused by a mountain lion and wanted to close the case without involving any other agencies. So what had changed so drastically between now and then? Interpol's involvement in such a matter was more than suspicious. Something didn't add up.

"The cops had to have had the rental under surveillance for some time, that much is certain. They jumped on Michael within two hours of our return and they knew we were in the house," said Irini, suddenly reappearing in the room now that the last police vehicle could be heard driving away.

"I'm sure they did," agreed Sheila.

The cops who'd interviewed her had indeed been surprised not to find Lucy and Irini inside the house, and had even searched the premises for the two women. They had no right to do so, but Sheila hadn't objected to the absence of a search warrant. She had nothing to hide and she found it entertaining to watch the officers going from room to room, scratching their heads, while the two vampires stood quietly in a corner of the living room, invisible to the human eye.

"What do we do now?" asked Lucy. "We're not going to let them put Michael in jail, are we?"

"Michael's more than capable of breaking out of any human jail, Lucy. He'll be breathing free air the minute he decides he's sick of their stupid games," answered Irini.

The vampire was correct, of course, but Sheila couldn't help worrying. She'd been around when Ez had mentioned the sudden disappearance of entire werewolf packs. And she remembered Michael telling Olivia to stay away from Jason Parrish, just in case... What if Parrish was linked to the werewolves' disappearances, and what if Michael was next on the list? Her teddy bear was as tough as they got, but sometimes he was too nice for his own good. By cooperating with this bullshit investigation, he might very well have walked into a trap from which he wouldn't get out.

"I must go back to the States right away. I need to use my weight as a journalist to pressure the authorities into releasing Michael. I don't think this arrest was even slightly legit."

"Agreed! There's something fishy about the whole thing," said Irini.

"The two of you can stay here in the rental. I just renewed the lease for another week. I know Michael wouldn't want Lucy to go back to

Vulpe's lair right away. Not until we figure out what the hell's going on."

Irini and Lucy accepted the offer, but Sheila could see in the elder's eyes that the woman had something else in mind altogether.

Sheila went to retrieve her computer from her bag and was logging into the airline website to change her return flight when Irini approached the table and looked down at the laptop. "I see you have a Mac. Good, that will make things easier."

Chapter 53

The gendarmerie's holding pen in which Michael had been placed was composed of three concrete walls and one made of dirty yellowed Plexiglas. The giant polymeric window was probably between a half and three-quarter inch in thickness, but Michael suspected he could effortlessly break through it if needed. At any rate, the lock on the door was unlikely to resist him long if he decided to put his muscles to work.

His cell companion, arrested for drunk driving, hadn't said a word since his arrival and was keeping well away from him. This suited Michael just fine; he wasn't in a chatty mood right now.

Michael had been locked up for two hours already when a delegation of four appeared on the other side of the Plexiglas. He immediately recognized the two Americans, but the two gendarmes in uniforms were newcomers.

"It's time to go, Biörn. Let's move." The man whose name was supposedly McDowell appeared to be in charge.

"Where are we going?"

"It's back to the States for you, Biörn. Where you'll stand trial for your crime."

As he approached the cell door, Michael quickly ran through his options. There was no doubt he could use this opportunity to knock everybody down and escape, but there were probably a dozen gendarmes between him and the door. A dozen innocents who would no doubt get hurt in the process. And once outside, what would he do? Steal a car, run? In either case he'd be chased, and more people would likely get injured.

He decided to continue cooperating for now. His beef was with the two Americans, especially that McDowell whose scent had been all over his cabin the day Bob had gone missing. If he left with them, it wouldn't be long before he found an opportunity for the three of them to have a nice chat.

The cell opened and the two Americans stepped inside. A pair of shiny handcuffs was hanging from Clark's right hand. Outside the cell, the two gendarmes had their hands on their sidearms, ready to take him out in case he tried anything. They all looked nervous, but the Americans more so than the others. Michael didn't wonder why: he already knew the answer. These Interpol agents understood what he was capable of, and he found the thought highly disturbing.

"Place your hands behind your back and turn around," ordered Clark.

Michael obeyed and slowly spun to face the back wall. Clark placed the handcuffs around his wrists, but Michael wasn't prepared for what came next: a sensation of mild strangulation as a collar snapped shut around his neck. Reacting on instinct, he spun around to face the agents and snapped the handcuffs chain as if it were made of glass while elbowing McDowell on the side of the head. The Interpol agent went down like a log before Michael realized what he was doing.

"Get on the ground now!" screamed the two gendarmes in French. Their guns were trained on his heart and Michael obeyed.

"Is alright colleague? a gendarme asked Clark in an English so approximative it was almost comical.

"I've never seen handcuffs break before," said the other whose mastery of the foreign language was far better.

"Me neither," admitted Clark, kneeling beside McDowell who was starting to regain consciousness. "But I've never put handcuffs on a giant his size either."

"What's that thing you put around his neck?" asked the gendarme.

"A shock collar designed to restrain people like him, those who can't be trusted with handcuffs..." said Clark. "Are you okay?" he asked McDowell, who was now sitting against the wall, massaging his jaw.

"I'm fine. He got me by surprise, but it won't happen again."

The man sounded more confident than he should have been. Maybe they didn't know what Michael was truly capable of after all.

But Michael last doubts evaporated when McDowell added, "He's going to behave now. This shock collar was built to take down a bear."

Michael walked out of the gendarmerie between Clark and McDowell and the three of them boarded a van where two more men awaited them. The two newcomers were American as well and Michael immediately identified the scent of the man behind the wheel; he, too, had visited his cabin the night Bob had disappeared.

Before Michael even had a chance to settle in his seat, the van started rolling as McDowell explained with palpable pleasure the intricacies of the collar around the prisoner's neck. For good measure, the man sitting on the passenger seat proceeded to demonstrate the power of the device to Michael by attaching a collar identical to his around an empty bottle of wine. He then pressed the button of the remote he held in his hand. This activated a torch inside the collar and within a second or two, the high-intensity flames had sliced the bottle in half. As the top moiety fell to the rug under the passenger's feet, the red-hot glass set fire to the synthetic fabric and after a few seconds of chaos, the rug was hurriedly thrown out the open window to avoid a disaster.

Michael just about died laughing. "Very impressive... Have you guys thought about taking your act on the road?"

The goons gave him dirty looks that failed to impress him. "You try anything at all and it's your head we'll be dumping through that window, understood?" barked the pyromaniac in a pathetic attempt at saving face.

But that only fueled Michael's laughter further and the ranger was soon forced to wipe tears from the corners of his eyes. In truth, his situation was far from humorous. Whoever these people were, they'd never set foot in an Interpol office, this much was certain. Michael chose to focus on the silver lining, though. Here was his chance to finally get some answers. These people knew what happened to Bob, and why. "I feel at a disadvantage here, guys—you know my name, but I don't know yours."

"Shut up, asshole!" said McDowell.

"I mean, it was nice of you to drop by my house a couple weeks ago, but you should have left a card or something so I could get back to you."

The four men looked at each other in silence as he continued, "That would have been the polite thing to do... Instead you left your two friends behind to rummage through my stuff like a couple of lowlife thugs. What were they looking for, by the way? I didn't get a chance to ask before killing them."

"You think you're tough, motherfucker? We'll see how tough you are when I press that fucking button," said the man in the passenger seat. His knuckles were white around the remote.

"I don't think so, Bozo. If you were allowed to kill me at whim, I'd be dead already." Giving the control to the man in the passenger seat had been a smart move; he sat too far away for Michael to have a chance to rush him without literally losing his head.

They finally reached their destination after two and a half hours: a hotel in the vicinity of Toulouse airport. Michael had spent the drive pushing all the men's buttons, but he still hadn't learned anything useful about his kidnappers, neither who they worked for nor what they wanted with him.

Though far smaller than any of the capital's, Toulouse-Blagnac International Airport was still one of the largest in the country and there was little doubt they'd be spending the night here before taking off the next day for the States.

His babysitters had reserved two adjacent double rooms with a communication door. The 3-star hotel wasn't the Ritz by any stretch of imagination, but it was definitely an upgrade over the holding pen. Michael dropped on the bed nearest the window with a loud sigh of relief, before propping his feet up on the bed frame and placing his hands under his head.

"What d'you think you're doing, asshole? This ain't your bed!" said

McDowell.

"Then move me."

McDowell pulled a gun equipped with a silencer and aimed it at Michael's head. "We can't kill you, but we can still shoot you…"

"I wouldn't do that if I were you. For one, you'd need to explain the blood on the sheet and carpet. That could get messy… And two, it would most likely trigger involuntary morphing, which in turn would trigger my collar…"

"I'm willing to take the chance."

"Be my guest." Michael had a bored look on his face as he watched McDowell pull the trigger.

Chapter 54

Hidden behind a grove of trees, the two wolves watched Jason Parrish exit his house and get onto his snowmobile. A moment later he was sliding down the road in the direction of the park's North Entrance where he'd likely take his breakfast in the small town of Gardiner. Gardiner didn't have nearly as much character as the town of West Yellowstone that lay at the park's West Entrance, but it was much closer to the Mammoth area where the majority of the park's employees resided.

Olivia and Daka had driven to Gardiner in the middle of the night and parked their car on a side street where it was unlikely to be noticed by park employees passing through town. They'd then headed towards the park, equipped with a small backpack containing a half dozen spy microphones. As a precaution, they'd purchased the devices online using a friend's credit card and had them delivered to his address.

Under the cover of darkness, they'd followed the main road a short while but had soon cut through the woods where, away from prying eyes, they'd both stripped naked and stuffed their clothes into the backpack.

Olivia had changed into her wolf first, and Daka had secured the bag onto her back before morphing himself. He'd initially objected to having his girlfriend bearing the load, but since Olivia's wolf was larger and Daka could change from his animal form to his human form instantly—as opposed to Olivia whose transformation sometimes took up to ten seconds—the debate had been quickly settled.

It had taken them nearly two hours to cover the distance from Gardiner to Mammoth. Moving through woods and prairies buried in tons of snow was hard work, but they'd still managed to reach the park's residential area three hours before dawn.

Bugging Jason's unlocked patrol car had been child's play. The snowmobile hadn't been much harder, though finding the right location to hide the mic had taken some time. They'd finally settled for a spot beneath the handlebar, hoping the mic wouldn't go flying at the first bump in the snow.

From now on, though, things were going to get a bit more complicated. Obviously they hadn't been able to bug Jason's house while he was sleeping there, and they'd clearly seen him locking his front door on his way out.

"What do we do?" asked Daka, standing naked between the branches of a snow-covered Douglas fir.

It took a few seconds for Olivia to morph back to her human self and answer, "I don't have a master key, but I believe Michael keeps one in his desk inside the ranger station."

"Doesn't look like the station's open yet. Can you get in?"

Olivia shook her head. Her wolf was well equipped against the biting cold of winter, but her naked human body wasn't, and her chattering teeth made the simple task of speaking difficult. "I can wait for someone to show up and walk in as if I was just coming for work," she managed to articulate, as Daka wrapped her in his arms to warm both their bodies. He'd taught her that in dire situations where cold posed a threat to survival, two naked bodies wrapped around each other provided much more warmth than the same bodies covered in clothes. Doubtful, Olivia had required a demonstration to be convinced, and many more since... just to confirm the technique still worked.

Olivia retrieved her clothes from the backpack and slipped into them while Daka morphed back into his furry alter ego. The first interpretive ranger showed up at the station ten minutes later: a woman by the name of Alison. Olivia waited another three minutes after the woman had unlocked the door and disappeared inside the office to follow her in.

The building only contained a handful of private offices—Jason Parrish's being one of them—and the majority of rangers shared a large open floor space. Michael's desk was located in the center of the room and Olivia had reached it by the time Alison came out of the break room carrying an empty coffee pot.

"Olivia! I didn't hear you come in. Where have you been? Jason's been looking for you."

"I took a few days off to visit some friends in Houston. What did he want?"

"I don't know. I think he was looking for Michael and hoped you knew where he was. You know how those two are... So you're back at work?"

"Not quite. I just stopped by because Michael asked me to water his plant and I can't seem to find my key for his house. I think he has a spare in his desk." Olivia had nonchalantly opened Michael's desk drawer while answering and was rummaging through it, looking bored. It was a good thing Alison didn't know much about Michael, who was as likely to have a plant in his cabin as he was to go on a vegetarian diet.

Olivia finally found his spare master key in the third drawer and pocketed it as Alison was coming back from the bathroom carrying the same pot now filled to the rim with water.

"Coffee will be done in ten minutes," announced the ranger before disappearing into the break room.

Olivia was about to leave when she remembered Jason's office. They'd completely forgotten about it, but there was no point in bugging the man's snowmobile while leaving his office without surveillance.

Based on the sounds coming from the break room, Alison was still busy preparing coffee. It was now or never!

Olivia approached Jason's office on her tiptoes and disappeared inside without making a sound. She hid one of the miniature microphones under a bookshelf and cautiously walked out of the room. As she stepped into the hallway, she nearly collided with Alison who was carrying dirty mugs.

"What were you doing in there?" The woman looked more curious than suspicious.

"I left a note on Jason's desk with my number in case he wants to get in touch," lied Olivia.

"He didn't have it?"

"I guess not, or else he would have called."

Alison shrugged and returned to her mug-washing mission while Olivia made a quick exit.

Olivia had already planted three bugs inside the house assigned to Jason and was placing the fourth and last one behind a cabinet in the kitchen when she heard a howl coming from outside… Daka! This was a warning.

She ran to the front door as fast as she could, but she knew it was already too late. The obnoxious noise that was getting louder by the second was that of a snowmobile engine. She carefully glanced through the window located by the front door as Jason was parking his snowmobile right in front of the house.

A quick look at her surroundings confirmed there was nowhere to hide. She hurriedly tiptoed her way to the closest room as she heard Jason's key turning in the lock.

Chapter 55

McDowell and Clark were sitting down at a table inside the hotel's restaurant. McDowell wasn't really sure what an *andouillette* actually was, but it sure was tasty. He'd have enjoyed spending a day or two relaxing and drinking wine before heading home, but it wasn't meant to be. Tomorrow, he'd be on a plane heading to Nevada.

The two other members of the team had already taken their meal and were back in the room, bear-sitting Michael Biörn. The asshole hadn't even flinched when the agent had pulled the trigger to shoot him in the face, as if he'd known all along that the gun's chamber was empty. It had pissed McDowell off, but it was of no consequence. Soon he'd be able to shoot the beast in the face five times a day if he felt like it. Inside the high-security building where they kept all the circus freaks, no one would give a damn about what happened to Biörn.

"Be discreet, but I think the chicks at that table over there are checking us out," said Clark, a glass of wine pressed against his lips as if he were drinking.

McDowell casually stretched in his chair, slowly turning his head in the direction indicated by his colleague. The table in question hosted three diners. Two were hot blondes who wouldn't have been out of place in the centerfold section of a Playboy magazine. The third one was a black beauty with boobs too big to fit in either one of his hands. "I think you're right," he said. "They *are* checking us out."

They continued their meals, glancing in the direction of the three women who on more than one occasion were caught looking back at them and even smiling.

The two agents were starting their desserts when the three ladies got up and headed for the door.

"I could have used some of that." Clark sounded regretful as he nodded towards the women.

"Who couldn't?"

McDowell had barely finished his sentence before one of the blondes approached their table. "My friends and me are going to a bar. Maybe you like to join?" She spoke in a heavy French accent, her smile as disarming as her tits.

"Sorry but we're working tonight," answered McDowell, his cock already pressing heavily against the seam of his jeans.

"That's too bad." He saw genuine disappointment in her big brown eyes as she offered him her hand to shake. "I'm Emilie and if you're change your mind, we'll be at the bar called 'L'extase' down the street."

With its small dance floor lost in a corner of the room and its black lights, the bar was halfway between a club and a proper drinking establishment. The three agents found the trio sitting by themselves at a table, but a number of male patrons were already orbiting around the women.

McDowell and Clark had encountered great difficulties convincing their two colleagues of the vital aspect of the current mission, and they'd only succeeded after offering to take one of them along. Peterson and Black had flipped a coin, and the loser was currently watching Biörn on his own. This was, of course, against protocol, but McDowell didn't give a shit. The only thing he could think of at the moment was the hot blonde who'd noticed them approaching and was waving at him. One man was all that was required to watch the asshole anyway. The collars rendered the freaks as harmless as declawed kitty cats.

McDowell and his friends introduced themselves to the three ladies before walking to the bar to order a first round. Getting hammered definitely wasn't a good idea, but a drink or two to loosen up the girls wouldn't hurt anyone.

An hour and a couple drinks later, he was dancing close up against Emilie, his cock harder than it'd been in a long time. She winked at him as her hand discreetly explored his crotch area.

"What are we going to do about this?" she asked, cupping him through the fabric of his jeans.

A moment later, she was leading him to the girls' bathroom under his teammates' envious eyes. Unfortunately for Clark and Peterson, the two other chicks didn't appear to be nearly as entrepreneurial as Emilie when it came to humping matters.

McDowell walked out of the bathroom ten minutes later with a giant grin on his face.

Chapter 56

Ezekiel had patrolled the perimeter of the vamps' compound a good half dozen times already, but the warlocks hadn't returned. It was nearing midnight now and he was getting tired.

He'd sensed the presence of the two dark practitioners the instant he'd arrived at the domain. A strong presence, powerful auras. Not nearly powerful enough to be responsible for the distortions of the magical field he'd been sensing for over a month, though; these two weren't the *entity*. But Ez was convinced they were part of the equation, maybe even a fragment of the *entity* itself...

Could the *entity* simply be a consortium of practitioners of the dark art? If this were the case, their numbers would have to be enormous—a real concern given the power of the two he'd so briefly seen that afternoon. He'd actually felt relieved to sense the energy split in two as he'd converged towards its source. If such a powerful energetic signature had belonged to a single individual, the foe would have been formidable— maybe too formidable for him to tackle on his own—but when he'd sensed the source of power separating, he'd known he was dealing with two enemies and he'd felt some relief. Neither one of them was as strong as Ezekiel himself, and the thought had felt strangely comforting.

He'd approached them cautiously, staff in hand and ready to use it, wondering whether the warlocks would dare starting something with all the werewolves patrolling the grounds. A battle between the warlocks and himself would no doubt have been noticed. It wasn't easy to remain invisible while fighting a wizard of the Second Circle.

The presence of the two inside the vamps' compound also seemed to confirm Ezekiel's theory. The fragments had to be here. What else would the warlocks be after? With all the activity around the artifact over the past few days, the coincidence was too unlikely. And this could only mean one thing: they would be back. They wouldn't give up on the artifact simply because Ezekiel happened to be in the way. They would return… and he needed to be ready for them.

Chapter 57

Michael sat frustrated against the headboard of the bed. He'd been alone with the man the others called Black for nearly three hours and still hadn't found on opportunity to escape. Black had dragged his armchair as far from Michael as possible and was relentlessly watching him, remote in hand, ready to chop his prisoner's head off at a moment's notice.

As if the demonstration of the collar's capabilities on the wine bottle hadn't been enough, Black had activated Michael's collar when the ranger had gotten up asking to use the restroom. In all fairness to the guard, Michael had ignored the first order to "get his ass back on the bed" before the searing pain around his neck had forced him to obey. The man had only depressed the remote's red button a fraction of a second, but Michael had nearly fainted with pain. It had taken several minutes for his body to heal completely and the pain to finally rescind.

"I know you weren't at my cabin that night," he said, catching Black off guard. "Clark wasn't there either. But Peterson and McDowell were there for certain."

"How d'you know that?" The words had poured out of the man's mouth automatically, and he didn't look happy about it.

"You think your side's the only one with spies?"

"What spies?" The man looked both doubtful and confused.

Michael could have told him the truth. He could have explained to his jailer that a bear had the most sensitive nose in the animal kingdom, that he never forgot a scent, but spies sounded better. He wanted to keep him on his toes. "It doesn't matter… But I know you're not one of those who kidnapped Robert Spencer and I'm not holding you directly responsible for his death."

"You think I give a rat's ass whether you hold me responsible or not?"

"Maybe not, but you should. I hold McDowell and Peterson directly responsible for Bob's death, for instance, and it's only a matter of time before I kill them."

"You're not in a position to make threats, asshole."

"You have no idea who you're dealing with, do you, kid? You guys are in way above your head here."

"We've been dealing with your kind for months and we've all survived so far…" Black was flashing a cocky smile at him.

"You've never dealt with my kind before, kid. I assure you. This is your last chance to do the right thing. Walk away now, while you still can. You don't have to die for this rotten cause, soldier. Bob didn't deserve to die."

"He wasn't supposed to. The team thought it was you they were grabbing." The man looked relieved, as if he had a weight off his chest.

This was the first time his kidnappers had admitted responsibility for what had happened to Bob. And it also confirmed what Michael had suspected for a while: his friend had never been the real target. He'd just been at the wrong place at the wrong time.

"And why did you have to kill the poor bastard?"

"I didn't have anything to with that! He was killed by one of them."

"One of them who?" asked Michael, but the man was done talking. He looked like he was going to be sick.

Despite Black's revelations, Michael still couldn't find anything linking the mercenaries to the Eye of the Phoenix. The two threats appeared to be originating from different points, just like Ez had said. Michael had been going over the new information in his head for nearly twenty minutes when his nose told him the other three had returned. It was another forty seconds before he heard their voices in the hallway and a full minute went by before they finally entered the bedroom.

"You missed some party, my friend!" announced McDowell, who had a grin going from one ear to the other.

"This jerk managed to screw one of the chicks in the bar's restroom," said Clark, nodding towards his friend and looking envious.

"She was so freaking hot, bro. I'd never touched a body like that before. And she moaned, my god, she moaned…"

McDowell spent the next ten minutes retelling his sexual encounter in vivid detail while completely ignoring Michael who'd finally decided to make a move when a knock came at the door.

Clark unholstered his gun and went to check the peephole. "It's the chick, your Emilie," he told McDowell, who looked as surprised as the others.

McDowell went to the door and opened it. An instant later a smoking blonde stood at his arm as he introduced her to Black whose mouth was open so wide it belonged in a Tex Avery cartoon.

The woman was indeed gorgeous with her lightly tanned skin and long blonde curls, but there was something definitely wrong with the picture. Her hair should have been black and very straight.

"Now's the time, baby," she told McDowell, who pulled his sidearm and shot his three colleagues in the head before they had a chance to understand what was happening. He then placed the gun in his own mouth and pulled the trigger.

"I'd suggest we get out through the window…" Irini told Michael. "How do you like the wig?"

Michael retrieved the collar's remote from under the bed where it had landed when Black had dropped it and pressed the release button. "I think I'll keep it as a souvenir. Let's go now," he said, opening the window.

Irini was right behind him. "Shit! I forgot…" She walked back to the center of the room and knelt beside Clark's body, searching the pocket of his winter coat.

"What are you doing?"

"Getting my phone back. How do you think we found you?" she answered, pulling an iPhone out of the dead man's pocket. "Have you ever heard of an app called *find my device*?"

Michael gave her a blank stare before jumping through the third-story window.

Irini's car was parked on a street adjacent to the hotel. Lucy was behind the wheel and she took off as soon as they got inside. They could already hear the police sirens getting closer. The quadruple murder-suicide hadn't gone unnoticed.

"I heard the gunshots from here," said Lucy, exiting a roundabout onto the freeway's access ramp. "Where to now?"

"We can't go back to the rental. That's the first place they'll be looking for me. I need to call Sheila and tell her to meet us somewhere safe."

There was only one problem with Michael's plan; his phone had been confiscated by the agents and he'd forgotten to retrieve it before leaving the hotel room. He still wasn't used to carrying the darned thing around and tended to leave the house without it more often than not, despite Sheila's repeated reminders. To make matters worse, he didn't have Sheila's new phone number memorized and the two vampires didn't have the journalist in their contacts either.

"We'll drop you off at a hotel and we'll go back to the rental to tell Sheila where to meet you. It will be safer than talking to her over the phone, anyway. Those guys' friends could have her cell tapped already. Apparently they know how to pull some strings…"

Michael nodded. The string-pulling power of these assholes had also been bugging him. Who could get Interpol credentials convincing enough to fool the French authorities into collaborating in an unlawful arrest? This had him worrying more than anything else for the simple reason that the riddle didn't have too many possible answers. It had to be some type of governmental organization, and the government in question in this instance was almost certainly the United States'. That or another country was doing an outstanding job framing the US for the operation.

"You got your phone back?" Lucy asked Irini.

"I did."

"What was it doing in McDowell's pocket?" asked Michael.

"I put it there when he and his buddy came inside the house to interrogate Sheila."

"I assume they never even realized the two of you were inside the house?"

"Of course not. Human minds are so easy to trick." It had only been six months since she'd been turned, but Lucy was already talking like a true vampire.

"After that, all we had to do was to log into my account on Sheila's Mac and follow my phone all the way to your hotel."

"When did you get a chance to enthrall McDowell?" asked Michael.

"We bumped into him at the hotel restaurant and I convinced him he really couldn't afford not to come and join us in a club later that evening. It was a simple suggestion, but I was able to capture his eyes long enough that I knew he'd be showing up. And then I finished the job at the bar."

"In the bathroom, I suppose?" Michael couldn't hide the disappointment in his voice. He couldn't help but see Wawetseka every time he looked at Irini. She looked exactly the same as the day she'd died under his surveillance all those centuries ago. And the idea that his little Wawetseka was the woman McDowell had bragged about to his friend made his stomach churn.

Irini had apparently read his mind, however. "The asshole never touched me, Michael. He only thinks he did. I've told you about induction before, remember? I may not be anywhere as good as Anastasia when it comes to implanting thoughts in a mind, but my skills are more than adequate to convince a jackass like McDowell he just had the thing he'd been dreaming about all night."

The news brought great relief to Michael, but he tried not to show it. "I can't believe those guys didn't recognize you. The rental was under surveillance, they must have seen you arriving with me at the house."

"They probably didn't get a good look at me. And at any rate, they would have been looking for a brunette and a redhead. Not two blondes and a black chick…"

"A black chick?"

"We recruited a friend for our little entrapment operation," chimed in Lucy.

"You mean you enthralled an innocent bystander." Michael wasn't pleased.

Irini was unfazed, however. "Yeah, that's another way of putting it."

They found a hotel open in the town of Périgeux, thirty minutes from Sheila's rental, and reserved a room using Lucy's fake passport. While Lucy and Michael headed to the room, Irini was already on her way to warn Sheila.

Michael took advantage of that time to take a shower, the wheels spinning in his head the whole time. He had two problems and needed to prioritize them. The goon squad would have to wait; for now he needed to help Ezekiel with the Eye of the Phoenix mystery. He had the feeling that once he figured out who'd been behind Lucy's framing, the rest of the pieces would fall into place.

He was clean and was dressed again in the only clothes he had available when he heard Lucy answering her phone in the adjacent bedroom.

He came out of the bathroom an instant later. "Was it Irini? Did she talk to Sheila?"

Lucy looked at him, embarrassed. "I'm sorry, Michael. The rental was empty. Sheila's gone."

Chapter 58

Crammed between the wall and the open door of Jason Parrish's bedroom, Olivia wondered when the man was finally going to leave the house. She'd been standing here for hours. What was he doing? Didn't he have a job to go to? Had he taken the day off? This would be her luck.

Daka hadn't manifested himself since Jason had returned and trapped her inside the house, but she knew the skinwalker was out there, waiting for her. Her boyfriend knew that technically she had nothing to fear from Jason Parrish; if push came to shove, she could knock the man out with a single finger. But that would also betray her not-so-human nature, and if Jason was indeed linked to the werewolves' disappearances Ez had mentioned, this was the type of advertising Olivia didn't need.

Killing the man would of course solve the issue, but they didn't have nearly enough evidence against him to justify such a thing. At least, that was the story Olivia liked to tell herself… In truth she doubted she'd be able to do it, even with all the proof in hand. It was one thing to kill in self-defense and another to murder just to cover your tracks.

She heard her phone ring and, for a second, she just about screamed at her own stupidity, but then she remembered that her phone had been safely left behind in Daka's car. This wasn't her mobile ringing—Jason simply happened to have the same ringtone as hers.

"Yes, Ma'am." She heard the ranger answer. "They're all dead? He killed them all?"

Olivia's werewolf possessed very decent hearing, but she was still too far from the phone to hear the other side of the conversation.

"It was one of ours? Why would he shoot his teammates and himself? That makes no sense… Could Biörn have talked him into doing this? Do you think werebears could have this kind of power over our minds?"

The conversation was getting interesting; they were talking about Michael. What had he gotten pulled into this time? Where was he, and what was he up to? Not looking into Bob's murder, that was for sure!

"Do we have any idea where he is at the moment? … Yes, I have his cell phone, but I doubt he'll answer. He suspects something about me, I'm sure that's why his pet werewolf has vanished. He must have told her to go into hiding."

So much for Olivia risking betraying her werewolf nature. There was nothing left to betray. The asshole already knew everything there was to know. At least she wouldn't need to use too much restraint when she punched his teeth out.

"No, Ma'am, I still have no idea where she is. She left the park, possibly the state by now ... Who? Houston, really? I wonder why."

What about Houston? What were they talking about? Houston was Lucy and Olivia's hometown. Did they think Olivia had gone back to Houston? Were they looking for her over there? She hoped they were...

"Yes, Ma'am. Absolutely! That would get Biörn's attention, no doubt about it."

Olivia didn't like the enthusiasm in Jason's voice. The jerk sounded far too happy.

Chapter 59

It was nearly 2 AM but neither Michael nor Lucy were sleeping. They sat on their respective hotel beds, Michael worrying about Sheila and Lucy playing with her phone.

Irini's characteristic smell suddenly tickled Michael's nostrils; finally, she was back. Unlike Lucy who barely possessed any vampire scent, Irini bore the odor associated with bloodsuckers of a certain age: a stench that accentuated with the passing years. But her particular aroma didn't really bother Michael anymore; it was Irini, after all, not a *real* vampire. At least that was what he told himself to justify his choice of company. He knew full well that the elder had taken countless innocent lives to satisfy her blood needs, and it wasn't because she'd converted to a different diet over the past six months that her sins were erased, but he preferred not thinking about these things.

"So?" Michael asked as soon as Irini entered the room.

"Nothing. I looked for Sheila's car at every hotel near Toulouse airport, but it wasn't there. She might have driven straight to Paris to catch a direct flight."

"You're sure she was heading back to the US?" asked Michael.

"She was trying to change her flight when we left the rental to chase after the van they'd thrown you in."

"Why did she want to go back if she knew you were planning to rescue me?"

The two vampires glanced at each other uneasily.

"What is it?" asked Michael.

"We told her we'd follow you from a distance. She didn't want us to go after the Interpol agents. She suspected something was fishy, but she wanted to solve it the proper way, the... legal way, apparently," answered Irini.

"Basically, she didn't want us to show up and slaughter all of them," added Lucy lightly. "Technically we respected her wish. They slaughtered each other and she never said anything about that…"

"Next time we should try to leave one of them alive. They tend to answer questions better that way," replied Michael in a tired voice. "If only I hadn't left my phone with those assholes."

"It's probably sitting in an evidence drawer as we speak," said Irini.

"Yep… It's going to be really tough for the cops to not believe I'm involved in this."

"Who cares?!" said Lucy.

"I do! Unlike the two of you, I have a legitimate life out there in the world. And so does your sister, by the w—" The thought of Olivia had stopped him dead in his tracks. "Olivia has Sheila's number programmed in her phone!"

"And I happen to have Olivia's number programmed in mine." Lucy was waving her phone, grinning.

"Call her, but don't tell her I'm with you. She doesn't know. I didn't want her to worry about your *predicament*."

"Lying to Olivia… really, Michael?" Lucy took an air of disappointment. "Don't get me wrong I do it all the time, but I didn't picture you as the lying type," she added, shaking her head.

Michael rolled his eyes. "Call your sister, Lucy."

Lucy dialed Olivia's number. It rang five times before the call went to voice mail. "Hey, sis," she said. "I hope everything's going well with you. I'm calling because I need Sheila's number and I thought you might have it. I don't want to ask Michael because you know how he is, always playing fifty questions and all… Anyway, text me her number when you get the message. Love you!"

Irini looked amused, but Michael was just staring at Lucy blankly.

"What? I was just trying to build you an alibi."

Before Michael could reply anything, Lucy's phone vibrated in her hand.

That didn't take long, thought Michael, but he was mistaken. The call wasn't from Olivia. Lucy had snatched the phone from the bed in an instant but not before he'd seen the name appearing on the device's oversized screen: Vlad. Unless Dracula had suddenly staged a comeback, Vlad was probably short for Vladislav. His suspicion was confirmed when Lucy excused herself and left the room as she answered the call.

She came back fifteen minutes later and, had she not been a vampire, she probably would have blushed under the inquisitive looks of Michael and Irini.

"Who was it?" said Irini.

"Why do you ask when you already know the answer?"

Irini just stared at her in silence.

"It was Vladislav. He wanted to make sure I was okay. He said he tried to come with you guys to rescue me, but Michael wouldn't let him." She was staring at Michael now, daring him to contradict her lover.

Michael didn't feel the need to justify himself, however, and simply ignored the question.

But Lucy wanted an answer. "Why?"

"Michael did what needed to be done. You could either get the help of Ezekiel and Tabitha or that of Vladislav. Not both. He made the right choice. End of the conversation!"

Lucy sighed. "Sorry, Michael, I didn't mean to—"

"That's alright," he interrupted before she could finish her sentence.

"And I never thanked you for fighting that hydra for me—you could have died."

"There's no need to thank me. I did what needed to be done at the time. That's all."

"Whatever you and Vladislav have going on, it needs to stop, Lucy. Anastasia will have your head for this."

"She's screwing Vulpe. She hasn't given a shit about her husband in months." Lucy sounded defensive.

"More like weeks, really, but that's not the point. It doesn't matter whoever she's screwing behind his back. I'm not talking about love here, just vengeance. You're having an affair with her husband, and now she knows it. She's not the forgiving kind, Lucy. And there's nothing I can do to protect you against her. She's much too close to Vulpe."

"Vlad will protect me."

"Like he protected you when Vaalt came to ask Vulpe for your head? Did he cover for you then? No! He didn't! Because he was afraid of his bitch of a wife, like you should be."

Lucy sighed heavily and sat back down on her bed, once again absorbed by her phone. "What's the plan now?" she asked without detaching her eyes from the screen.

"You should get some sleep, Michael," said Irini. "Until Olivia texts Sheila's number, there's nothing we can do."

She had a point. He hadn't gotten much sleep over the past couple days and he had the feeling he was going to need all his strength before this whole thing was over.

He nodded in agreement and took off his shoes before lying down on the bed, still dressed in the clothes he'd been wearing for two straight days. He would need to get new ones at some point soon or the enemy, praeternatural or not, would smell him coming from a mile away.

Irini announced she was going to shower before switching off the bedroom light so Michael could get some rest. He was the only one present who needed light in the first place, after all.

He lay there a few minutes, eyes shut, trying to will himself to sleep, but to no avail. He had far too many matters on his mind. Sheila was at the forefront of his concerns, but worrying about her wouldn't be a productive use of his time so he tried once more to focus on the case at hand.

Someone had impersonated Lucy to steal both Vulpe's and Lord

Vaalt's fragments of the Eye of the Phoenix. The chameleon Seemak was the logical culprit, of course, but he'd have been unable to penetrate Lord Vaalt's defenses since the chamber had been protected against his kind. That didn't mean he couldn't have impersonated Lucy to steal Vulpe's fragment, but it made it less likely. Even with Victor's help, how could Seemak have learned the safe's combination? Victor wasn't supposed to have access to Vulpe's apartment, Irini had already checked on this, and the consequences for him would have been dire if he'd been caught snooping around in there. Apparently Vulpe was very protective of his quarters, maybe because of the books he kept in his library—as Michael had expected, Irini's request to borrow one of the books for herself had been denied.

So who had stolen Vulpe's artifact? Odds were the same person had impersonated Lucy for both robberies, but in this case, it couldn't be a chameleon. What could impersonate someone well enough to fool a chameleon? Michael didn't have the answer to that question. According to Ez, as far as wizards were concerned, it would take someone from the Second Circle or above to perform such a trick, but Michael strongly doubted Tabitha or Methuselah were behind this, and there were no First Circle practitioners alive. Unless… could it be that Lucy herself had stolen Vaalt's artifact? Could she have been enthralled by Victor to do the job so he wouldn't get caught? She'd been with Vladislav during the first robbery, but Michael had carefully looked at Lucy's schedule on the day Lord Vaalt had been robbed and he had found a few holes in it. Holes that Lucy had been unable to fill. It was, of course, incredibly difficult to remember one's day minute by minute, but if she'd been enthralled that would explain a lot. The only problem was that a vampire couldn't be enthralled… Lucy was a hybrid, but he wasn't sure it made a difference in that matter. This was something he would need to look into. If Lucy had stolen the second fragment, it was possible Seemak had stolen the first, impersonating her in preparation for the second robbery? No, it didn't make sense. He wouldn't have framed her in this case. He would have needed her alive to commit the second robbery. And there was another element that didn't fit his theory. Victor couldn't have enthralled Lucy and sent her to steal Vaalt's artifact. He'd already been dead by then.

He heard Irini stepping out of the shower in the bathroom. He wasn't even slightly tired anymore.

Lucy's phone started vibrating a minute later. "It's Olivia calling back."

Michael was on his feet in an instant.

"Hey, sis. What's up?" said Lucy, trying to sound casual.

"You called me, remember? What do you need Sheila's number for?" Olivia could be heard saying on the other end of the line.

"A story she might be interested in reporting. I wanted to give her the heads up." Lucy sounded almost convincing.

"That's kind of you, especially given that you barely know the woman... What's the story about?"

Lucy gave Michael a pleading look and he gestured for her to come up with something: something he hoped would be remotely credible.

"Sex trafficking in Romania," offered Lucy.

"You usually lie better than this, Luce. Did Michael put you up to this?"

"What? No? What? ... I haven't seen him in six months!" Lucy sounded outraged.

"Oh really? So you happen to casually want to chat with his girlfriend? Your comment about him always playing fifty questions was a dead giveaway. I know your sense of humor, Luce. Is he sitting next to you?"

Lucy took a second too long to answer.

"Pass him the phone. I have something he'll want to hear."

Chapter 60

Sheila's plane had just landed at George Bush Intercontinental Airport in Houston and was taxiing towards Terminal E, the mandatory stop for international arrivals.

She'd spent a good part of the flight debating how to tackle the problem. Should she directly go to the US Interpol office nearest Houston and introduce herself as a journalist enquiring about the legitimacy of Michael's arrest? Should she try to talk to Jason Parrish to see what he had to say for himself? She knew better than to meet the man one on one, but there was little he could do to her over the phone, and she might be able to trick him into revealing something useful. It was of capital importance that she figured out where Michael was going to be detained awaiting his hearing.

Talking to her own boss would probably be a good starting point. He'd written several pieces on police brutality and abuse of power among government officials and could have some good advice to offer.

She switched her phone back on and soon the flow of data that had been interrupted during the nine-hour flight poured into her device. A dozen voicemails and text messages from friends, work and a couple unknown numbers flooded her inbox, and that was on top of the twenty plus emails she'd received during that time.

With the exception of a couple spam messages that had found their way through the Houston Post automated filters, they were all legitimate work emails, the majority of which consisted of automatic alerts sent by international news outlets.

One of the headlines immediately caught her eye: *Four Americans shot dead in Toulouse*. She clicked the link and started reading.

The French police responded to several gun shots being fired in a hotel in the suburbs of Toulouse, the country's fourth largest city. When the authorities arrived at the location, they found a scene of utter chaos. The hotel parking lot was jampacked with people, some trying to flee the danger zone, others waiting to see what excitement came next. After conducting a thorough search of the hotel, the police finally discovered the macabre scene in a room located on the third floor: the bodies of four men who had been shot dead.

At this point, the police haven't released the identities of the victims, but a source close to the case has confirmed that the four men were American officials. Our source also informed us that the police's current working hypothesis is that one of the men had shot the other three before turning his weapon on himself. The four victims hadn't been seen or heard arguing prior to the incident, and the motive of this apparent murder-suicide remains unclear at the moment.

The article mentioned no names, but Sheila couldn't help wondering whether this had anything to do with Michael. If he were being escorted back to the US to await trial, as the Interpol agents had stated, Toulouse was most likely where they would have been catching their flight first to Paris and from there to the US. The fact the victims were government officials was also rather suspicious. The murder-suicide story didn't sound like Michael, though; when her boyfriend killed someone, he didn't use a gun and didn't stage the crime scene. He either burnt the place down, called Ez to clean up, or simply left things the way they were.

The whole story sounded more like Irini. So much for her promise of *following Michael at a distance, just to keep an eye on him*. The vamp had most likely enthralled the men into killing each other. She wondered how Michael was going to take it.

On the plus side, it was probable Sheila no longer had to worry about freeing him. Her relief was short-lived, though. If Michael had escaped and was found responsible for the quadruple homicide, he would be a fugitive for the rest of his life. Having a werebear as a boyfriend already involved a lot of concessions, and Sheila didn't think their relationship would survive if Michael decided to add *fugitive from the law* to his already disturbing résumé.

The plane made it to the gate and Sheila retrieved her carry-on from the overhead compartment and followed her fellow passengers to the dreaded immigration lines.

The queues were far from being the worst she'd seen but she estimated it would still be a good twenty-five minutes before she was granted access to the *Land of the Free*.

Ignoring the multiple signs expressly forbidding the use of cellular phones in this part of the airport, she followed the example of her fellow travelers and took this opportunity to check her messages.

She was shocked to hear Michael's voice associated with a number she didn't recognize: Sheila, this is Michael. I lost my phone and I'm calling you from Lucy's. Where are you? Whatever you do, don't go back to Houston. We have reasons to believe it's not safe for you over there. If you're already on your way to the US, don't go to your house, no matter what. Don't even leave the airport. Get on another flight and come back here right away. We'll pick you up in Paris.

As usual, Michael's message was short and to the point. No explanations, no indication of where he might be or what had happened to the Interpol agents... typical! And why would she be in danger in Houston? She wanted to call him back, but it would have to wait a few minutes; the border patrol officer currently giving her the stink eye was a good deterrent. Calling her fugitive of a boyfriend while standing in the no-phone zone wasn't the best idea.

Sheila finally made it to the booth at the front of the line and handed her passport to a smiling agent who proceeded to swipe the document into his electronic reader.

"Were you travelling for business or pleasure?" he asked while Sheila's information loaded onto his monitor.

"Pleasure."

"One of these days, I'll go to France. My wife always says—"

The agent stopped in mid-sentence and Sheila immediately noticed a change in his attitude. The relaxed, pleasant man had disappeared. The twin who'd replaced him looked solemn and business-like. He typed a few things on his keyboard, but Sheila had the distinct feeling he was avoiding making eye contact.

"Is there a problem, officer?" she asked finally.

Busy typing apparently endless queries on his keyboard, he ignored her for about thirty seconds. By the time he finally returned his attention to her, Sheila was sandwiched between two other officers who'd approached her from opposite directions.

"Ma'am, there is an alert from the Department of Homeland Security attached to your passport. I must ask you to follow these two gentlemen."

Sheila barely heard the end of the man's sentence. Her mind was reeling, Michael's warning replaying in her head. But he'd been wrong about one thing... even the airport hadn't been safe.

Chapter 61

Sheila had never been in an interrogation room and had no reference, but the place looked nothing like those she'd seen on television. On the other hand, she wasn't in a police station, either. At least she didn't think so. In truth, she had no idea where she was at the moment.

The two border patrol agents had escorted her from the control booth to the office area of the terminal and delivered her to two Homeland Security personnel who'd apparently been waiting for her. They'd worn no uniforms but there had been something about the way they held themselves that had betrayed their military affiliation. Whether that affiliation was past or present, Sheila wasn't sure. All she knew was that these two were as likely to work for Homeland Security as the jackasses in France were to belong to Interpol.

Ignoring her questions and her outrage with equal dexterity, the two had pushed her into a van where she'd been handcuffed to a rail. The drive had been short, however. A moment later she'd been thrown into a private jet.

Three hours later, they'd landed on an airstrip in the middle of the desert. There were many deserts three hours away from Houston and Sheila wasn't enough of an expert on the subject to recognize that particular one. The only certainty was that they'd been flying west. Which meant she could be in Arizona, Nevada, California, Utah, or even Mexico…

The airstrip was in the middle of nowhere and, for a second, she worried they'd brought her here to bury her body. They didn't need to put her on a plane for that, though; they could have thrown her into the bayou in Houston and called it a day. Still, she'd been relieved when she'd seen a metallic door at the base of a cliff wall. The door had opened onto an elevator and, after a long descent, here she was.

The door of the interrogation room swung open, and two men walked in. One of them had the same military stiffness as the two who'd brought her in, but the other walked with animal grace. His mane of hair fell nearly over his eyes and was in stark contrast with his companion's crew cut.

"Who are you and what am I doing here?" This was at least the twelfth time she'd asked the question and she no longer expected any answer, but the military-type surprised her.

"You can call me Captain Brown, and you're here because of your relationship with Michael Biörn," he said, sitting down opposite her at the concrete table in the middle of the room. His companion remained standing by the door.

"You're telling me I was arrested and brought here simply because of who I'm dating?" She hoped her voice conveyed all the outrage and none of the fear she currently felt.

Brown ignored the question. "We need to get in touch with Michael Biörn, but he doesn't currently have his phone with him. Do you know how to reach him?"

This time it was Sheila's turn to ignore the question. She was sitting very straight in the uncomfortable metal chair, staring at the man, arms crossed over her chest.

"I'm going to need you to unlock your phone, Ma'am," said the man, sliding her phone across the table.

She looked at the device but made no move towards it.

Brown nodded slightly and the move caught Sheila off guard. What was he nodding about? He turned his head towards his silent partner and that's when Sheila noticed the earpiece Brown was wearing. He was receiving information from someone outside the room.

"Miss Wang, we need you to unlock this phone and it would be better for everyone involved if you did it willingly." There was almost a plea in his voice.

Still Sheila didn't move, and after a half minute Brown turned to his companion and the latter left the wall and walked straight to Sheila. He wrapped his hand around her neck and lifted her in the air, her feet dangling while her hands clawed at her aggressor's hand. Her neck was bearing the weight of her own body and she was worried it might snap, but she was even more concerned about the lack of oxygen she was experiencing. Soon she stopped fighting, she had no air left in her longs, no oxygen to power her muscles. She was about to pass out when the man released her throat and she collapsed to the ground.

She lay there an instant, gasping for breath, before Brown asked again. "Please unlock your phone, Miss Wang. We have no beef with you, but your boyfriend is a dangerous individual and there is nothing we won't do to get to him."

Sheila remained motionless, wishing Michael were here right now. Just to show them how truly dangerous he was.

When after a minute she still hadn't moved, the silent man bent down to grab her by the hair and pull her back on her feet. That's when she noticed the weird diadem around the man's neck. His hair had hidden it up to now, but it was definitely there, pressing against the base of his cranium. On second thought, the man's eyes were strange as well, unfocused, as if he were on drugs. Before she could wonder why, the man started morphing into a mountain lion under her very eyes.

Sheila had witnessed more than her fair share of werebeings' transformations, but that didn't make this one any less terrifying. She grabbed her phone as the beast completed his morphing and unlocked it.

Brown spent the next ten minutes snooping through her contacts and messages while she sat on her chair under the watchful eyes of the lion that stood three feet away. She couldn't believe that praeternaturals were involved in this. That they would collaborate with these men, whoever they might be, to betray other praeternaturals.

Finally Brown found the message Michael had sent her from Lucy's phone and carefully listened to it. "Who's Lucy?" he asked.

Sheila didn't answer and he didn't push the issue. "You're going to call her phone and ask to talk to Biörn."

Sheila shook her head vehemently, but she already knew she would obey.

"Please, Ma'am, don't make me do this. I don't enjoy hurting you." He actually sounded sincere.

Sheila briefly considered her options and dialed Lucy's number.

It was Michael who answered on the second ring. "Sheila! You got my message? Did you book a flight to come back?"

"No, Michael, they were waiting for me at the airport. I'm in an underground desert facil—"

Brown ripped the phone out of her hand before she could finish but Sheila wasn't deterred and she simply screamed the end of her message, "underground desert facility. They have werecougars working for them."

The mountain lion had regained his human form and wrapped his hand tightly around her mouth to silence her.

"Mr Biörn. You will have heard that your friend is healthy for now. Whether she remains that way is up to you."

Sheila couldn't hear Michael's reply but Brown looked puzzled. "Did you hear me, Biörn?"

She hadn't heard Michael's reply because he hadn't said anything.

"Miss Wang will be freed in exchange for your full cooperation. I'm sending you GPS coordinates. Meet me there at precisely 11 PM two days from now. We've already reserved you a seat on a flight leaving from Paris tomorrow. Do we have an understanding?"

Sheila heard nothing but crickets coming from Michael's side of the conversation.

"You have two days to get here, Biörn. If you don't show up, she dies. Understood?"

"I'll be there. But if you don't bring her to the rendezvous, I'll know, and I'll walk. You can't fool me," she finally heard Michael replying. "In the meantime, I suggest you go buy yourself a casket. You'll need it soon."

Chapter 62

Michael and Lucy had been watching the morning news in their hotel room when Sheila's number had appeared on the vampire's cell phone. The news report had confirmed Michael's suspicions about the legality of the Interpol operation that had placed him into custody. The story was still developing, but the US Interpol office was denying having sent any agents by those four names to France and called their credentials fabricated.

To make matters more interesting, a cursory examination of the bodies by a forensic team had revealed matching implants in the men's mouths. Further examinations were on the way, but a source close to the case had revealed to a television reporter that the implants resembled those used by some spies. The news hadn't surprised Michael. One of the two assholes he'd caught rummaging his cabin had committed suicide under his very eyes by biting on such an implant.

"What are you going to do?" asked Lucy, as Irini entered the room carrying breakfast for everybody.

Lucy briefly informed her mentor of the phone call they'd received, and the two vampires turned their attention to Michael.

"So?" asked Irini.

"I'm going to go, of course. It's not like I have a choice," replied Michael, his anger threatening to explode at the faces of the two women who'd done nothing to deserve his wrath.

"You *can't* go," said Irini. "Those coordinates are located fifty miles south of Las Vegas... They've set the meeting in the middle of the desert for a reason. It's an ambush. They'll have an army waiting for you there. And possibly an army of praeternaturals if Sheila's right about the cougars."

"It changes noth—"

Lucy's phone interrupted him mid-sentence but this time Ezekiel's name appeared on the screen. She showed it to Michael, baffled. "I don't understand. I don't have Ezekiel's number in my phone."

The detail appeared irrelevant to Michael. If Ez wanted to let you know the call was from him, whether he was in your contacts or not made no difference.

"Hello?" answered Lucy tentatively as she turned on the device's speaker.

"Hello, Lucy. Could you please hand the phone to Michael?" It was definitely Ez's voice.

The wizard didn't bother explaining how he knew Lucy and Michael were together, and Michael didn't bother asking. He wasn't in the mood for Ez's sense of humor. "This is Michael. You're on speaker, Ez."

"Good! I need you to meet me in front of Vulpe's compound as soon as possible."

"I can't." Michael proceeded to update the wizard on Sheila's situation.

"It's very unfortunate for Sheila. I love the kid and I would hate to see anything bad happening to her, but I need you here with me right away, Michael." The wizard sounded deadly serious.

"I can't! Do you hear me? They'll kill her if I don't go!"

"And if you don't come and help me, there is no telling how many innocents will die. If the *entity* takes possession of the Eye of the Phoenix, countless lives will be forfeited."

"Why now? What makes you think it's going after the Eye of the Phoenix now?"

"I've been camping around the compound for two straight days now. And two warlocks keep popping in and out with increasing frequency. They're scouting the perimeter but disappear as soon as I get close to them. They will make a move soon, I know it."

"And what can I do against warlocks, Ez? Ask Tabitha to help you."

"Tabitha is in Australia searching for Methuselah at the moment. We lost contact with him twelve hours ago. This has never happened before, Michael. I wouldn't ask you if it weren't important. We need to get into Vulpe's castle and find out where the fragments are hidden before the warlocks take the offensive."

"What about the faes? Can't they assist? Vaalt should have a vested interest in stopping those warlocks."

There was a sigh on the other end of the line. "I've already requested Lord Vaalt's assistance."

"And?"

"And he laughed and hung up the phone!"

"I assume that means he won't help… And how do you propose I get into the castle? Unlike you I can't walk through walls, and I didn't exactly leave on friendly terms the last time I visited the vamps…"

"I was thinking Irini could intercede in your favor." The wizard sounded uneasy.

Michael was torn. For Ez to admit he required Irini's help, the situation had to be dire indeed, but he simply couldn't abandon Sheila to the savages who'd fed Bob to a mountain lion.

"I know you'll make the right choice, Michael," said Ez before ending the call.

Michael let out a loud roar into which he put all his anger and frustration. The ruckus was clearly going to piss off the neighbors this early in the morning, but the two vampires were smart enough not to mention it to him.

"Lucy and I will go rescue Sheila while you go help Ezekiel," said Irini.

"Sheila needs me."

"It sounds like the world needs you more. We can take care of a few humans. They'll never see us coming," she said, winking at him.

"These aren't your average humans. They have praeternaturals at their side and your mind tricks won't work on werecougars or whatever else they may have on payroll. The two of you will be significantly outgunned."

They argued back and forth for another ten minutes before being interrupted by Lucy entering the room holding her phone. Michael hadn't even noticed that the young woman had left in the first place.

"I have a solution," she announced.

"A solution to what?" Irini looked perplexed.

"A solution to everything. I just called Vladislav and explained the situation."

"You what?" interjected Michael.

"Vlad will talk to Vulpe and make sure you and Ez are granted safe-passage inside the castle. He will also let us borrow the Covenant's private jet and a few men to go rescue Lucy. I suspect a dozen trained and armed vampires will be more than a match for Sheila's kidnappers."

Michael considered his options a moment. Neither one was good, but it didn't matter. He was out of time.

Chapter 63

Michael and Ezekiel stood together a quarter mile outside the Eastern Covenant compound, waiting for Michael's phone to ring. He'd stopped to purchase a disposable phone on his way to the rendezvous point. Since the two vampires had gone straight to a small airport to board the Covenant's private jet and go rescue Sheila, Michael had been forced to rent a car under an assumed identity provided by Irini.

It had been the most difficult decision of his life—or at least of the past couple hundred years—but in the end he'd decided to entrust Sheila's fate to the vamps while he'd accompany Ezekiel in what the wizard had warned him could very well be the fight of his life.

The *entity* hadn't shown itself yet, but he'd sent his two warlocks on numerous recon missions around the castle, and Ez was afraid these flash visits had the sole purpose of preparing the terrain for the arrival of their master.

"So you think the master of those two is the *entity* responsible for the magical field distortions you've been sensing?"

"I do."

"How did you even learn about his existence?"

"That's the one thing Lord Vaalt told me after laughing his ass off and before hanging up."

"How does he know?"

"Apparently Seemak admitted to it under torture, but Vaalt decided to sit on the information until now. It's the master who sent Seemak to steal the fragments in the first place."

"And knowing all this, Vaalt still won't help you fight him? I'm starting to think he's afraid of that master and would rather see you take care of the problem for him."

"It's very possible, but one thing is certain: if the master shows up with the two warlocks, I'll never be able to defeat them on my own." Ezekiel looked uncharacteristically glum. "We must act now and locate the three fragments before their arrival. If I have the Eye of the Phoenix in my possession, maybe we stand a chance. I count on you to figure out where they are, my friend. If anyone can break this riddle, it's you."

Michael wasn't sharing the wizard's confidence, however. He still had no idea who had framed Lucy and therefore who was in possession of the fragments. Or whether the fragments were even in the castle for that matter... although Ez appeared pretty convinced that's what the warlocks were after. Michael felt like the answer to the puzzle was on the tip of his tongue, but some of the pieces simply didn't fit.

"Who do you have your money on, Michael? Who killed Seemak? Who has the fragments in their possession?"

Michael shrugged. "I'm not sure, Ez. Given where we are and the fact that only vampires were in the room when you sensed the presence of one of the fragments the last time we were here, it's fair to assume we're looking for a vamp. But which one?"

He had barely finished his sentence before he thought about Seemak. What if a chameleon had been hiding in the lot that day, masquerading as a vampire?

His phone vibrated in his pocket at the same instant and he answered. The discussion was brief and to the point.

"It was Vladislav. He talked to Vulpe. We are expected."

They were met at the door by a vampire and the same four werewolves Michael had molested on his previous visit to the castle. The wolves were staring threateningly, but none of them made a move towards him. The enthralled creatures weren't able to defy orders.

The vampire confirmed their identities and escorted them inside the castle. The sun was still high in the sky and the vamp looked like a ninja in his black daysuit designed to protect him from harmful UV radiation.

They were once again shown to the castle's reception hall where two dozen elders were waiting for them. This was unexpected. At this time of day the majority of vampires should still be sleeping. The fact they weren't suggested they'd been woken up for the occasion. The question was why. Was this an ambush to catch Michael Biörn, Dragos' slayer, or were they preparing for a potential attack from the warlocks?

All eyes were on Michael and Ez as they walked the fifty feet from the door to the center of the room where Vulpe sat in the company of his wife and brother. Anastasia stood between Vladislav and Vulpe's chairs, halfway between her husband and her lover—assuming that the rumors were correct, and she was indeed Vulpe's mistress.

"The three fragments are here, Michael. In this room. I can feel their combined power. But I don't know where. The waves are so strong that they flood the entire room. Be on your guard. We have no friends here and some of the best inducers and enthrallers in the world are among the crowd. Some of them good enough to convince you to drop your pants if they so wished." The voice had come from inside Michael's head and he knew who it belonged to. It wasn't the first time the wizard had communicated with him through telepathy, but Michael was unable to reciprocate.

"We've never met, but I know your name, Ezekiel of the Second Circle. So, when Vladislav told me you wanted to warn me of our impending doom, my interest was piqued. I understand your presence here relates to the Eye of the Phoenix?"

"That is correct, Vulpe. The artifact has already been stolen from you once, and I have reason to believe that powerful warlocks intend to steal it again in the coming hours."

"Powerful warlocks? And how would they know it's here in my possession?" The vampire was staring at Michael, the unspoken accusation hanging in the air.

"You know as well as I do that Lord Vaalt's artifact was also stolen," replied Ez. "And whether a fae enrolled a vampire to help him steal the artifacts or vice versa is completely irrelevant. The only thing that matters is the fact that the warlocks were pulling the strings in the background. They were the ones after the artifacts from the beginning."

Michael saw the slightest hint of a smile appear on Anastasia's lips. The world's best inducer seemed pleased with what she was hearing. The world's best inducer... Ezekiel's statement came back to his mind: *Good enough to convince you to drop your pants...* At this instant, the pieces of the puzzle finally clicked in place. He knew who had impersonated Lucy. He knew who'd stolen the artifacts. He wasn't certain why, but he could guess. The oldest motive in the book: power. Power, and jealousy.

"What you don't know, Vulpe," he heard Ezekiel say, "is that the pendant hanging from your neck is actually a fake. The real fragment is present in this room, however. Along with the other two. This is why you are in danger. Because you've been deceived, and the warlocks will stop at nothing to put their hands on the complete artifact."

Vulpe gave the wizard a skeptical look. "And why would someone go to the trouble of hiding a fake fragment in Lucy's belongings?"

"For the same reason someone would make sure Lucy was seen in your room that night," intervened Michael. "To frame her, and to make you believe the real artifact had been recovered. This guaranteed that you would stop looking for it. This is just my guess, mind you. If you want the real reason, you should ask the person who stole the artifact in the first place. He's sitting right next to you. Vladislav! Did I capture your line of thought correctly?"

All eyes went to Vladislav who looked amused. "This is how you thank me for loaning you a plane and granting you access to the castle? You accuse me of stealing from my brother, bear?"

"I'm not accusing anyone of anything. Just stating a fact. Of course, you didn't do it alone. Your wife helped you quite a bit, didn't she? I assume this is another one of the fragments." Michael pointed at the ruby-colored piece of jewelry resting on Anastasia's chest. "Where is yours, Vladislav? Don't you also usually wear a pendant for social occasions such as these? A pyramidal emerald, if I recall properly."

Vladislav was still smiling, but Anastasia's smirk had been wiped clean off her face by Michael's accusatory words.

"Where is your pyramid, brother?" Vulpe's tone was cold as ice.

Still smiling, Vladislav reached inside his shirt collar but the pendant he retrieved wasn't a pyramidal emerald. The jewel had the color of citrine and a hollow center encircled by two half moons.

"That looks familiar," said Ezekiel. "I'm afraid I'm going to need that, Vladislav."

But before Ez could reach for the pendant, Cristos stormed into the room. "We're under attack, my liege. Sorcerers have breached the perimeter and are converging on the drawbridge."

Chapter 64

"Send all men and wolves to defend the perimeter," ordered Vulpe. "You stay here, wizard, in case they get through."

But Ezekiel was paying no attention to the leader. His eyes were riveted on the red, translucent oval shape flying towards Vladislav: Anastasia's jewel. Ez cast a spell but missed his target by a hair and the oval landed on Vladislav's chest where it immediately took its place at the hollow center of the citrine ellipse.

"Too late," muttered the wizard, aiming his staff towards the vampire whose appearance had changed in a fraction of a second. Vladislav was now as big as a troll but retained a human appearance, albeit grossly deformed.

Michael immediately realized what was happening; the reunified Eye of the Phoenix conferred the powers of the faes upon the vampire. Vladislav remained a bloodsucker, but he could tap into the faculties of any fae that came to his mind. Currently he was as big and strong as a troll, but a troll with magical powers equivalent to those of Lord Vaalt himself.

Before Ez could cast his first attack, a loud commotion came from the back of the room and Michael turned just in time to see a woman wave a wand towards Ezekiel. Reacting on instinct, Michael dove towards his friend and the two of them crashed to the ground as the spell flew above their heads, nipping Vladislav's troll in his fleshy love handle.

The troll didn't even appear to notice he'd been hit. He waved a hand towards the warlock, and a shard of ice shaped like a lightning bolt and as long as a car flew out of it and headed straight for the wand lady. She side-stepped the incoming object easily, however, and it impaled two vampires standing behind her.

"I think your warlock friends have joined the party," said Michael, frantically searching the room for the other warlock and their master.

The scene was pure chaos. The initial shock having passed, everyone was now fighting on one side or another. What should have been a simple fight between Ezekiel and an outclassed vampire elder had turned into a three-way battle with warlocks on one side, Michael, Ez and the majority of the Eastern Covenant on the second, and rogue vampires on the third—because it was becoming increasingly clear that Anastasia and Vladislav hadn't been conspiring alone. Nearly half of the vamps in the room were fighting on their side. What the couple had been preparing for was quite simply a coup to dethrone Vulpe, and they'd already converted a number of the elders to their cause.

As he morphed into his bear, Michael saw a green beam of light fly out of Ezekiel's staff and rush to the center of the room where it was met with an equally bright beam of yellow light. The two attacks canceled each other out, but Michael had now identified the target of Ezekiel's wrath: a man dressed in a black robe and waving a wand as long as Michael's forearm.

The battle was still raging between Vladislav and the female warlock, and since Ez was busying himself with the male, Michael decided to help hunt the rogues.

A number of vampires already lay slain on the ground, their heads detached from their bodies, but the battle was nowhere close to over. From the corner of his eye the bear saw Vulpe and his wife Milena battling a group of five rogues, but Anastasia wasn't among them. Where had the queen bitch gone?

His nose gave him the answer a second later. The vampire stench was overwhelming in the reception hall, but Anastasia's distinctive odor had suddenly overpowered the others. Michael's bear did a one-eighty faster than any eight-hundred-pound creature should be able to move and slashed at Anastasia who'd been ready to pounce on his back. The razor-sharp claws caught the vampire across the chest, tearing the expensive fabric of her evening dress and ripping off the pendant that had borne a third of the Eye of the Phoenix a moment earlier. The bloodsucker hissed in anger as much as in pain.

Anastasia was quite possibly the oldest vampire Michael had ever faced, older than Dragos, even. Underestimating her would be a fatal mistake.

The woman flashed a set of canines that would have made a werewolf proud before jumping over him to once again try and attack him from behind. Using his powerful back legs as springs, Michael uncoiled into the air, his front paws reaching for the sky in the hope of intercepting the flying vamp. But bears weren't jumpers and despite his effort Anastasia easily cleared the obstacle and landed behind him.

He spun around just in time to receive her foot on the side of the head. The powerful kick would have broken the neck of any mortal creature, but fortunately Michael didn't qualify. He reciprocated with a swift strike of his front paw but missed the mark entirely. She was simply too fast; he would need to be smarter than that to catch her off guard.

The battle was still raging both inside the reception hall and outside the castle walls where the staccato of automatic weapons could be heard every few seconds. The sorcerers had no doubt attacked the outside perimeter to create a diversion—but a diversion that kept Cristos' men plenty busy.

Michael lost sight of Anastasia for an instant, but the searing pain he felt as her claws sliced through the flesh of his neck told her she was on his right. Before he could even react, he felt the same searing pain on the left side of his neck and then on his back, his face, and his back again. The vamp was like a tornado, incredibly fast and unstoppable.

Against enemies such as Anastasia, skinwalkers typically tag-teamed their preys, but Michael had nobody to do the tag-teaming with, so he tried something else. Ignoring the jabs of the woman, he went for another target. Two vampires were fighting beside him and, pouncing on the one he hoped was on Vladislav's side, he sank his fangs deep into the bloodsucker's neck and shook vigorously. As the man's head rolled to the ground, Anastasia jumped onto Michael's back, and he felt her arms wrap into a choke-hold around his massive neck.

She'd taken the bait, but now he needed to do something about it, and quick. He'd hoped to receive some assistance from the opponent of the vamp he'd decapitated, but he received none. Instead, the ungrateful bloodsucker chose to attack the female warlock instead and soon met his end.

The bear's paws couldn't reach Anastasia who kept dodging them while squeezing tighter and tighter. Oxygen was getting scarce and Michael was desperately scanning the room in search of an ally. He found Ezekiel, but the wizard was still too busy battling the male warlock to notice his predicament. If Michael's bear didn't get rid of the pesky vamp now, he'd pass out and then die of asphyxiation. That would be a first for him and not a particularly worrisome way to die under other circumstances, but he had no doubt Anastasia would take advantage of this opportunity to separate his head from the rest of his body and make his passing more… permanent. He'd just ruined her little coup, and she struck him as vindictive.

His muscles, starving for oxygen, were starting to weaken. Time was running out… That's when an idea came to him. A long shot, but worth a try. Using the claws of his right paw, he skewered the woman's arm at the level of her elbow but didn't obtain the result he was hoping for. His second attempt succeeded, however; the claws sliced through the articulation's tendons, separating arm and forearm and releasing the chokehold at the same instant. Anastasia's shriek of hatred and rage was deafening, but Michael didn't lose focus. Before the severed forearm even hit the ground, he used his claws to skewer the part still attached to her elbow through the biceps and gave a powerful tug in the direction of the floor, bringing the woman's neck within reach of his lethal jaws. Her screams quickly died in her torn throat as her head joined her forearm at the bear's feet. He then took a moment to dig her heart out of her chest and pulverize it under the weight of his back paw before returning to the fray.

With few of Vladislav's wannabe conspirators still standing, the battlefield was getting quieter. Vulpe had turned his destructive power against his brother, who was still battling the female warlock, so Michael opted to assist Ez. He easily located the wizard, but the latter needed no help. Ezekiel was finishing off the male warlock using a fire spell Michael had never seen before. The human-shaped pyre blinked in and out of the room a few times, appearing more consumed by the magical fire with each reappearance. Eventually the warlock collapsed to the ground and finished burning, as the smell of charring flesh invaded the bear's nostrils. Apparently, roasted warlocks smelled like chicken.

Michael was on the other side of the room when he saw Vladislav casting a spell that sent Vulpe crashing against a wall. But the Covenant leader had distracted his brother just long enough for the surviving warlock to take advantage of the situation and cast a spell that Vladislav failed to counter. As the wave of energy hit him square in the chest, his trollish body deformed under the impact before collapsing.

The traitor had barely hit the ground when the warlock vanished, only to reappear a split second later at his side. She reached for the vampire's pendant and ripped it off his neck just as Ezekiel's spell was rushing towards her. She vanished a moment later but not before the wizard's attack reached the pendant.

Michael saw a flash of citrine spinning high into the air. By the time the fragment was on its way down, Ez was underneath it and snatched it before it hit the ground.

Chapter 65

Ezekiel's hand was clenched around the half-moon jewel, while Michael's bear stood by his side. Michael had retained his animal form in case any of Vulpe's men decided to settle old counts with him now that the main threat had been, at least temporarily, dispatched.

"It belongs to me, wizard. I suggest you hand it over now, and you and your friend be on your way."

"I'm afraid I can't do that, Vulpe. It wouldn't be safe here. The warlocks would be back sooner or later and we can't afford for them to have the missing piece," said Ez, before adding in a more reproachful tone, "They already hold two of the three fragments, thanks to you and your brother."

"I believe my traitor of a brother bears the sole responsibility of this debacle, and he will answer for his crime and those of his wife since she's no longer able to amend for her faults," said Vulpe, staring his brother down. Vladislav had already largely recovered from the warlock's attack but was ignoring his brother's comment. Tightly surrounded by four of Cristos' men, the traitor was sending daggers at Michael, his wife's killer. The bear wasn't worried, however. Vladislav was just one more name to an already exceedingly long list of *immortal* enemies.

"If you hadn't attacked your brother while he was battling the warlock, I could have neutralized her before she had a chance to defeat him and take off with her loot." Ezekiel's patience was clearly running thin with this lot. It was time to take their leave.

Cristos arrived at this instant to give his report: a welcome intermission that would hopefully relieve some of the tension in the room.

According to Cristos, the battle outside the castle's wall had been as fierce as the one waged inside. The vampire had lost no less than eleven wolves and five of his bloodsucking brothers in the onslaught. The sorcerers' diversion had proven both efficient and deadly. With the nine that had fallen fighting in the reception hall, it made a total of fourteen dead vamps: a substantial loss to the Covenant, given the number of powerful elders among the casualties.

Michael shed no tears, though. As far as he was concerned, it was good riddance.

"You see what you've done, brother? Why all this waste?" Vulpe sounded disgusted.

"If you need to ask, you're even dumber than you look, *brother*. I did it because I was tired of living in your shadow, of course. I've been a vampire just as long as you have and I've always been the second, simply because I was born two years after you."

"And how did you convince the other traitors to follow you? How did you convince Anastasia?"

Vladislav flashed a humorless smile. "Convince Anastasia? It was her idea in the first place, *brother*. You truly believe you could have bedded my wife if there hadn't been something in it for me?"

Vulpe looked confused, but Michael knew exactly what his brother meant by that.

"You think you're so smart, but this whole time she's been wearing her own fragment of the artifact right under your nose and you never even noticed. We've known about yours for years, but stealing it wouldn't have done us much good without the third piece, so we left it alone, biding our time in your shadow. But then Victor came to me a few weeks ago with the most exciting news. Some fae had contacted him to enroll his help in stealing both your artifact and the one held by Lord Vaalt. You can imagine my delight… I convinced him to learn more about it before going to you with the information, and that's exactly what he did."

"But you killed him before he had a chance to tell me anything," said Vulpe.

"Yes, I did. Victor was a loyal servant, but he couldn't be trusted with a coup, so I did what needed to be done."

Vulpe gestured towards his brother, but he was addressing the guards. "Take him away."

"We'll be leaving too. My friend has a flight to catch," said Ezekiel, patting Michael's bear on the shoulder.

Michael expected more protests or some threat from Vulpe, but then the vamps' leader surprised him. "I've heard of your troubles, and since you did me a service in revealing Vladislav as a traitor, I'd like to offer you our private jet to make the trip under the radar. The pilot knows the way. I believe he dropped off Irini and Lucy at the same place no later than yesterday."

Chapter 66

Michael was getting close to the rendez-vous point now. As he surveyed the desert stretching out around him, he wondered where the hell the enemy was going to come from.

Vulpe's plane had dropped him off on a private airstrip three hundred miles away around noon and, after jumping into the jeep that had been arranged for him, Michael had driven straight to Vegas. He'd reached Sin City in under five hours and, after a copious dinner, he'd wasted a couple more hours hiding in a casino.

With its crowd and constant noise, Las Vegas was just about his least favorite city on the planet, but it was a good place to hide, and Michael didn't want his enemies to know where he was before the time came to meet with them. It was clear by now that they had the US government's sizable resources at their disposal and weren't shy about using all the leverage they could get. And for Sheila's sake, he couldn't afford being captured before the arranged meeting.

He was far from certain the jackasses would actually bring Sheila to the rendezvous, but he was convinced that it would be disastrous for the journalist if they were to catch him before he got there.

He was about thirty minutes from the indicated coordinates and driving through the desert, miles from anything resembling a road, when he stopped the jeep and got out. He'd chosen to approach the target location from this specific direction for two reasons. First, his enemies would be expecting him to drive on the road, and he wanted to keep them on their toes. Second, he needed to travel in a direction downwind of where he was heading: a precaution designed to mask his approach in case other praeternaturals were part of the reception committee.

He took a few steps straight towards him to get away from the odors of warm plastic and rubber associated with the car, before smelling the air. He immediately picked up the scent he was looking for... Sheila's. They had brought her to the rendezvous, and they were already there, waiting for him.

He got back in his jeep and headed straight to the meeting. He didn't want to be late.

Michael was about three hundred yards from the indicated coordinates when he went over a hill and finally saw a van and two large SUVs parked on the sand in the distance. He rolled to a stop a hundred and fifty yards from the vehicles and cautiously got out of the jeep, scanning his surroundings for the ambush he fully expected. He saw nothing unusual, which wasn't surprising coming from professionals, and detected no human odors other than Sheila's. This was more surprising. Jason Parrish's friends were using damn good scent concealers. Much better than the stuff worn by hunters.

In the distance, he heard the van's door sliding open and two men came out, holding assault rifles. Then came Sheila, her hands handcuffed in front of her. What came out of the van next wasn't much of a surprise to Michael, who'd smelled the mountain lion upon his first stop thirty minutes earlier. There had been a remote chance the scent had belonged to some wild cat roaming the area, but now the more likely explanation had been confirmed. They'd brought a werecougar with them. Was that supposed to impress him?

A half dozen other men wearing full body armor and armed to the teeth came out of the two SUVs and took up defensive positions. Their weapons were trained towards the ground in a non-threatening fashion, but it didn't matter. Michael knew full well that the danger didn't come from the men he could see.

He was about to get back into the jeep to close the distance when the first round hit him square in the jaw, shattering his teeth to smithereens. He received three more bullets in the chest before the fifth round finally went through his brain and he collapsed to the ground.

Only a minute or so had passed when he finally came back to life and noticed he'd been shot at least twice more through the heart—probably to buy his murderers the time necessary to secure the familiar collar he felt around his neck.

Lying on the ground, eyes trained towards the starry sky, he counted no less than six rifles trained towards him as one of the men re-explained to him the nature of the remote-controlled piece of jewelry he'd been fitted with.

Michael rolled onto his side and spat out a mouthful of shattered teeth. This brought laughter from a couple of the guys, but they quickly stopped when he flashed them a smile with his brand-new set.

"You have me. Now you can let the girl go."

"If it were up to me, I would. I swear it's true. But it's not up to me, and the girl has to come with us," said the man holding the remote.

Michael recognized the voice immediately. He was the one who'd called him on the phone with the ultimatum.

"Wrong answer," said Michael. "By the way, did you pick your casket yet?"

The man gave him a sad smile, and then the remote was ripped out of his hand by Irini's invisible hand. Invisible to the human's eye, at least, because Michael had seen her standing among them all along.

Before the human even registered the loss of his toy, all his men were disarmed in a flash, and soon he was the only one without a vampire sucking on his neck.

The sight of the bloodsuckers draining the life out of the mercenaries didn't bother Michael nearly as much as it should have. These guys had it coming.

The leader started running towards the van, screaming "Shoot them!" to the darkness. But the darkness did not reply. All his snipers had already been dispatched by the vamps.

"I told you what was coming to you, asshole. You should have listened." Michael was quietly walking towards the running man.

"My cougar will kill her if you get any closer, Biörn."

Now *that* was a real threat and it gave Michael pause, but not for long. A split second later, Lucy was swooping Sheila off her feet and carrying her towards Michael at a pace even the mountain lion was having a hard time matching. He would have caught up with her eventually... had Michael not been in the way.

Unfortunately for the lion, Michael had fully recovered and changed into his bear by the time the two praeternaturals met in an avalanche of fangs and claws.

The fight was short-lived, however, and not even the mercenary leader looked surprised when the bear beheaded the cat.

Michael was staring at the carcass of the defeated cat when he noticed the weird diadem-looking device around the cat's neck. What in heaven was that thing supposed to be? He morphed back into his human form and, not giving a damn about his total absence of clothes, walked straight to the mercenary leader to obtain some long overdue answers.

The man didn't even try to run. He just stared straight in front of him. Michael was only ten feet away when the man collapsed to the ground. The bitter almond scent that reached Michael's nostrils told him everything he needed to know about his enemy's cause of death.

Epilogue

Michael's jaw just about dropped when he and Sheila entered the house, and if the expression on his girlfriend's face were any indication, she was as impressed as he was with the sight. Olivia was visibly amused by their reaction. Having arrived a few hours earlier, the young woman had already had some time to recover from the initial shock everyone no doubt felt when stepping into a place like this.

From inside, the house looked like it had been carved out of a tree and furnished with whatever material the builder had found in the immediate vicinity. Which was, of course, close to the truth, except that the elves had assembled the local rocks, wood essences and other vegetal materials into something absolutely breathtaking. With its stream running through the living room, and colorful flowers and plants growing on the walls, the house literally looked alive.

Given the resources of the people after them, Michael, Sheila, Olivia, and Daka had decided to lay low for a while. And since an elvish city was a good place to hide from an organization that had eyes everywhere, Ez had interceded to High King Dariel in their favor, and the elf had granted the group asylum.

I-Naur-Tal, the fiery city, was located in Montana, a mere two hours north of Yellowstone, but it was protected by powerful elvish magic and was therefore absolutely undetectable by humans. Even Michael, who'd known the area well, had been unaware of its existence until a couple years earlier when Ez had introduced him to Dariel.

Michael had been back to the city a few times since but had never spent significant amounts of time within its walls. Until now…

Still gawking at his surroundings, he walked to a chair resembling a mushroom and settled down in it just as Ezekiel was making his entry.

"Good afternoon, my friends," said the wizard in a booming theatrical voice. Defeating one of the warlocks and preventing the enemy from acquiring the Eye of the Phoenix had apparently improved his mood.

Greetings and pleasantries were exchanged but soon it was time to get back to serious matters.

"I'm glad to see you back in one piece, Sheila. I'm telling you, hanging around this individual isn't as safe as one would think," said Ez, gesturing towards Michael.

"Any news on that front, Ez? Do we know who these people are?" asked Michael.

The wizard shook his head. "Not yet. It's becoming pretty clear that they're part of the US government, but we have no indication which branch they belong to. Most likely a top-secret agency unknown by most of the bickering paper-pushers sitting in Washington."

"Whatever the agency may be, these men's willingness to commit suicide rather than being taken is very concerning. It's one thing to have a cyanide implant in your mouth and another to actually use it. And now I've seen two of these men choosing suicide over answering my questions."

"Do you blame them? These men know what you are, Michael. For a human, I'm sure the perspective of being questioned by a werebear is a powerful motivation to take one's own life," replied the wizard.

Michael wasn't convinced but dropped the issue. "What about the warlocks? Any news on that front?"

Ezekiel inhaled deeply as he took a seat. "I have some news, but it isn't good. I'm sure you all know by now that I killed one of them in Vulpe's castle, but the second managed to escape with two of the Eye of the Phoenix' fragments. What you don't know yet is that our side suffered a massive loss as well. Methuselah is dead. Tabitha found his body half-buried in the Australian outback."

The group was shell-shocked. Methuselah was one of the three most powerful wizards on the planet, and now he was gone.

"How did he die?" asked Michael.

"He lost a battle against the warlocks' master. The residual energy around his body leaves no doubt about it."

"Who is this master? How could he defeat Methuselah?" The question came from Sheila.

"We still don't know who he is, but we now have a good idea of what he is. In truth, I think the Second Circle has known the answer all along, we just refused to admit it."

"What is he?" asked Olivia.

"I just came back from the faes where I left the third fragment of the artifact with Lord Vaalt for safe keeping. I had a long chat with him and it became clear to me that he doesn't perceive the master's energetic signature, the distortion of the magical field, nearly as intensely as Tabitha and I do. This suggests the type of magic involved isn't earth-bound. Which also rules out a rogue elf. If you add to this the fact the *entity* was able to defeat Methuselah one on one, it leaves only one possibility. We're dealing with a mage. A wizard of the First Circle."

They all looked at each other, trying to gauge what the information really meant.

"Wouldn't a mage fight on your side, Ez?" Michael asked finally.

"You would think so, but apparently we're dealing with a dark mage. A practitioner who chose the dark side after they reincarnated into a mage."

"How can this happen?" said Michael.

"It's a simple matter of choice. Once you have the power you can use it for good or evil. A wizard has free will, Michael. Why a mage would choose the dark side is beyond me, but that's beside the point. The master hasn't been around very long—a few months at most, or we'd have felt his or her presence earlier—but based on the warlocks and sorcerers who attacked the vamps' compound, he's recruiting heavily."

"Recruiting for what?" asked Michael, but he already knew the answer.

"World domination... What else?"

The atmosphere in the room suddenly became oppressing as if the master stood here with them, but it was only his ghost.

"Talking about vamps, where's your sister?" Ezekiel asked Olivia.

"She went back to France with Irini. She doesn't have much to fear from the jerks who are hunting us down, and Vulpe's court is well protected. At least against humans..."

Ezekiel nodded and turned to Michael. "You never told me how you figured out it was Vladislav who was after the Eye of the Phoenix."

"I mostly got lucky, Ez. I came to the realization right there in Vulpe's reception hall. I'd been suspecting Anastasia for a while, but it hadn't occurred to me that her husband might be in on it. They were seemingly at each other's throat so it appeared unlikely they'd be conspiring to overthrow Vulpe. Especially since he was supposedly Anastasia's lover."

"Great job summarizing why you shouldn't have suspected him, Michael. How about you get to the point where you did start suspecting him?" said Ezekiel.

"I was getting to that... There was one thing I found interesting about the feud between Vladislav and his wife; it appeared to be fairly recent and had gotten a lot worse over the past few weeks. Why? Maybe because Vulpe was bedding Anastasia at the same time Vladislav and Lucy were having an affair... These would have been legitimate reasons to be at each other's throat, but it could also have been a big act aimed at deceiving. But if that were the case, aimed at deceiving who, and why? If you put this question in the perspective of the robberies, it's possible to draw some hypotheses. What if Anastasia had an ulterior motive for seducing Vulpe? What if it were a way of getting close to him to steal his safe combination?"

"Is that what she did?" asked Ez.

"Yep. She hid a fiber-optic camera behind books on his bookshelf. The fiber was aimed towards the safe. I suspected as much when I found a small rectangle where dust hadn't collected behind the books, and this was confirmed when Cristos' men searched Anastasia's quarters after her death. They found the camera, though she'd been careful to not keep track of the recording on her computer or Vladislav's."

"And how did you know the camera belonged to her?" asked Ez.

"I didn't know for a fact, but there were a few signs pointing in that direction. She had one of Vulpe's books in her room. A book that belonged on the shelf where the camera had been dissimulated. And Vulpe is very protective of his books. To be able to borrow one, you would have to be in his good grace. I tested that hypothesis with Irini and it was confirmed. Irini wasn't close enough to Vulpe to be allowed to borrow his books. Since Anastasia had the intimacy required to borrow Vulpe's books, that gave her a perfect opportunity to discreetly hide and then remove the camera while the leader stood in the very same room."

"Okay, so Anastasia might have had the means to learn the safe combination. That's all you had on her?" asked Ez.

"Not quite. She was also the one who ordered the slave to light the fire in Vulpe's room an hour earlier on the day of the robbery. Had she not made that request, the slave would have never walked in on the thief inside Vulpe's apartments. In turn, Lucy would have never been accused of the crime, and the fake pendant would have never been found hidden among her stuff. For Lucy to get caught, as was clearly intended by planting a fake in her belongings, the servant needed to go into that room an hour earlier. Once again more than suggesting Anastasia's involvement."

"Enough with Anastasia, call me convinced of her guilt, but who actually stole the fragment from Vulpe's safe? Anastasia looks nothing like Lucy, and vampires can't adopt someone else's physical appearance."

"That one baffled me for a long time, but only because I wrongly assumed that the same person impersonated Lucy to steal both Vulpe's and Lord Vaalt's fragments."

"That's not the case?" The wizard looked baffled.

"Definitely not. Vladislav himself stole Lord Vaalt's fragment."

"How? He can no more change appearance than his wife."

"That's where you're wrong, Ez," said Michael teasingly. "Anyone with two fragments of the Eye of the Phoenix is imbued with the same powers as any nearby fae, and after stealing Vulpe's, Vladislav and Anastasia had indeed two fragments at their disposal. As you know, Anastasia had the ruby-colored fragment in her possession for a long time—"

"But you didn't know that. Michael!"

"I suspected as much... For one thing, I'd seen her retrieving her pendant from the safe located in the apartments she shared with her husband. According to Irini, no vampire would bother locking away an object of purely monetary value. An invaluable fae artifact, on the other hand, would definitely justify such precautions. And finally, keep in mind that only one fragment was stolen from the faes."

"So?"

"So if three fragments were in Vulpe's castle, as you were convinced of, and only one had been stolen from Lord Vaalt's, it meant the other two had been with the vampires all along."

"Okay, fine..." conceded the wizard.

"I'm glad we agree on this point. So, Vladislav had two fragments at his disposal and all he needed was a chameleon nearby to absorb the fae's power and shapeshift into anyone he liked... So why not change into Lucy? When Victor told Vladislav a chameleon had approached him to help steal the two fragments, Vladislav couldn't believe his good fortune. The fact he was Victor's maker should have put me on his trail much faster, but what can I say, I'm slow. Anyway, we knew that Victor had been killed prior to his last meeting with Seemak, so we were definitely dealing with an impostor. When I asked you, Ez, what level of a wizard would be able to shapeshift into someone else, you told me it would take a member of the Second Circle or a warlock. Neither of which fit the bill."

"What do you mean by that?"

"I mean that I couldn't picture Tabitha or Methuselah adopting Lucy's appearance to commit a robbery and if a warlock had done it, the loot wouldn't have remained in Vulpe's castle. Furthermore, Vaalt's chamber was protected against chameleons' intrusion for this very reason; he didn't want a chameleon impersonating him to go rob him blind. Which only left two possibilities: either Lucy had done it, or another vampire had impersonated Lucy by using the power of the two fragments. Since Lucy appeared to have a fairly solid alibi for the second robbery, I followed the *other vampire* lead. All Vladislav needed to be able to adopt Lucy's appearance was a chameleon to be nearby, and since the robbery was committed with Seemak's assistance, he definitely had access to the chameleon he needed."

"It could have been Anastasia impersonating Lucy, couldn't it?" pointed out Sheila.

"I suppose it could have been, but it made little difference."

"On the contrary, my young friend!" interjected the wizard. "Based on your demonstration, Anastasia is a more likely culprit, which would mean you still have no evidence incriminating Vladislav."

Michael gave him an enigmatic smile. "Oh, but I do. This brings me to the first robbery. Who do you think stole Vulpe's fragment?" He paused for effect, daring Ezekiel to venture a guess, but the wizard didn't take the bait. "Fine, I'll tell you, *old* friend. It couldn't be Vladislav or Anastasia since they only had one fragment at this point and wouldn't have been able to adopt Lucy's appearance. And if a chameleon had committed the deed, the fragment would have once again never landed in Vladislav's hands... In the end, there was only one person who could have done it. The most obvious one of them all... Lucy!"

"Are you kidding? Luce would never have done such a thing. And she wouldn't lie to you about it." Olivia was looking at him with outrage.

"Lucy never lied to me, Olivia. It's not a lie if she believed she was telling the truth. Anastasia induced Lucy into believing she was having an affair with Vladislav. She implanted false memories in your sister's mind. For instance, Lucy was adamant she'd spent a whole day with Vladislav until Irini reminded her she'd actually been out of town with her on that day. Why was Lucy confused? Simply because the memory of being with Vladislav wasn't real in the first place. None of her memories of time spent with him were. Anastasia implanted those memories in her mind and enthralled her into stealing Vulpe's fragment for them."

"But vampires can't be enthralled," said Olivia.

"Except that Lucy isn't a true vampire, and she's also been enthralled prior to becoming a vampire. I'm not sure which one of those factors is responsible, but Lucy could be and was enthralled by Anastasia. She was given the safe's combination and instructed what to do when she got caught by the servant."

"But why?" asked Olivia.

"Because it provided Vladislav and his wife with a great alibi. They couldn't have done it since they looked nothing like her. And the alibi only got better when Vladislav falsely confessed to his affair with Lucy in front of his wife, supposedly to save his lover. Who could have imagined this was a diversion?"

"You... apparently," said Ezekiel.

"But it took me a while... The confession had a secondary objective as well. He needed to get Lucy off the hook. He needed her alive and free since he was planning on impersonating her for the second robbery."

"Another sleight of hand, I suppose?"

"You suppose correctly. Lucy was his favorite pawn in the complex game of chess he was playing against his brother and Lord Vaalt. He never loved her or had any interest in her other than as a sacrificial lamb. He never tried to rescue her when the faes demanded she be surrendered to them. He even denied her an alibi when Vulpe asked him if they'd been together at the time of Lord Vaalt's robbery. By then Vladislav wanted Lucy gone; he had no more need of her and she'd become a liability. When he showed up at my house with Irini to supposedly help rescue Lucy from the faes, I suspect he was actually hoping to derail the rescue mission and have her killed."

Michael's demonstration had convinced everyone, and they were discussing dinner options when Daka came out of an adjacent room.

"Daka? I didn't know you were here," said Sheila.

"I was keeping our guest company," replied the skinwalker, before turning to Michael. "He just woke up."

Michael nodded and headed for the room Daka had just exited. He pushed the door open and stared in silence at the swollen face of the man tied up to the bed.

The eyes of Jason Parrish went wide when he recognized Michael. He clacked his teeth together loudly a few times as if to bite on an invisible object, but nothing happened.

"Are you looking for this?" Michael pointed at a dental implant on the dresser, well out of reach. "Unlike your buddies, you're not taking the easy way out, Jason. I'm going to ask you some questions and believe me, you're going to answer."

The end

This story will be concluded in BROKEN ALLIANCE

A word from the author

I hope you enjoyed this book, and I wanted to thank you for being one of my readers.

With over 300,000 books published in the US every year, new authors face an uphill battle when it comes to making their work visible to the public. So, if you enjoy my stories, I would greatly appreciate if you could help me get the word out.

If you believe Michael Biörn deserves to be discovered by a wider audience, please tell your friends about the books. This would make a real difference and help me publish more stories at a faster pace. Even a simple post on social media or liking my Michael Biörn Novels Facebook page would make a significant difference.

Of course, if you truly love these novels and decided to write a brief review for any of the books on Amazon, I'd be eternally grateful. Whatever you choose to do, thanks again for reading my stories; it means a lot to me.

Thanks,
Marc

Michael's back story

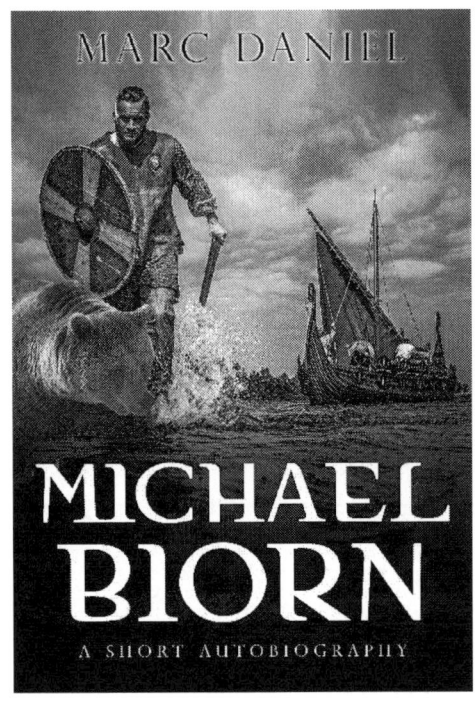

Download your free copy at:

http://bit.ly/MichaelBiornBackStory

Marc Daniel

After spending significant amounts of time in Ohio, France, and Montana, Marc is currently living in Houston with his wife and three dogs.

When he's not writing, cooking dinner or playing with his dogs, Marc enjoys woodworking, going to the theater and escaping the city to reconnect with nature.

Contact information:
marc@marcdaniel-books.com
www.marcdaniel-books.com
https://www.facebook.com/MichaelBiornNovels
@MarcDanielBooks

Printed in Great Britain
by Amazon